Where You Lead

LESLEA WAHL

This book is dedicated to the men in my life:

To my father, the hardest working and most interesting man I know, whose adventurous true-life tales continue to astound and inspire me.

To my husband who moved this Colorado girl to the excitement and chaos of Washington, DC to begin our very own life of adventure.

To my sons:

JWahl—my DC baby who sparked my interest in history by always sharing the exciting, little-known details he learned.

Jaco—whose inventive spirit has made him the perfect collaborator to brainstorm with about unique ideas for scenes.

Copyright ©2018 Leslea Wahl
Second Edition October 2025
ISBN: 979-8-9869037-9-8

Cover illustration ©2018 Elaina Lee/For the Muse Designs.

Praise for *Where You Lead*

Where You Lead by Leslea Wahl is a mix of mystery, danger, and a "treasure hunt" adventure with a hint of romance. Plunged into the heart of Washington D.C., faith-filled characters Eve and Nick believe they are on a mission from God. I enjoyed the Civil War trivia and seeing the museums and monuments of our nation's capital through the eyes of these characters. Even more, I loved the beautiful message that spoke through the pages: we all need the courage to say "yes" to God's will, whether in big, life-changing moments or the little ways of everyday life. This story is sure to entertain teens and young adults.

~Theresa Linden, author of award-winning *Roland West, Loner*

Few authors are as talented in the genre of young adult fiction as Leslea Wahl. Two things especially amaze me about Wahl's books. First is her delightful ability to get into the heads and hearts of today's teenagers, delving straight into the way teenagers think and act. Reading her stories brings me back to high school and make me feel the pain and the joys and the uncertainties and the struggles of being young all over again. The other thing I especially admire is Wahl's facility with blending the Catholic Faith with her mystery plots. She never preaches but rather immerses her characters into exciting situations which make them grow unexpectedly in the love of God and neighbor. The world needs more books like this for today's Catholic teens!

~ Susan Peek, bestselling author of *God's Forgotten Friends: Lives of Little Known Saints series*

Awards for **Where You Lead**

Catholic Press Association Second Place Book Award

Illumination Christian Book Award Silver Medal

Colorado Independent Press Association Award

Moonbeam Children's Book Award Bronze Medal

Royal Dragonfly Award First Place, Young Adult Fiction

Independent Author Network Award Finalist

Chanticleer International Book Awards, Dante Rossetti
Award Finalist

Contents

Chapter One

"Excuse me. Are you all right?"

A soft voice echoed through her head. Eve turned to face the wide-eyed woman standing next to her.

"What?"

"Are you okay? You've been standing here staring at your reflection since I entered."

Eve glanced around. A row of bathroom stalls and a pair of paper towel dispensers on the wall. A public bathroom.

"Oh. Ah. Yeah, I'm fine." Maybe a little dizzy and confused, but otherwise fine.

"Are you sure?" The wide eyes narrowed into slits as the woman's forehead crinkled.

"Yeah." She watched the water pouring from the faucet she stood in front of. "Um, where am I?"

Okay, maybe not completely fine.

"We're at the Pizza Barn." The woman stared at her the way you might look at a stray dog, with equal parts concern, compassion, caution, and fear.

"Oh, right. Got it, thanks." The Pizza Barn? When had she come to the Pizza Barn? She smiled, hoping that would appease the woman's concern.

No such luck. The woman continued to stare.

Eve turned her attention to the task of washing her shaking hands, trying to convey normalcy. Move along, please. Nothing to see here. It's totally normal for a teenage girl not to know where she is. Happens all the time.

The strategy worked. After another moment of intense scrutiny, the woman left.

Eve's gaze travelled from the closing bathroom door to the mirror. Yikes. No wonder the woman had stared: she bore a disturbing resemblance to the Ghost of Christmas Past. That would make anyone nervous. Stark lighting might work for those born with a warm complexion, but harsh lights are not a friend to pale skin and reddish hair. Light freckles stood out like bright red cactus blossoms against pale desert sand.

The cold water she splashed on her face sent a shiver down her spine. What happened? Why couldn't she remember coming here? Could dehydration cause confusion? Better order a large glass of water.

She threw away her wadded-up paper towel. She pushed through the bathroom door, and her empty stomach lurched at the mouth-watering aroma of hot pizza.

As she walked through the dining area, an odd déjà vu sensation passed over her, like she'd been here and done this all before. Not too surprising. All Pizza Barn locations across the country were the same: the kitchens in the back corner, the walls all painted the same bold red, the enlarged photographs that decorated the dining area were the same, the booths and tables all identical. Even the bathrooms were always located in the same spot. She knew the layout well, as she'd spent a lot of time at the Pizza Barn in her hometown of Albuquerque, New Mexico, before she moved.

There was one difference though—Nick. Her heart fluttered when she spotted him at a booth along the wall, his back to her. His head, with that thick dark hair, bent forward as he scanned his phone. Before joining him, she paused at the juke box. Just like in New Mexico, this one was full of '50s songs. Shaking off her unsettled feeling, she inserted a coin and chose their favorite Elvis tune. She'd never understood why most teens didn't like this kind of music. They were classics for a reason.

As the King of Rock and Roll began his serenade, she couldn't help but smile, thinking how blessed she was to now live in this new state with a new boyfriend who appreciated her. She and Nick had an amazing connection. They just "got" each other. She said a silent prayer of thanks, then slid into the booth, transfixed by his hands. She reached out and wrapped her fingers around his.

The hands flinched and jerked free of her grip.

Startled, she looked up and peered into the eyes of a stranger.

What?

She recoiled in shock as she glanced around the nearly empty restaurant.

"Can I help you?" The boy, who was most definitely not Nick, watched her through wide, startled eyes.

Eve stared back, unsure how to answer.

His eyes narrowed. "Are you all right? Are you sick?"

Maybe. She wrapped an arm around her abdomen as a wave of nausea washed over her. She had felt certain that this boy was—

"Where's Nick?" The words barely made it out of her dry mouth.

"Sorry, I don't know anyone named Nick." Not-Nick glanced over his shoulder. "Um, my takeout's ready now."

Before she could think of anything else to ask, he slid out of the booth, leaving her alone.

With trembling fingers, she eased back the red-checkered curtain from the window and gaped at the cars in the parking lot. They all bore New Mexico license plates. A quick scan of the street, and she knew her location—Albuquerque. She grasped the edge of the table, afraid she might faint. Why was she in Albuquerque? She and her family had moved. Hadn't they? The wonderful aroma of cooking pizzas turned her stomach. Suddenly, she wasn't sure of anything.

When she closed her eyes, she could see Nick smiling at her. She pictured him reaching for her hand and them strolling along, fingers laced together.

But who was Nick?

Chapter Two

"Nurse Kauffman?" Eve knocked on the open door of the nurse's office.

The school nurse of her small Catholic high school looked up from her paperwork. "Oh, hi, Eve. Come on in."

After a sleepless night plagued by visions of the mysterious Nick, the time had come to seek answers from a professional. Eve handed the nurse a baggie of her homemade chocolate chip cookies.

"Wow. These look delicious. Thanks." Nurse Kauffman opened the little bag, closed her eyes, and inhaled the scent of the cookies.

"They're homemade." Sheesh. Why did she feel it necessary to state that fact?

"I didn't know you were such a baker."

She shrugged. "It's kinda become my go-to thing over the last few months."

Nurse Kauffman set the cookies aside and tucked a wayward strand of blond hair behind her ear. "What can I help you with?" She leaned forward and lowered her voice. "Cramps?"

"No. Why do you ask?" Eve perched on the edge of the hard, plastic chair in front of the nurse's desk.

"There aren't a lot of reasons teenage girls come to see me. It's usually either cramps or migraines. I see all kinds of interesting ailments and accidents from the elementary students next door, but don't get a lot of visits from you high schoolers."

"Oh. Well, I don't have cramps or a migraine." The chair wasn't meant to be sat on for more than a few seconds. Eve shifted uncomfortably. Time to spit this out. "There's something else I wanted to ask you about."

"Sure, hon."

"Yesterday, something strange happened to me." She hesitated. How do you explain the unexplainable?

"Oh. Some kind of *female* problem?" The nurse directed all her attention to Eve.

"No. Well, I don't know. I kind of had this memory of someone. It wasn't real but felt really real." So real that whenever she closed her eyes, the image of "Nick" caused her pulse to spasm.

Nurse Kauffman peered at her. "I see. First, let me say, this is a safe place. You can confide in me."

Eve nodded. Wasn't that what she was doing?

"Have you taken any drugs?"

She jerked back. "No! Absolutely not." *That's her first thought? Really?* Although . . . the possibility of someone slipping her a hallucinogen might be worth pondering. She cleared her throat. "Actually, I was wondering if maybe I could be suffering from a brain aneurysm or something?"

That question resulted in a thorough examination of her head, a vision test, and a series of questions to determine if she had a concussion. All of which turned out normal, and she was given a clean bill of health.

Nurse Kauffman sat back at her desk and reached for the bag of cookies. "Well, you seem fine. Why don't you take an aspirin and let me know how you feel tomorrow? We can go from there. And if you do start having cramps, let me know."

"Thanks." For nothing.

Time for Plan B.

Eve left the clinic and headed for the office across the hall. Hopefully, the counselor could offer more help—she couldn't possibly be any less helpful.

Ms. Martinez's long, manicured finger motioned her in, her smile growing as she eyed the bag of cookies in Eve's hand. While the counselor dove into the sweet treats, Eve tried to explain the situation. Again.

"Hmm, that's unusual."

"I know, weird, huh? Have you ever heard of something like this before?" *Please say, yes, it happens all the time, no need to worry about your sanity. Please.*

"Not exactly." The counselor wiped the crumbs off her hands. She reached for a book on the shelf behind her and flipped through it.

"Let's see. This could be a psychological manifestation of an issue you're facing. Are there any problems at home?"

"I don't think so." She stared at the woman, now contemplating a whole new quandary—to mention or not to mention the crumbs sprinkled across her sweater. Would it be ruder to point out her messy eating habits or to let her spend the rest of the day covered in crumbs?

"Eve?"

"Oh, yes?"

The counselor watched her for a moment then closed the book.

"I must confess I've been concerned about you this year. You haven't been the same outgoing girl since your friend Mindy left."

Eve stiffened. "Mindy? This has nothing to do with Mindy."

"Are you sure? I know things have been difficult for you since she moved away to South America. Becoming missionaries was a great opportunity for her family, but it's probably been hard on you. And then your sister headed off to college. You might be feeling a little abandoned, and understandably so."

She stared at the counselor for a moment. Was she that transparent? Sure, she was a little lonely but that had nothing to do with the situation at hand. "Just because the two people in the world that I used to be with all day every day have left, and I have no friends or anyone to do anything with, doesn't mean I would dream up make-believe boyfriends." At least she hoped it didn't.

Ms. Martinez held her in a piercing gaze. Eve squirmed, unnerved.

"I just haven't felt like myself since Mindy left." Was it really that difficult to understand that losing a best friend was like losing a part of yourself? "But I'm fine. I don't need friends. I only have a year and a half until I'm off to college. Besides, I have plenty to keep me busy with my reading and baking." She winced. She'd just described her seventy-five-year-old grandma.

"There are some nice girls in your class. You should try hanging out with them."

She sighed. "It's not that simple. Mindy and I were best friends since kindergarten. We did *everything* together, and eventually the other girls stopped hanging out with us. I don't blame them. We completely isolated ourselves, but now that Mindy's gone, it's pretty lonely.

I've tried sitting with the others at lunch, but the conversation always ends up being about things they've all done together or some kind of inside joke that I'm not a part of." Amazing how depressing a lunchroom full of kids could be.

Ms. Martinez nodded. "I see. Why don't you make an appointment to come in again? We'll discuss your personal life in more detail."

Strike two.

"Sure, sounds great." Not. Why wouldn't anyone take her seriously? Something was wrong, and it wasn't because she had cramps or was lonely.

Her next stop was the rectory. She'd never had an actual conversation with Father Romero, but the elderly priest seemed pretty cool. His homilies were always easy to understand and usually humorous. And when she'd gone to confession, he'd never been all judgy-like. Surely, he'd have some kind of insight.

"Hi, Father." Eve handed him her last bag of cookies. The soothing scent of incense calmed her nerves. Something about the dark wood and the shelves of books filled her with hope.

"Eve, you look horrible." He crinkled his already wrinkled forehead in concern.

Geez. "No offense, Father, but you really don't have the best bedside manner."

He smiled, then placed the bag on his desk as if it were made of delicate glass and might shatter into a million pieces. "You obviously have something on your mind. What can I do for you?" When he raised his glasses onto his head, they disappeared into his thick, white hair. His cardigan looked so soft, she resisted the urge to reach out and touch it.

Eve sat on the couch and stared at the corner of his desk. Finally, she drew a deep breath and dove into her story . . . for the third time. "Umm. Yesterday, I had this vision-like thing." She wiped her palms on her plaid skirt. "I thought I had moved away from here and was dating a guy named Nick. I know it sounds crazy, but the feelings were so real. In fact, I freaked out some poor guy at the Pizza Barn, thinking he was Nick." She forced herself to look at Father Romero to gauge his reaction.

She had to give the man credit when he didn't stare at her like she was insane.

"I know it's been hard on you since Mindy and Brooke left. Maybe you should join a few clubs to build up a new group of friends."

Her insides fell like a ruined soufflé. Him, too? Really?

"Yeah, maybe, but that doesn't answer my question."

"Which is what?"

"Am I going crazy?" *Please say no, please say no.*

His bushy white eyebrows arched. "You're sure you don't know this Nick?"

Eve let out the breath she didn't even know she was holding. "I'm positive I've never met him. Yet, I feel like I know him well, like we have this whole history together." Her shoulders collapsed. "It doesn't make any sense."

"You said you thought your family had moved away. Have your parents recently discussed moving?" His chair squeaked in protest when he relaxed against the back.

"No. My dad loves being a professor here at the college. He'd never want to move. Be honest, Father." She picked at her clear nail polish. "Do you think something's wrong with me? Could . . . could I be possessed or something?"

She half expected him to roll his eyes and tell her she was being ridiculous, but instead his smile was full of warmth and compassion.

"No. I don't want you to worry. Dreams can be extremely realistic. I don't know you too well, but I have observed a few things over the years. I remember many afternoons when you and your friend Mindy unintentionally interrupted my prayer time with your giggles while you walked down the hallway to the library. That joyous sound, full of such innocence and happiness, always made me smile. I also recall the time you and Mindy started the clothing and toy drive for the family in town who lost their house in a fire. You have an amazing spirit, Eve—not only thoughtful and generous but happy and caring as well. I think losing your friend and your sister has been hard on you, and whether you realize it or not, you have been sad and a bit depressed. I want you to focus once again on what is good in your life and not dwell on the past. You have a lot to share with the world, and if you keep dwelling on what you've lost, you will miss the beauty and good around you."

"That's great advice, but it's not really why I came to see you. Something is terribly wrong with me." She bit her lip, trying to stop the tears that threatened to fill her eyes. "I know this doesn't make sense, but I think Nick needs me for some reason. I have this pull toward him, deep in my soul. My feelings inside keep getting stronger, and I know I'm supposed to do something, but I have no idea what."

The priest looked toward the crucifix on the wall, almost in an attitude of prayer. After a moment his compassionate smile fell. He slowly turned his gaze on Eve once again.

A chill ran down her spine. He knew something . . . and she feared the worst. Her fingernails dug into the cushioned arms of the chair as she braced herself for whatever he was about to say.

He studied her face for a moment then cleared his throat.

"Do you remember the story of Samuel? From the Bible?"

Her head tilted as she stared at the elderly priest. A Bible story? Really?

He ignored her questioning look and continued. "As a boy, Samuel lived with the priest, Eli. Samuel kept hearing his name being called in the middle of the night. He thought it was Eli, but the old priest kept sending him back to bed. Finally, Eli understood and told the boy the next time he heard his name called to answer, 'Speak, Lord, your servant is listening.' Do you remember that?"

The meaning of the story slowly dawned on her. Was he serious? "You think God is sending me a message about some cute boy?"

She was not expecting that. "Why would God talk to *me*? I mean, there are a lot more competent people in the world who could do His work."

He reached out and took her hands. "God uses everyone."

"But I'm only a student." Great, another useless visit.

He shrugged. "Saint Joan of Arc was only thirteen when He called her to drive out the English from French territory." His eyes drifted to the cross around her neck. "I believe your faith is strong. I suggest praying for your answer."

She nodded, not sure he'd helped at all. In fact, he'd come up with an even crazier suggestion than her stressed mind had imagined.

"Thanks, Father, I'll think about what you said."

Eve left the rectory, disheartened. *Three strikes, girl. You're out.*

Chapter Three

They were in a park. Eve loved the way sunlight shone off Nick's dark hair as he tossed a flying disc to her. She caught it and flung it back, but her aim was off. Oops! Hard to keep her mind in the game with her eyes on the red castle behind Nick. So beautiful . . . so majestic.

She woke with a horrible pain in her neck. Because she fell asleep on her algebra book or a symptom of her glitchy mind? Could she somehow be haunted by someone else's memories?

She flipped to an empty page in her notebook and began to sketch the handsome features that filled her mind almost every moment. The physical aspects weren't hard to capture, but how to depict kindness and strength? Or the way his smile made her insides all gooey?

One thing was clear: her thoughts were vividly real. They didn't feel like a dream, more like memories. She'd once heard déjà vu was caused by a thought going to the wrong part of your brain, somehow making its way to the memory part before the present part. Could something like that be happening?

Her algebra homework abandoned, she spent the rest of the afternoon searching through internet sites about mind control, out-of-body experiences, and alternate universes. While nothing matched her symptoms, she did discover there were some seriously freaky people out there.

***

That night at dinner, she showed her parents the sketch of Nick. Her hopes evaporated when they both looked blankly at the rendering. She shoved the drawing in her pocket, surprised but glad when neither of them questioned why their daughter was sketching pictures of some random guy. She soon found out why.

Her mom's intense gaze was the first indication of trouble.

"Tennis lessons at the rec center are starting up again soon. Should I sign you up?"

Not again. This was the last thing she needed. "No. I lost my doubles partner when Mindy left. My tennis career is over."

"That's why you should go, so you can find a new partner before tennis season begins."

"No, thanks." Eve took a bite of her dinner, not missing the loaded glance between her parents.

Her mom tried again. "I heard the auditions for the school musical are next week. Maybe you should try out."

The school musical? "I don't sing, or dance, or act." Couldn't she just let this go?

Another glance between the parents. "It might be a nice way to meet new people."

Her dad cleared his throat. "Your mom's right. Since Mindy left, you haven't been yourself. Maybe trying a new activity is a good idea."

This tag teaming was not cool. "I don't need a new activity." Except maybe if the activity involved determining whether Nick really existed or was a figment of her imagination.

"Honey, we're worried." Mom seemed to be choosing her words with great care. "You've lost your spunk. You've always been so outgoing, it's hard to see you isolating yourself this much."

"Just because I like being alone and reading books all the time doesn't mean I'm isolating myself."

The glance again. Her parents seemed unable to keep their eyes off each other tonight.

Eve sighed. Even she knew how weak her protest sounded.

Mom was nothing if not persistent. Better to tell her what she wanted to hear. "Fine. I'll think about joining a club or something."

"Good." Mom's triumphant smile marked the end of the uncomfortable conversation.

Her dad shifted topics to other events of the day. "I've been reading up on some of the more interesting congressional races across the country."

Having a history professor for a dad made for some extremely boring dinner conversations. Eve swirled peas into the white mound of mashed potatoes on her plate, shifting her thoughts back to Nick. As she considered the possibility of being a time traveler, a wave of dizziness made the room spin.

Nick threw a flying disc to her. She caught it then flung it back to him. A red castle stood regally behind him. She turned to the right, and a white obelisk came into view. The Washington Monument. Washington, D.C.?

"Oh!" Her head jerked up. The sudden outburst interrupted her parents' boring conversation. "Have we ever been to D.C.?"

"Washington, D.C.? Your father and I have been there, but you girls haven't." Mom handed her the bread-basket.

She had a location! It had to mean something.

"Is there any way we could take a trip to D.C. now?" Maybe they'd agree. After all, they'd just told her she needed a new interest.

Dad's eyebrows rose. "Now? No way. I'm in the middle of my semester. Maybe this summer."

Her shoulders slumped. "I don't think I can wait till then." She couldn't keep having these haunting visions. Somehow, she had to figure out what was happening to her. "What about going during Christmas break? Brooke could meet us there."

Mom shook her head. "Honey, this is your sister's first year away from home. I'm sure she'd like to come here for Christmas."

Ignoring her mom, Eve turned big puppy-dog eyes on Dad.

"Come on, there's a lot of cool history stuff in D.C."

"You sound just like Gabe," Dad grumbled.

"Who's Gabe?"

He stuffed a forkful of food in his mouth, so Mom answered for him. "A colleague of your Dad's who's been trying to convince him to teach at his university."

This was the first she'd heard of it. "Which university?" She took a bite of her dinner.

"Georgetown."

Eve stopped chewing. "Is that in D.C.?"

"Yes."

She nearly spit her half-chewed bite of pork chop out on the table. "*What?* Someone offered you a job in Washington, D.C.?" This could not be a coincidence.

Dad shrugged. "That was a while ago. Early in the summer. He asked me to fill a position in the history department. Can you please pass the pepper?"

She ignored his request. This was not some casual comment he could just shrug off. "Why didn't you take the job?"

With a sharp look in her direction, he reached across her to grab the pepper himself. "Clearly, it's not the time to uproot our family. Your sister just started college. If we moved, she would feel abandoned, like she has no home to come back to. And you have two years left of high school. There will be plenty of time to further my career in a few years." He turned to the task of seasoning his food.

Eve pushed away hers, unable to eat another bite. "Dad, do you think the position is still available?"

"I doubt it. I'm sure they've filled it by now. Why?"

She fingered her cross necklace. "Because I think it would be cool to move to D.C."

Both parents stared at her, their faces frozen in mid-chew.

Her mother's eyebrows creased in concern. "You've never lived outside of Albuquerque. Why would you want to move back east? It's a whole new world."

Chapter Four

"Let me get this straight. You called because you've been daydreaming about a boy?"

Desperate to talk with someone she could trust, Eve had called her sister. She'd tried Mindy first, but the internet connection was so horrible in South America, she hadn't been able to reach her. Of course, she wasn't about to tell Brooke that she'd been the second-choice confidant.

Eve paced across her room. The space wasn't very large, so it was more like walking in a small circle. "I think I'm losing my mind."

Her sister laughed. "Well, I could've told you that years ago."

"Come on, I'm serious. I'm having these intense visions about this guy."

"As much as I'm enjoying your dramatic hysteria, I must state the obvious. Daydreaming about a boy is rather normal for a teenaged girl."

Eve flopped down on her bed. "It's not a daydream. I think he's real and lives in Washington, D.C., and I think I'm supposed to help him somehow."

"Some stranger you've never met, in a place you've never been, needs your help?"

Why was she having such trouble getting anyone to understand her desperation? "I don't know! That's what's driving me crazy. But I've got to get there somehow. I've looked up leadership conferences to attend, but you know how those are. I'd never be able to sneak off to search for some mystery boy. And I brought up visiting there this fall, but Mom and Dad shot that idea down."

"I'm sorry, sis, I don't know what to tell you. This all sounds pretty odd. I know you don't know him very well, but Father Romero helped me out with a few problems. Maybe you should talk with him."

She sighed. Another dead end. "I did, and he started talking nonsense about me being called by God. You know, like Samuel in the Bible, 'Speak Lord, your servant is listening.'"

She was prepared for her sister's laughter, but not the unnerving silence from her end.

"Come on, you don't honestly think I'm being called by God?"

"It does happen, you know."

Eve was about to argue until she thought about all the crazy ideas she'd come up with to explain what was happening. Would this be any crazier?

"In one of my religion classes, we talked about people who had unusual experiences when God was leading them. Take Father's advice and pray. Tell God you're listening. What do you have to lose?"

Panic surged through her. She wanted to discover who Nick was, but being called by God? That was more than she'd bargained for. Still, did she have a choice? If she ignored it, she might never feel normal again.

"All right." Her grumbling response indicated an acceptance of Brooke's advice.

That night as she lay in bed, bundled under her warm blankets, Eve fingered her gold cross and prayed.

Okay, God, here I am. You've got my attention. In fact, I hope this is You trying to get me to do something, otherwise my next stop might be the state mental hospital. I don't know how this works but . . . speak Lord, I'm listening. I trust You and will go where You lead.

A sense of calm washed over her. Maybe she'd finally figured it out? But with the calmness came a sense of urgency.

She must get to D.C. and find Nick.

Her thoughts flashed to her dad. This was all happening because he'd turned down that job offer. If they had moved to Washington, D.C. back then, like they were clearly supposed to have done, things would be going just fine. Her parents somehow messed up God's plan, and now it was up to her to put it back on track.

The gravity of that knowledge was like a punch to the stomach, leaving her gasping for breath.

Okay, seriously, God? I'm only a teenager. How am I supposed to get to D.C. and meet a guy named Nick without so much as a last name to go on?

Could she say no? Maybe politely decline? *Thanks, God, for thinking of me, but I'm gonna have to say no. This is all a little above my pay grade. I'll just keep my nice, quiet life for now.*

Another thought bulldozed its way into her head. She knew what she had to do. Geez, this being a servant stuff was tough work.

She threw the covers back, crawled out of bed, and tiptoed to her dad's office. She scanned through his emails, searching for the name Gabe. Finally! There it

was. Dad's correspondence from the summer . . . with
Gabe McIntire.

Eve said a quick prayer that she could accomplish the
task at hand without lying. She copied his email address,
then composed a message from her own account.

Dear Mr. McIntire,

*I am Grant Donahue's daughter. I've just started
my college search and might be interested in
attending Georgetown University. I understand
you and my father are colleagues. I wanted to
reach out and introduce myself because I thought
you might be a great contact and source of
information if I have any questions during this
process.*

*By the way, I heard that you had offered my dad
a position in the history department this past
summer. Has that position been filled? Just
between the two of us, I think Dad has some
regrets about not taking the position.*

Thank you for your time.

Eve Donahue

She stared at the message a moment then prayed.
*Hey, God, I'm totally excited to be Your servant and all, but if
I'm supposed to get my family to move to D.C., I'm going to need
a little help.*

Send.

Chapter Five

Eve had gotten pretty good at pushing the images of Nick to the back of her mind. After all, she'd tried everything she could think of to get to D.C. Now she had to be patient and wait. But tonight, it was no easy task. Attempting to do her homework in the kitchen was nearly impossible. The tantalizing scent of the bubbling lasagna baking in the oven made her think of the Pizza Barn.

She'd just slammed her math book shut in protest when Dad burst through the door.

"You won't believe this." His wide eyes were excited and perplexed at the same time.

Mom set down the knife she was holding. "What's wrong? You don't look good."

Dad ran his fingers through his brown hair. It shot out in a million different directions, rather like a startled hedgehog.

"I got a message from Gabe this afternoon."

Clutching her pencil, Eve closed her eyes. This was the moment of truth. She was about to find out if this was indeed God's plan. She sure hoped so, because this whole thing was too complicated. She needed His help to pull it off.

"He offered me a job."

Her eyes popped open as a chill ran down her spine. Oh my gosh, this was actually happening.

After a moment, Mom broke the silence that had filled the kitchen. "Again? I thought he filled the position."

"He did hire someone for the spot he talked to me about this summer, but a new position opened up." He sank into the chair across from Eve. "This morning, one of his female professors approached him. She's pregnant and just found out she's having triplets. She'll need to be on bed rest for months and doesn't really want to come back full time after the babies are born."

Eve glanced at the ceiling. *Just this morning? Wow, God, Your timing is perfect.*

"And get this." His lips curved up into a small smile. "The position focuses on the Civil War."

"That's always been your passion." Now it was her mom's turn to sink into a chair.

"It has?" *Since when?* "I thought you specialized in Western culture and Native American history."

Dad's gaze fixed on Mom's face. "That's the position that was open here, but I've always been fascinated with the intricacies of the Civil War. I know this is terrible timing, and I'll probably need to refuse him again, but I'm sure he won't ask a third time. And to be offered something at such a prestigious university is incredible."

"Are you crazy?"

Both parents snapped their heads toward her at the sudden outburst.

"Dad, you have to accept." Eve had only been thinking about getting herself to D.C., but clearly this position would be a fantastic opportunity for her dad. Most importantly, this was so much bigger than either of them.

God was directing them; her parents had to agree. "I've been telling you that I'm ready for a new adventure, and I know Brooke is also on board. This sounds like an amazing opportunity for you. And Mom, there are a ton of museums there. Surely you could find a similar job to yours at one of them."

Her parents focused on each other again, communicating with their eyes.

Hang on, Nick. I'm on my way.

Chapter Six

Eve thought she knew what city life would be like. After all, she had envisioned it for months now. But as her family exited the Capital Beltway which circled the greater D.C. area and made their way down Connecticut Avenue, all the horn blasts and zooming taxi cabs were more than a little intimidating. After they had spent so much time driving through the heartland of America, across New Mexico, Colorado, Nebraska, Iowa, Illinois, Ohio, Pennsylvania, and Maryland, the hustle of the metropolis was a shock to all of them.

"I still can't believe how quickly we got this move together." Brooke shifted in her seat.

Eve looked at her sister. How was she taking credit for any of this? "We? You didn't do anything."

"Hey, why should I have helped with any of it? It wasn't my idea to move halfway across the country."

Hard to argue with that.

They were finally on the last leg of their journey after spending Christmas in Iowa with their grandparents three days ago.

Mom turned to look at them in the back seat of the family car. "I know how you feel. It all happened so fast."

"Yeah, like it was God's plan."

Eve grinned at the wink her sister gave her.

"We're getting close now." Dad spoke a little absently as he navigated through the crazy traffic. "I'm taking a little detour to Massachusetts Avenue. I want to drive by the Naval Observatory, which happens to be the home of the Vice President."

"Oh, wow." For once, Eve joined in her dad's enthusiasm about historical places. She was excited to see her new city.

"When we drive past the row of embassies, we could play a game to see who's first to figure out which embassy belongs to which country based solely on the flags that hang out front."

Eve shared another look with her sister. Okay, so maybe she wasn't quite as enthusiastic as he was.

Police cars barricaded the road around the VP's residence. They watched in fascination as a line of secret service limos poured out from the gate of the Naval Observatory and turned onto the major thoroughfare.

"I don't think we want to be stuck behind that motorcade. I'll just head back to Connecticut Avenue." Dad made a quick turn onto a side street.

"Dad!" Eve screeched in terror. "You're going the wrong way—this is a one-way street!" She watched in horror as an oncoming car barreled toward them.

"No, I'm not." His answer was strained.

No way was this meant to be anything other than one way. The street was insanely narrow. How could both cars possibly fit?

Dad's knuckles turned white as he inched down the road, almost scraping the vehicles parked at the curb. A lady in a luxury car rolled down her window and yelled at them, emphasizing her anger with a surprising hand gesture.

Brooke gasped. "Wow. Welcome to the big city."

Oh boy. This was not what Eve had expected. What had she gotten them into? Well, it was a little too late to turn back now.

"These old roads were made for horses and carriages, not for two cars to drive down. To say nothing of all the parked cars along the curb." Mom's smile clearly aimed for "reassuring," but the strain etched on her face belied the effort.

They all breathed a sigh of relief when they made their way back to the much wider Connecticut Avenue and joined the mass of cars streaming into the heart of D.C. They relaxed a little as the shops and apartments zipped by. As they neared their new home, they entered a circular path of crazy traffic, which the friendly phone navigator called Dupont Circle. Eve would have named it Dante's Inferno Round-About.

She'd seen a few of these dangerous traffic junctions before. Out West they weren't very popular. Occasionally, when a couple of not-so-busy roads intersected, the transportation department would leap into action and build a traffic circle. Cars would then gingerly ease into the merry-go-round of moving vehicles and exit onto another road.

Dupont Circle could best be described as a cesspool of swirling chaos. Hundreds of cars moved in mass confusion. Drivers cut each other off, blared their horns, slammed on brakes, veered back and forth between the inner and outer lanes, and clustered together at the various stoplights. Eve clasped Brooke's hand as the insane frenzy took place around them. Fresh out of optimism, she was sure one of the maniac drivers would plow into them, cause a massive pileup, and send them all to the hospital. Not a great way to spend their first night in the city. Mom even abandoned her calm façade. She gasped a few times, white as the proverbial bedsheet, and finally started reciting the Rosary.

They ended up driving around the massive circle three times before it spit them out onto P Street. By then, Mom's white-knuckled fingers gouged little dents in the dashboard, and Dad's jaw resembled carved granite.

Eve eased up on Brooke's hand. *Thank you, God, for keeping us safe. I'd never question Your divine plan or anything, but are You sure this is where You want us? I don't know how well we're going to fit in.*

Dad lifted a shaking hand and pointed out the red brick building to their right. "There's the back of our apartment building."

Real estate in D.C. being much more expensive than in New Mexico meant they'd no longer live in a single-family, suburban home with a yard. Their new home was an apartment in the city. Her parents figured this would be better, with no yard to maintain and an easy commute to work and school.

Eve considered it a cool adventure to live in the city. Very cosmopolitan.

As he turned onto another narrow, brick-paved street, and made his way to the front of the building, Dad let out a loud sigh.

Brooke patted his shoulder. "Well, we made it."

"Barely."

"This place is insane." Eve rolled her shoulders, trying to loosen the knots that had formed.

Her sister grinned. "Well, you wanted an adventure."

"Yes, an *exciting* adventure, not a *traumatic* one."

Mom turned in her seat to look at them. The color had returned to her cheeks. "Who's ready to check out the new apartment?"

Brooke raised her hand. "I, for one, can't wait to get out of this car."

Eve nodded. They'd spent too much time in the car over the last two weeks. Now, after the harrowing experience of D.C. traffic, she was more than ready to see their new home.

Their excitement diminished as they spent another twenty minutes driving around, searching for a place to park. Street parking was limited in front of the row houses that fit together like puzzle pieces. Eventually, they found a spot, but Eve did not share Dad's confidence that it was large enough to parallel park in. Dad soon proved that skill was not his strong suit. As he backed in and out edging the family car into the small space, the drivers behind them blared their horns. Eve vowed not to drive anytime soon.

Inside the apartment building, they were greeted by Mrs. Rosenbaum. The plump apartment manager sported a smile and a purple suit. She introduced them to LaVonne, the beaming woman who manned the front desk.

Mom took the key Mrs. Rosenbaum handed her. "You probably don't get many people moving in during the holidays."

"Actually, this time of year is a busy relocation time here. The new members of Congress and their staff all move into town before the new year."

"Oh. I hadn't thought of that."

Mrs. Rosenbaum gave one quick nod. "You'll soon find that life here revolves around politics." She held out a piece of paper. "Here is the code for the underground garage. Also, don't leave your car parked on the street. You'll be ticketed if you don't have a permit sticker."

Dad grimaced. "Excuse me then. I'll meet you girls upstairs."

As he scurried out to extract the car from the hard-earned parking spot, Eve and Brooke followed their mom to a charmingly old-fashioned elevator and rode up six floors. Mom told them that constituted a tall structure in Washington. No buildings were allowed to be taller than the monuments.

They stopped at a door while Mom inserted the key. Eve held her breath. This was it! Their new home! The door swung open, and Eve stood there, mesmerized as sunlight streamed in through tall windows overlooking the city. She wandered closer and touched the glass, taking in the amazing view. To the left, the Washington Monument pointed to the heavens. She scanned the city. A boy named Nick lived out there. Somewhere. And somehow, she was going to find him.

Pulling herself from the window, she joined Brooke to explore the apartment. Cool architectural details highlighted the spacious living room, and an interesting pattern of wood parquet flooring ran throughout the apartment. A hallway to the left led to Dad's new office and two bedrooms, one for her parents and one she'd share with Brooke when they were both home. The right-side hall led to the kitchen and dining room.

Perfect.

Dad finally entered the apartment, a piece of paper gripped between thumb and fingers, a wry half-grin on his face. "Here's our welcome gift from the city: a thirty-dollar ticket for illegal parking."

"Why exactly are you baking Christmas cookies five days after Christmas?"

Eve shooed Dad's hand away from the stack of decorated sugar cookies.

"Brooke and I thought we'd take them to the neighbors and introduce ourselves."

"That's a nice idea. But surely you can spare one or two for your old man." He snatched two frosted stars before the girls could protest.

An elderly gentleman opened the first door they knocked on. He grudgingly accepted the plate, then peered suspiciously under the foil. Eve didn't agree with Brooke that he'd throw them in the trash.

The next door they rapped on never opened, but an eyeball stared at them through the peephole. They introduced themselves, but whoever belonged to the eyeball only yelled for them to leave the plate of cookies in the hallway.

A young mother with a baby on her hip and dark circles under her eyes was so thrilled with the plate of cookies that she insisted on giving them something in return. Sweet, but what would they do with a half-dead poinsettia?

The next person they met, a middle-aged man, warned them that someone on the floor liked to steal newspapers. He explained how he woke up at 4:30 every morning so he would hear the paper being delivered and could snatch it before someone else did.

Their last stop was across the hall from their apartment.

Eve rapped her knuckles against the door three times. Both girls grinned when the triple knock elicited a soft, irritated moan from inside, followed by the shuffle of slow footsteps. The door opened a crack, just enough to reveal half a wrinkly face and one squinty eye.

"What is that?" An elderly woman's voice—and not a very pleasant one. The single eye visible through the barely open door fixed on the plate of cookies in Eve's hand.

"Cookies. We wanted to introduce ourselves." Eve flashed her friendliest smile.

"Why?"

She glanced at Brooke. Her sister shrugged. *Thanks. You're a big help.*

"Because we just moved in across the hall. I'm Eve and this is my sister, Brooke."

The eye in the partial face blinked but never wavered. Half a pair of shriveled lips remained pursed.

"What's your name?" Eve posed the question around a stifled sigh. This wasn't going well. *I can't believe I'm standing here talking to the sliver of a head.*

"Mrs. Grant. Are those Christmas cookies?"

"Yes. We bake them every year. We didn't get a chance to do it before Christmas this year because we were moving, so we thought we'd make them now."

"I don't celebrate Christmas."

"Oh, are you Jewish?" Maybe giving Christmas cookies to a non-Christian person wasn't politically correct.

"No. I'm not religious."

"Oh. Okay. Well, enjoy the cookies anyway." Eve bumped the plate against the crack in the door.

The lady sighed then widened the gap enough to snatch the plate, after which she shut the door in their faces.

"Happy Holidays," Brooke murmured.

Chapter Seven

"Let me know as soon as you find Nick."

Eve glanced at her parents, but they were too busy shoving Brooke's suitcases into the car to pay attention. Her secret remained safe.

She wrapped her arms around her sister. "You'll be the first to know. Have fun at school this semester."

Mixed emotions flooded over her as her parents drove away, whisking Brooke off to the airport. With Christmas break over, her new life awaited. Starting in the middle of her junior year would be a challenge. Still, how could she not be excited about this new chapter in her life?

Her main focus would be finding Nick. That's why she was here. But where did she even begin to search for him?

When she walked back into the apartment building, the rather large but extremely sweet and all-knowing receptionist motioned Eve toward her. Nothing happened in this building without LaVonne Sherman's knowledge. She greeted every resident with a warm smile and a friendly chat. Definitely the go-to person.

"Girl, you sure do look fabulous in hats!" LaVonne's loud voice echoed across the foyer. "Not everyone can pull off that look so smoothly."

Eve touched the cheery wool hat perched over her curls. She'd thought it looked quite fetching. Nice to know someone else appreciated it too.

"Thanks, Ms. LaVonne. To tell you the truth, I've never really been a hat person, but ever since I moved here, my hair has been all Medusa-like, with a mind of its own."

LaVonne nodded, her enormous hoop earrings bobbing along. "It's the humidity, sugar. If you think your hair's wild now, just wait till this summer."

"Gee, that's nice. Something to look forward to." She turned toward the elevator.

"Do you like pets?" LaVonne's question stopped her departure. "I bet you're an animal person."

"Yeah. I used to pet sit back in New Mexico." Animals were the best. They never excluded anyone.

"Well, hon, if you're brave enough to talk to her, Mrs. Grant could sure use some help with her cats."

A shiver coursed through Eve. The memory of the slammed door in her face remained fresh in her mind. "I don't think I possess that kind of courage."

LaVonne let out a hearty laugh. "Oh, honey, her bark is far worse than her bite. Although if you tell her I said that, I will throw you under the bus in a heartbeat and deny every word. I don't want that woman on my bad side."

She nodded. "I understand. Don't worry, it's our little secret."

"I know it's hard to believe, but she used to be quite active and outgoing. She worked at the Smithsonian for years and was involved with all kinds of organizations around town. But the poor thing's had a rough spell of it the last few years. She could use a friendly face, whether she's willing to admit it or not."

Mrs. Grant hadn't appeared to care much for Eve's friendly face. "I don't know. Honestly, I've kinda become a bit of an introvert lately."

"Well, that's perfect!" LaVonne clapped her hands. Her inch-long fingernails clicked together. *How on earth does she get any work done with those things in the way?* "She's not much of a people person either. You could maybe pop in and visit the cats once in a while."

Eve wasn't so sure about the idea. Maybe if she agreed, LaVonne would recommend her pet-sitting services to others, and she could earn some spending money. "I guess I could try, but if you don't see me for a couple of days, please send a rescue team."

The receptionist's loud laughter brought a smile to her face.

On the elevator ride up to the sixth floor, Eve gathered her courage. Seriously, how bad could it be? Mrs. Grant was a little old lady, not a Gorgon.

She knocked. Slow, shuffling feet made their way across the apartment. The door opened a crack, and one wrinkly eye peered out. *Déjà vu.*

"What?"

She smiled brightly. "Hi, Mrs. Grant. Remember me? I'm Eve. I live across the hall."

"So?"

She swallowed hard, then lifted her chin. "I heard you have some cats. Do you ever need any help with them? I love animals."

The eye squinted. "You a Yankee or a Confederate?"

Eve flinched, baffled. "Excuse me?"

"You slow or something? Yankee or Confederate?"

"Um, you do know the Civil War's been over for like a hundred and fifty years, right?" Maybe Mrs. Grant wasn't just lonely and grumpy. Maybe her problem was . . . well, all in the head.

"Of course, I know that," snapped Mrs. Grant. "What's wrong with you?"

What was wrong with *her?*

"It's a simple question." Mrs. Grant emphasized each word like she was trying to explain something to a small child. "Are your people from the North or the South?"

With no idea how to answer the question, Eve took a guess. "My people. Well, I'm from New Mexico, which wasn't a state yet during the Civil War. My parents are from Iowa. So, I guess maybe the North?"

"Hmmph."

She must've hit on the right answer. The apartment door opened, so apparently it wasn't *not* the right answer.

Mrs. Grant turned out to be quite tiny and thin. Curly gray hair hugged her head. Pearls accompanied a pink housecoat. Her eyes followed Eve's every movement, and her lips pinched together, creating even more lines on her wrinkled face.

Eve walked past her unwilling hostess into an apartment that felt more like an antique store. She was pretty sure she'd seen some of the furniture in one of those movies from the turn of the century. Lace doilies covered upholstered armrests on the chairs while fragile knick-knacks graced the tables and shelves. Photographs in vintage frames lined the fireplace mantel.

The pictures appeared to be of Mrs. Grant and maybe a husband and son. Judging by the backgrounds in the photos, the family must have traveled a lot. What had happened to the happy woman in the photos to make her the curmudgeonly person she was now?

"Do you always wear a cross?" The elderly woman demanded. Her inquiries had a way of sounding oddly accusatory.

Eve touched her cross necklace. "Yes, I try to."

"Why?"

She'd never had to explain her faith before and found it rather unnerving. "To show I'm a Christian."

"You really believe in God?"

Finally, a question that was easy to answer, especially after the last few months. "Yes, ma'am. I feel Him guiding me through my life."

Mrs. Grant's suspicious gaze raked Eve's face before she abruptly changed the subject. "Where do you go to school?"

"I'll be starting this week at Georgetown Visitation Prep School."

Silence.

"It's an all-girls high school next to the University."

"I never said it wasn't."

The retirement center where Eve and her class sometimes visited back home had been full of warm and fuzzy senior citizens. This woman was more like a prickly cactus you wanted to avoid.

LaVonne's words whispered through Eve's mind, and she decided to keep trying.

"So, would you be interested in some help with your cats?"

Mrs. Grant crossed bony arms over her chest. "Why would I trust you with my precious cats?"

Was a good deed really worth this interrogation?

"I'm extremely responsible. I took care of pets for years back in Albuquerque. I'll play with them, keep them company, make sure they have enough food and water, and even clean their litter box."

"And take them for walks."

"Walks?" Was this lady serious?

"Are you sure you're not slow?" Eyes narrowed, the persnickety woman all but snarled. "You don't seem very 'with it' sometimes."

Of all the neighbors LaVonne could've asked her to visit, why did it have to be this odd woman? "I just never heard of a cat who liked to take walks."

"My Tyler does. He likes to walk up and down the hallway."

A cat who likes to walk? "Oh, well, sure. I could take him on walks. How many cats do you have?"

"Two. Tyler and Lizzie."

The two cats appeared out of nowhere, most likely awakened by the sound of their names. A big ball of orange fur with a head and legs rubbed insistently against Eve's legs. The other cat, a thin gray feline, stared from a distance.

"I like their names." Eve bent to scratch the orange furball's head.

"That one is Tyler. My son named him. The gray one is Lizzie. She's named after Elizabeth Bennett, although she's kind of nasty. I should've named her after Lizzie Borden." Mrs. Grant scanned Eve up and down then added, "I'm sure you don't know who either of them are."

Eve smiled, triumphant. "Of course, I do. Elizabeth Bennett from *Pride and Prejudice* and ax murderer Lizzie Borden."

The antique chair creaked as Mrs. Grant lowered herself into it. "Hmm . . . there might be hope for you yet."

Okay, God, now what? I've been in D.C. for a few weeks and I'm no closer to finding Nick than before I dragged my parents halfway across the country. Do You have any idea how many teenage guys live in Washington? Well, yeah, I suppose You do since You're God. Not complaining here, 'cause I'm super stoked to help You out, but I have no idea where to begin my search. A little guidance might be helpful. Thanks! Amen.

Getting her family to move here should have been the tough part, but she was stumped. What was her next move? She watched for Nick everywhere she went but how in the world would she find him among the millions who lived and worked inside "the Beltway" (which was how the locals referred to the D.C. area)?

That cold January evening, after she'd finished her homework, she sank into the sofa cushions and rested her head against a pillow. Another boring night watching television with her parents.

Dad grabbed the remote and started flipping through channels like he did every night.

And there he was.

Eve gasped and sprang forward. Nick. On the TV. No one could possibly mistake that handsome face. Her heart hammered against her chest.

Dad glanced at her then aimed the remote, ready to switch channels.

"Wait!" She snatched the device out of his hand to turn up the volume.

A reporter talked about the new congressional freshman class. Images of Nick and what must be his family accompanied the story. The report centered around John Hammond, the newly elected senator from Virginia. Eve tried to concentrate on what the reporter said so she'd have some clues to go on, but her excitement at seeing Nick's face made it hard to focus. Her cheeks burned as she studied his dark hair and chocolatey brown eyes, which were even more amazing in high definition than they had been in her visions. He really did exist! He was a real person and he lived here! But how would she find him?

She ignored Dad's questioning look, then rushed down the hall to her room and computer. Now that she had Nick's father's name, hundreds of stories appeared. John Hammond, an engineer with no history in politics, out of the blue decided to make a difference and run for the Senate. His down-to-earth style and large family of six kids annoyed some but thrilled others. He'd shocked everyone by easily defeating the long-time incumbent.

None of the articles she found on the internet provided a lot of information about Nick. Just that he was the oldest of the six Hammond children and attended St. Mary's Catholic school in Alexandria. A quick search mapped out Alexandria on the other side of the Potomac.

Eve closed her eyes. She had found him.

Chapter Eight

"He's real! I found him. He's real!" Eve's excitement reached a new level when Brooke answered her phone. This news was too big to share over text.

"I'm sorry. Who're we talking about?"

"Don't be annoying. I need to share my joy!"

"Your joy?"

"*Brooooooke!*" Why were older sisters such a pain?

"I'm sorry. Are you serious? You sure you found him? Not just someone who slightly resembles him, but him?"

"I'm positive. His name is Nick Hammond, and he's a senator's son. I'm heading out to go meet him right now." Just saying it gave her goosebumps.

"Shouldn't you be in school?" Brooke let out an exaggerated gasp. "Ohhh, is good-girl Eve skipping school to meet up with a boy?"

"No. Some kind of teacher meeting changed the schedule, so I had a half day. Nick's school is across the river; I just need to figure out how to get there. The Metro has a stop nearby, but I'm thinking maybe I should be safe and take a cab or something."

"You should take the Metro. You're embarking on a new adventure so be adventurous."

What a great idea. "You're right. Well, wish me luck."

"Just be yourself. And call later with all the details."

***

Eve skipped out of the apartment and turned right toward Dumbarton Bridge and the perils of Dupont Circle. Giant buffalo statues adorned each corner of the unique bridge. Dad had told her that when the city planners wanted to connect Q Street in Georgetown and Q Street on the other side of Rock Creek, they didn't line up. The only way to connect them was to build a bridge with a curve.

Once over the bridge, she waved at the armed guard at one of the embassies. He didn't return her greeting. How cool would it be to live in such a huge mansion?

As she neared Dupont Circle, things got increasingly busier. The circle was designed like a giant wheel, with the streets as spokes converging in the center. Restaurants, bars, and shops crowded every street around it. She finally located the giant "M," the symbol for the Metro, and took a deep breath. She fingered the bag of cookies in her pocket, seeking strength from her gift for Nick. *Come on. Embrace the adventure.* Every day, thousands of people ride these trains . . . it can't be that difficult.

An escalator carried her deep underground. This subway was nothing like the New York subway depicted in movies. No disgusting smells or signs of rats anywhere.

Unsure of her next move, she watched people scurry around her, passing through the electronic gate with ease. The giant map on the wall, which looked like a knot of colored yarn, was no help at all.

Just pick someone and follow them. Stop wasting time.

An elderly couple with matching canes shuffled by, moving in slow motion compared to all the other passengers: the ideal candidates. Soon (well, soon for a snail), her new Metro card in hand, she boarded and found a seat. The train flew down the track, but an examination of the colorful knot disguised as a map told her she'd need to transfer tracks to reach her destination. *Oh, Lord, give me strength.*

When she stepped off the bus across the street from Nick's school, she felt like kissing the ground . . . and then disowning her sister for suggesting she take the Metro. After getting lost in a swarm of people while trying to change trains at Metro Center, almost missing her stop at King Street, and then dealing with the crankiest and slowest bus driver in all of D.C., she finally made it with minutes to spare. Would she ever get used to city life?

But she had no time to dwell on that.

St. Mary's Catholic School where Nick attended, was a pretty red-brick building that boasted a white cupola. A beautiful cross topped the structure.

Eve crossed her arms and leaned against a tree to wait. Too nonchalant. Maybe she should put her hands on her hips. No, too awkward. *You're about to meet the person who will change your life forever. Figure out how to stand!*

She paced. *Right, that works.* The moment she'd worked so hard for was about to happen. The months of planning and cajoling all led up to this moment. No pressure.

The school bell rang. Her stomach lurched. *Please don't throw up.*

She stood frozen in place as students poured out of the building. Uh oh. What if the school had more than one exit, and she missed Nick? What if he was staying after school and not leaving now? Maybe he wasn't even here today. Panic inched up her throat as her gaze darted across the sea of faces. Then she saw him.

Her handsome Nick, whose face had tormented her for months, stood across the street. He was taller than she'd thought and had a slim, athletic body. He walked with another guy, about his own height but stockier, like a football player. Both wore the typical private school uniform of polo shirts neatly tucked into khaki pants. Nick laughed at something his friend said. Her pulse quickened. Could any smile be more adorable?

"Nick!" She darted around the vehicles in the carline and ran across the street. "Nick!"

He and his friend stopped in their tracks and watched her.

"Nick! It's me!" She hurried toward him.

He froze. No recognition crossed his face. He actually looked a little wary.

"Nick, it's me, Eve. I'm here to help you."

He took a step back. "With what?"

"Umm, I'm not sure." She bit her lip.

His friend nudged him. "Great, another whacko."

Ignore the big brute. "I brought Snickerdoodles."

"Excuse me?" He shot a look to his friend.

She pulled the bag from her coat pocket. "Cookies. I made you cookies." Yeesh! Brooke had advised her to be herself, but seriously! How awkward could she get?

"Um, hi, Eve. It's nice to meet you." He cautiously accepted the bag of goodies.

The truth came crashing down. "You don't know who I am?" How was that possible?

He hesitated. "No. Should I?"

Her heart sank. This couldn't be happening. After all she went through to get here, she'd never once considered that he might not have a clue who she was. Who knew this vision thing didn't work both ways? Everything blurred as tears welled up in her eyes.

"Whoa," said the friend.

"Listen, I'm sorry, Eve." Nick's voice was calm and soothing. "I meet a lot of people and have a terrible memory. Maybe you could help me out here and tell me where we met."

She sniffed back the tears. "We haven't, but I think we might be soulmates."

"Oh boy." His friend grabbed his arm. "Let's get out of here. They just keep getting crazier."

Nick shrugged out of the hold, keeping his eyes on her. "Jace, can you give us a minute, please?"

"Are you sure?" Jace scanned her from head to toe.

"Yeah." Nick nodded his assurance.

"Okay. I'll be right over here . . . watching." Jace shot her a suspicious look, then took a few steps back.

Eve sniffled. "What's his problem?"

A tiny smirk crossed Nick's face. Her heart fluttered. Oh my gosh, he was so cute.

"He's a little overprotective. Ever since my dad jumped into politics and pictures of our family have been in the news, I've had some interesting admirers."

"Stalkers." Annoying Jace. *Eavesdropper.*

Her eyes flew wide. "You think I'm some crazy stalker?"

Nick grimaced. "Well, the thought crossed my mind."

"I'm not." How could he think that?

"You seem nice, but so did the girl we ended up having to get a restraining order for."

She swallowed the lump forming in her throat. "Sorry to ambush you like this. I thought you'd recognize me."

"Why? Are you famous?"

His head tilt made her insides jump. She wanted to reach out and touch him but resisted the temptation. Bodyguard Jace might slam her to the ground or something.

"No. It's just that I've had this overwhelming feeling I had to meet you."

She ignored the coughing fit that overtook Jace out of nowhere. How could she make Nick understand without sounding criminally insane?

"I pictured your face and knew we had this connection."

Alarm crossed Nick's face. "Okay, well, I've got to go, but it was nice meeting you."

He and Jace hurried off before Eve could think of anything else to say.

Chapter Nine

"So, you're telling me *all* these buildings are part of the Smithsonian Museum?" Eve and her mom walked along "the Mall," the huge grassy field anchored at one end by the Washington Monument with the United States Capitol residing at the other. Both sides of the grassy expanse were lined by large buildings which all housed museums.

"Yep." Her mom pointed off to the left. "The most popular ones are the Air and Space Museum, up that way. Natural History is across the way, and down there is American History."

"Wow. I had no idea there were this many." It was Friday afternoon, and they were about to explore one of the many collections.

"See the beautiful red building? That's the original building built by James Smithson." Mom pointed to the red castle. Eve knew the building from her visions of Nick.

"Mom, do you believe certain people are meant to meet? That God brings them together?"

Her mom linked arms with her, pulling her close. "Sure. Sometimes, though, we need a little coaxing, not knowing what's good for us. For instance, Dad asked me out four times before I finally said yes."

Maybe Nick would take some convincing as well.

Her mother's words were similar to Brooke's advice that Eve needed to run into him again and just be herself. Get to know him naturally. And under no circumstances mention the term soulmates.

Eve thought back to her conversation with her big sister after the ill-fated encounter a few days ago. Thank goodness, they hadn't Facetimed. Picturing Brooke smacking her palm into her forehead and shaking her head as Eve replayed her encounter with Nick had been painful enough. Actually seeing her reaction would have been excruciating.

But none of this helped her fix the situation. How could she somehow see him again without terrifying him in the process?

"You were right, sweetheart, this move was a wonderful opportunity. I love exploring all these museums and galleries with you." Mom rattled on about what they would see at today's stop, the Hirshhorn Sculpture Museum. She'd made a list of places around the metro area for the two of them to tour. She always brought along her resume to drop off, still in search of a job.

But it was hard to enjoy the mother-daughter outing. The epic failure of her encounter with Nick a few days before still burned in her mind. She kept thinking about his dark brown eyes, which unfortunately held a hint of fear when she'd seen them. Though his friend seemed like a bit of a tool, Nick himself had been nice, even if he thought she was mentally unstable.

"Do you know what you're going to wear to the event tonight?" Mom asked as they neared the museum.

"Oh, I almost forgot about it." They were attending some fancy shindig for the university. Their lives were so different here; it was fun to have something to dress up for. Maybe it would take her mind off the Nick fiasco.

***

The event turned out to be at The Kennedy Center, the huge theater complex along the Potomac River. Besides being a memorial to President Kennedy, it housed six theaters, including an opera house and symphony hall.

The Georgetown gala was set up in the long foyer which ran the entire length of the building in front of the three main theaters. An enormous bust of President Kennedy sat in the center of the long hall. Mom claimed it was actually long enough that the Washington Monument could lay down in it. That seemed impossible.

Eve wandered around the huge crowd of mingling adults. Why'd she bother coming? This event was just a cocktail party for grown-ups who liked to chat. In other words, boring.

She squeezed through the crowd at the bar to order a soda. When she turned around with drink in hand, she bumped into the person behind her, spilling the liquid all over his dark suit.

"Oh, I'm so sorry." She glanced up at a familiar face. "Nick!"

Chapter Ten

Nick scanned the area for an escape route. But he was trapped. There was nowhere to go without plowing into hundreds of well-dressed people and making a scene. So, he turned back toward the crazy girl who had tracked him down at his school earlier in the week.

"Eve, right?"

"You remembered." Her eyes lit up.

"Hard to forget." Was it possible that she had followed him here?

"Relax, I'm not stalking you. My dad works for Georgetown."

His eyes probably gave away his suspicions.

She glanced at his damp suit. "Oh, gosh. I'm so sorry." She began dabbing his chest with her cocktail napkin.

"Don't worry about it." *Just grab a drink then walk away.*

Wide eyes looked up at him. "Well, at least let me buy you a drink."

"From the free open bar?"

"Exactly!" She beamed.

She turned and ordered two sodas. It would be rude to ditch her now. *New plan. Chat politely for a few minutes then disappear.*

He led the way out of the crowded bar area.

As they walked, she handed him one of the drinks. "So, you know why I'm here. What brings you to this elegant soiree?"

Now that they were not smashed up against each other, he could see her dress. It looked like something from the roaring '20s, blue with swaying fringe, nothing like the black, form-fitting dresses girls usually wore to events like this.

"My dad's an alumnus of Georgetown. He insisted I come along to meet the dean and some of the professors."

She smiled. "It's nice to see someone my own age. I didn't realize it would basically be all adults when I agreed to tag along. Not that I had any other plans for the evening."

"Not much of a social life?" He took a sip of his soda.

"We only moved here a few weeks ago so I don't know anyone. Except you." Her smile widened.

He involuntarily stiffened.

"Hey, I'm sorry I ambushed you the other day." As she apologized, her cheeks turned the same shade as her unruly red curls.

Maybe he'd misread the weird incident at school. She seemed fairly normal tonight. Besides, what could she possibly do to him? She was like five-feet-two. He glanced around. She was right. This event was boring.

"Come on, let me show you something." He led her away from the party, down the Hall of Nations.

"Whoa." She stared in awe at the cavernous hallway. Hundreds of flags from all the countries around the world hung from the ceiling as they walked to a bank of elevators.

"Where are we going?"

"To my favorite part of the building. The Terrace Level." Now that he'd decided her sanity was probably intact, he had to admit she was cute, although not like the typical polished D.C. girl. The saying "marching to the beat of your own drum," came to mind.

When they exited the elevator and ventured out onto the terrace which circled the entire building, Eve's face lit up.

"This is amazing." Her tone was almost reverent as she took in the views of the city lights and monuments.

Coming up here was always the best part of the night when his parents brought him to a show.

They strolled along the perimeter in silence, enjoying the views from every angle. When they turned the corner, Georgetown University's dark spires, lit from below, reached up to the night sky.

She gasped. "Oh, it's so beautiful."

He stopped under a heat lamp. Hopefully his wet shirt would dry quickly.

"So, where'd you move from?"

"The Land of Enchantment."

Maybe he'd been too quick with gauging her mental stability. "Um, okay."

She glanced at him then laughed. "New Mexico. That's its nickname."

"Oh, right." Learn something new. "Wow, that's quite a move."

"Yep. I'm still adjusting. This city is huge. But I love the monuments and all the history." Her eyes sparkled as she looked out over the city.

Nick grinned at her enthusiasm.

"That's Virginia on the other side of the river?"

"Yep." He pointed to the left. "Memorial Bridge is down that way. It leads straight to the Lincoln Memorial." Surprised by his desire to impress her, he then pointed the other way toward the university. "That bridge leading into Georgetown is the Key Bridge, named after Francis Scott Key."

"The author of The Star-Spangled Banner."

He smiled. "Very good, you know your history."

"You pick up a few things when your dad's a history professor. I can't get over how old everything around here is." She peered down at the massive river. "I also can't believe the size of the Potomac. It's enormous."

"No rivers in New Mexico?" His family had taken a trip out West a few years ago but hadn't visited New Mexico.

"Nothing this large. The Rio Grande is a little stream compared to this. I mean, look at the size of the boat out there." She pointed to a dinner cruiser. "Our rivers are only wide enough to raft in."

The way her eyes lit up with this joyous sparkle intrigued him. "See that green and white building at the base of the Key Bridge? That's where I row from."

"Row?" Her forehead crinkled.

"I'm on a crew team."

"A what team?"

"Crew." Nick stared at her. She had to be teasing.

"Is that slang for your homies?" She looked confused.

"What?" His turn to be confused.

"Your friends, your bros, your crew?"

His eyebrows furrowed. "Have you seriously never heard of a crew team?" He couldn't believe someone didn't know what rowing was. In the spring and summer, crew teams always dotted the river.

She shrugged.

"Sorry, but I assumed there were crew teams everywhere." He leaned against the railing. "It's a team that rows a long boat down a river or across a lake."

She giggled. "Your big sport is rowing a boat? My grandpa has a little wooden rowboat he takes out on the lake near his house in Iowa. But I don't think anyone would call it a sport."

Nick laughed out loud. "It's a precision team sport."

"I'll take your word for it."

Her frown caused a twinge of guilt for laughing. "It's kinda hard to explain. Keep an eye out for the teams on the Potomac this spring. You'll see plenty of them when the weather warms up. So, what brought you here from New Mexico?"

"Um . . . " Her face paled.

"It can't be that bad."

She bit her lip. "No. My dad got a job at Georgetown."

"Very cool." He was glad he'd given her a chance. Talking with her was so much better than mingling with the adults downstairs. "Hey, can I ask what all that talk the other day about soulmates was about?" Nick could hardly believe the girl who showed up at his school holding a bag of cookies and this girl were one and the same.

She drew a deep breath. "Please don't think I'm insane again, but the oddest thing happened a few months ago."

Before he could answer, she rattled off some story about a Pizza Barn and how she had seen his face and knew his name and had this strong connection with him. Unease crept through his body as she talked about a vision of them throwing a flying disc in front of the Smithsonian Castle. He kept staring throughout the part when she told her priest she thought something might be wrong with her, and how this Father Romero suggested maybe it was like Samuel in the Bible and told her to pray, "Speak, Lord, your servant is listening."

Despite the heat from the lamp, Nick's insides had turned to ice. When her story ended, she looked at him, her eyes wide, waiting for his response.

What could he possibly say to all that? He watched her a moment longer then glanced at his watch. "Um, great seeing you again, but I've got to go."

He turned and walked away, leaving her alone on the massive terrace.

Chapter Eleven

Not many guys hung around Eve's all-girls high school. Which didn't seem to make a lot of sense. Wouldn't that be the perfect place to meet a girl? Regardless, none were usually anywhere to be seen.

Except for this mid-February day. When she and her classmates left the building, several guys stood around with flowers and boxes of chocolates. Valentine's Day brought out the boyfriends. She tried to ignore the twinges of jealousy coursing through her body as girls rushed to embrace their beaus. She could buy her own chocolates. Who needed a boy?

Then she saw *him,* standing across the street, hands in the pockets of his mid-length wool coat, the collar popped up around his neck. Like the scene from some movie, the cute guy at long last realizing he has feelings for the girl and shows up to lay his heart on the line. She pulled off her gloves and pinched herself to make sure this romantic Valentine's Day scene was actually happening.

Her arm now stung, but he still stood there, watching her.

Okay, God, can I get a little assistance here so I don't blow this again?

With a wave of her fingers, she crossed the street.

"Hi. What're you doing here?"

Nick glanced at his shoes then back at her face. "I had to talk to you."

Amazing how one single sentence could send a girl's heart racing.

"How'd you find me?" Maybe he'd finally had a vision too.

"Turns out there aren't a lot of Georgetown history professors who just moved here from New Mexico. I told your dad's secretary I was a friend visiting D.C. and wanted to find you."

No vision, just intellect. Who cared? He was here now. But why? "You wanted to find me?"

Another glance at his shoes. "Yeah, I haven't been able to get you out of my mind."

"*Really?*" She felt the heat of a blush. It had been a few weeks since their encounter on the terrace at the Kennedy Center. He had looked amazing that night in his suit, but she could still feel the sting of rejection as he'd walked away from her.

"Oh, um, not like that." He stumbled on his words. "I mean, your story is kind of unbelievable."

She nodded, despising the heat in her cheeks. Yeah, she was fully aware she'd screwed up. He obviously hadn't had similar visions, so blurting out such a crazy story had freaked him out. Of course it had. That's why she had decided to stay away from Nick until she could figure out what to do. Being God's servant wasn't as easy as it might sound.

He shivered. "It's a little cold out here. Can we talk somewhere warmer?"

Eve led him to the student union at the university. More couples, flowers, and hearts. No escaping romance today. They claimed two open chairs in the lounge area. Why was he here? Surely, he wouldn't have come in person to deliver a restraining order. But whatever the reason, he was nervous. He had avoided eye contact since they left her school and now concentrated on his hands as he rubbed them together.

She kept quiet and waited for his explanation, hoping not to mess anything up again.

After an eternity, he took a deep breath and looked up at her. "Did all that stuff you told me really happen?"

"Yes, exactly as I told you." This time she wasn't nervous. She knew somehow this was God's plan and prepared herself for whatever Nick's reaction would be.

"Why do you think we're soulmates?" He continued to watch her.

"I don't know, but why else would God want *us* to meet?"

"I just think that's . . . unlikely."

Ouch. "You don't think I could be your soulmate?" Painful words to hear on Valentine's Day while surrounded by happy couples.

He briefly shut his eyes. "No, no, no. It's not *that.* It's just that, well, it seems like an awful lot of work, you know? Uprooting your whole family and moving halfway across the country just to have us *meet.* I mean, God could have led us to the same college in a year and a half."

Hmm. Okay, he made a good point. Nick and his logic. "I'm telling you the truth about what happened. If you have a better explanation, I'd love to hear it."

He stared at his hands in silence.

Why didn't he just spit it out? Maybe he needed some encouraging. "I don't think you went to all the trouble of tracking me down just to disprove my theory," she tried.

A shake of his head. "I think maybe it's something bigger than simply you and I meeting one another."

"Like what?"

"That day at my school, you said something about coming to help me with something."

"Yeah. I had a feeling you needed my help. Are you having some kind of problem?"

"Not that I know of, but, well . . ." He ran his hand through his hair. "Something sort of similar happened to me last year."

He pulled a folded sheet of paper from his pocket and handed it to her.

Election Night

I have no idea why I'm writing this. But I've put my family on this trajectory, and I'm not sure if it was the right decision. It looks like Dad's about to become the next senator of Virginia, and that scares me. Why did I set this in motion?

It seemed like a great idea a year ago. But seeing how politics can destroy people, I'm not so sure anymore. We've all lost friends and had lies told about us. Is it worth it?

But when my parents became so involved in the campaign of the outsider who was trying to beat the incumbent senator, I couldn't help becoming intrigued as well. I heard them discussing how the current senator had held the seat for decades, that he only followed the party line (probably like a lot of politicians) and didn't do what was right for Virginia. That he didn't care about the rest of the state who didn't live and breathe Beltway politics.

It was exciting when they started helping organize rallies and fundraisers for their outsider candidate. Everything they said made sense, and I wanted to help. They'd never seemed that interested in politics, but maybe it was just because the campaign manager was my dad's college roommate. Who knows why, but it was fun to see them so into it.

Then the scandal broke. The candidate they had been so passionate about had been caught stealing campaign contributions, and it quickly became clear that this guy's political aspirations were over. Dad took it hard. He had believed in the guy, and I knew he felt discouraged for the state and all the residents who didn't have a voice.

I'm not sure why it bothered me that he was so upset. And I probably should've ignored the crazy thought that popped into my head. But the idea wouldn't go away. Dad needed to run for the Senate seat.

Why I couldn't let it go is a mystery. That stupid thought just kept floating around my mind, and the more I thought about it, the more I realized he would be perfect for Virginia. I felt like I was supposed to convince him to run.

I asked him if he'd ever thought of running for office. But he said no, he would never want to run. His exact words were, "We'll just have to pray for someone honest and good to run." I argued with him that he was the honest and good person who would make a difference. But he remained adamant that it wasn't a good idea, that he had no experience, and that the turmoil of a campaign would be hard on our family. Don't know why I didn't listen.

I'll never forget the day it all changed. The phone rang, and the caller ID identified the caller as Dad's friend, the campaign manager. I answered and told him my idea. He chuckled, but within the week, the state party began calling my dad, trying to convince him to run. After another week of family meetings, prayers, and discussion, he agreed.

Things started out great but then turned ugly. The opposition tried to smear him through distorted facts and lies. Reporters began to follow us. Our large family intrigued people for some reason, and we were suddenly thrown into the spotlight. Girls I didn't know sent me creepy notes and photos, and one started following me so much, we had to take action.

But Dad connected with the people. His ideas and lack of political experience excited them, mostly the voters located outside the D.C. area, and he started to soar in the polls. The everyman vs. the career politician.

That brings us to tonight, election night. I write this as the results are starting to come in. I'm still not sure I made the right decision, but Dad is a good man, and if anyone can make a real difference, it's my dad.

Chapter Twelve

Nick chewed on the inside of his cheek while Eve read. His insides bounced around like a pinball game. How would she react? Since that night at the Kennedy Center, he'd been debating whether to share his story with her. He'd never told anyone what had been eating at him for months. Yet he felt this overwhelming urge to tell Eve. She of all people would understand. Hopefully.

When she finished reading, her gaze met his. "So that's how your dad became a senator? You convinced him to run?"

Nick nodded. "It was like this force compelled me to do it. I never thought about it being God leading me until you told me your story." Every time some critical or negative campaign slur was flung their way, he'd felt responsible for putting his family through so much. But this new idea—that God had led him—changed everything. Maybe he could finally stop feeling so guilty.

Having someone to talk to about this was such a relief. "I'm sorry I was so rude to you at the Kennedy Center when I left you alone on the terrace. What you said freaked me out. Then I started to wonder if God had guided me to get my dad to run for Senate." Her smile coaxed him to continue. "I've been praying about it since that night, and now I'm sure it was God. But honestly, I thought I'd completed my goal when my dad won. Now I wonder if we're supposed to do something else . . . together."

"So, God has called us both? Why would He choose us?" She handed the paper back to him.

"Why does He choose anyone? He's used more unlikely characters than two Catholic teenagers: tax collectors, fishermen, shepherds, Christian persecutors."

"True." She curled her legs beneath her, cozying up in the lounge chair.

"I just have no idea what He's calling us to do." Seriously, where were they supposed to go from here?

"We're smart. We can figure this out."

The excitement in her voice made him smile.

Trying to figure this out meant they'd need to spend more time together. He couldn't deny the idea had a lot of appeal. He studied her face as she stared off in the distance, lost in thought. She wasn't wearing as much makeup today, making her freckles more noticeable. He'd always liked freckles.

Her gaze suddenly swung back to him. Oops! She'd caught him watching her.

He cleared his throat. "Well, you felt pulled here. It must be something in D.C."

"Yes, and we both have a connection to Georgetown."

He glanced around the student union. "That's true. Maybe something's wrong or corrupt here at the university."

She wrapped one of her curls around her finger. "Seems strange though to recruit two high school students when there's a small army of priests on campus."

"Yeah." He sank back in his chair.

"And besides, it doesn't explain why your dad had to be a senator."

Good point. "Maybe it has to do with the government."

She rolled her eyes. "Come on. How on earth would we affect anything in the federal government?"

"I don't know, but He's leading us to something." *Come on, God. You're going to have to help us out a little here.*

"Well, what government committee is your dad involved in?" She leaned toward him.

"He's on the Foreign Relations Committee."

"Great. So, it might not even be our country with the problem we somehow have to fix?"

They sat in silence. This was impossible. Of all the problems in the world, how would they ever pinpoint the one they were supposed to somehow solve? And even if they did, how would they fix it? He closed his eyes. Why was this happening? Would he ever be able to be a regular teenager again?

"Hey, Nick, can I ask you a question?"

He opened his eyes. She was watching him, her pretty smile replaced with a serious look. "Sure, what?"

"What did you do with the cookies I baked for you? You know, the ones I gave you when I came to your school?"

"What?" *Oh, dang.* Should he lie? No, better to just man up. "Oh, um. Well, Jace threw them in a dumpster. He was afraid they might have been poisoned."

Her face fell, and, for Nick, it was like a punch to the gut.

"Sorry."

"No, it's okay." She gave him one of her warm smiles. "I'll just have to bake you some more."

"Thanks. That would be nice." Amazing how much had changed since that first meeting.

"Can I ask you another question?" She bit her lip.

"Sure?"

"Do you know it's Valentine's Day?"

Valentine's Day? He glanced around, for the first time noticing the red and pink balloons, the flowers and hearts surrounding them. How had he not realized what day it was? The most romantic day of the year. What an idiot.

He shook his head. "I had no idea. I'm sorry. Am I keeping you from something?"

A smile spread across her face. "No. But I can't think of a better way to spend the afternoon than with you, figuring out a potential international crisis that needs divine intervention."

He liked the way her enthusiasm lit up the room.

Chapter Thirteen

Father Romero,

I met him! Nick! He really exists! In fact, he's sitting here in my living room right now. When I first met him, he questioned my sanity (telling him I thought we were soulmates kinda freaked him out), but it turns out he had a similar experience. Although he didn't have a crazy vision, only a strong feeling. (By the way, this seems to be the usual way people are led to something. Don't know why I had to think I was losing my mind, but I digress.) We think God wants us to work together on something. We're still trying to figure out what. Will keep you posted.

Eve

Eve,

It's so good to hear from you. I've been thinking about you a lot. I'm glad you met Nick. It must be a relief to know he's indeed real. I think it's extraordinary you both believe you are called for a purpose.

However, I do feel the need to caution you on a few things. Even though God has led you to Nick for some reason, I don't think you should assume it's for romantic purposes. Putting that kind of pressure on your relationship could be harmful and a distraction to whatever it is you are being called to do.

Also, please be careful and keep praying for guidance throughout your journey. And you are right, a vision is not a usual happening, but it's not unheard of either. St. Angela Merici experienced a vision of her deceased sister telling her about her future. Keep in mind, gifts are given for a reason, for a spiritual good to be attained. There is some extraordinary purpose for which you have been called, such as leading others to Christ and ensuring their eternal salvation.

I will pray that purpose becomes clear. Remember, I'm always here for you if you have concerns or questions. God's blessings.

Father Romero

Eternal salvation? Yeesh! No pressure there.

While she was supposed to be doing some research into what her joint mission with Nick might be, she'd been unable to concentrate. After sneaking a photo of Nick to send Brooke, she'd sent a quick message to let Father Romero know she hadn't been crazy after all.

She looked up from her laptop to watch Nick type something into his computer. His brow furrowed in concentration. After all those months of trying to find him, here he was, sitting on her couch. Unbelievable! Father Romero was right though: Nick might not be her one and only. Still, it was a relief to have found him and to have someone to hang out with.

He glanced up, like he sensed her watching him. Her insides did a flip.

"Thanks for letting us work here. I love your family's apartment." His eyes scanned the room.

"So do I. The view is awesome." She tore her eyes off his face and watched as the daylight diminished over the monuments. The city lights were beginning to sparkle in the twilight. "I'm sure you get used to seeing all the sites every day, but I still can't believe I live here."

"The view's great, but I meant how quiet it is. You can actually concentrate here and get a lot done."

"Your house isn't quiet?" She set aside her laptop, glad for a break after the hours they'd spent searching the web looking into world news.

"Hardly. There's never a quiet moment with five younger siblings around. Sometimes I go to the library just so I can get my homework done."

How fun would it be to have a big family? Always someone to hang out with, never a worry about being lonely. Things got so quiet around here that when her mom wasn't home to chat with, she often turned on a radio or the TV to drown out the silence.

"I don't know about you." He stood to stretch. "But I can't see where all this searching has helped at all. I still have no idea what we're supposed to be looking for."

She watched him, still amazed he was here. "It's like searching for a Native American artifact when we don't even know which reservation it's on."

Just then the front door of the apartment opened, and Eve's parents walked in. They were in the middle of a conversation but stopped midsentence when they saw Nick.

"Oh. Hi." Mom stammered the greeting, obviously surprised to find a strange young man in her apartment.

"Hi, Mr. and Mrs. Donahue, I'm Nick Hammond. It's a pleasure to meet you." Nick smoothly reached out his hand in greeting.

"Mom, Dad, this is Nick." Her introduction only caused more confusion on their faces.

"Nice to meet you." Dad shook Nick's hand. "What're you kids up to?" His eyes flicked down to the laptops.

"We're studying." She knew her vague answer didn't really clear things up.

"Oh. And how did you meet?"

An obvious question since they'd only been in the city less than two months, and she attended an all-girls school. How would she have met a boy? But she was at a complete blank on what to say. Divine intervention seemed hard to explain.

Nick easily took charge.

"We met at the Georgetown event at the Kennedy Center a couple weeks back."

"Speaking of the Kennedy Center." Mom suddenly seemed less concerned about the handsome boy standing in her living room. "I'll be starting work there next week."

"Oh, that's great, Mom. But it's a theater, not a museum."

"Actually, it has quite a display of art, items given to the center when it first opened. Since the theater serves as a memorial to President Kennedy, countries gave gifts to honor the late president. Anyway, they were searching for someone with museum experience to oversee the collection. They also hope to start bringing in exhibits."

"Cool."

"Congratulations, Mrs. Donahue. What a wonderful opportunity." Nick's gracious response sounded all adult-like.

"Thank you, Nick. I'm very excited."

Eve smiled, impressed with how smooth and in control Nick could be.

"Returning to our previous subject," Dad interrupted. "You said you two met at the Georgetown event. Does one of your parents work at the university, too?"

Eve threw a look at her dad. Geez, how embarrassing could he be?

"No, sir. But my dad graduated from there and would love for me to attend."

"Nick's dad is John Hammond, the new senator from Virginia." She enjoyed the shocked looks that transformed her parents' faces. Even though they were new to the area, Senator Hammond's story still dominated the local news.

Mom was the first to react. "Wow. From what I've heard, you've had an exciting few months."

"Yes, it's been an amazing experience." He offered them a charming smile which turned Eve's insides to mush.

Dad turned to her. "That's so strange. Eve, you and I are invited to a dinner party next week at the Endelbourg Embassy."

"An embassy? Why?"

"The ambassador's chief of staff called my office today. For some reason, he's fascinated with our Civil War history and wants to discuss a few things. He mentioned the ambassador has a teenage daughter, and when I told him about you, he insisted you join me at a dinner party they are hosting next week. The strange part is that he mentioned he had invited Senator Hammond as well."

She shot a look at Nick. He grinned. *Oh my gosh. Could this be the clue we've been searching for?*

"Wow, that sounds fantastic." She mentally scanned her closet. What was the appropriate attire for dinner at an embassy? Something like this would never happen in a million years back in Albuquerque. Wait till she told Brooke.

"Speaking of dinner, would you like to stay and eat with us, Nick?"

Smooth move, Mom.

"Thank you for the offer, but my dad's driver is coming to pick me up soon."

Darn.

He glanced at his watch. "Actually, I should be heading down. He'll be here any minute, and I don't want to keep him waiting."

"A driver?" Impressive.

"A nice little security perk." Nick grinned as he gathered his computer and coat.

Eve walked him out. The moment they were alone in the hallway, he turned toward her.

"Endelbourg? This has got to be the connection."

"But what on earth could we do? I don't even know where Endelbourg is." World geography was not her thing. Why would God think she could help with a country she knew nothing about?

Before they had a chance to formulate their next move, the elevator door slid open. Nick held the door as Mrs. Grant shuffled out carrying two bags of groceries.

"Hi, Mrs. Grant. Would you like me to help you with the bags?"

"Do I look like I can't carry my own groceries?"

"I thought they might be heavy." She was in too good a mood to let Mrs. Grant get to her.

"You just want a tip, but I'm not made of money, so forget it."

"I don't want a tip. I'm being neighborly."

"Humph."

"You know, on my way home from school I pass a few small markets. If you let me know what you need, I could stop and pick up some items for you."

Mrs. Grant eyed her suspiciously then continued on toward her apartment.

As they got on the elevator, Nick grinned at her.

She shrugged. "Believe it or not, that was one of our more cordial conversations."

"Wow. Anyway, I don't know much about Endelbourg either. I think it's in Eastern Europe somewhere. But this has to be it. One year ago, neither of us would ever have been invited to an embassy for dinner. This has got to be the reason for everything we've been through." His enthusiasm was contagious. And somehow made him look even more handsome.

"Well, if God went to this much trouble to put us here at this precise time, we'd better figure out what we're supposed to accomplish."

He nodded. "If you're not busy, I could come over after school again tomorrow, and we can search for information about Endelbourg."

A brilliant idea popped into her head. "Since you came here this time, do you want me to come to your house instead?"

His eyebrows arched. "Really?"

"Absolutely." She was curious about his family and wanted to meet them.

They exited the elevator and walked toward the front door of the building.

"I'm not sure you know what you're getting yourself into, but okay. Why don't I meet you at the King Street Metro stop after school?"

"Great! It's a . . ." *Date?* Better not push it. "It's a plan." Too bad he couldn't stay for dinner. They may not be destined to be together forever, but it was so nice to have someone to hang out with.

A large black Town Car pulled into the circle drive in front of the building. Nick walked toward the sedan. But before he climbed in, he turned back and smiled.

"Happy Valentine's Day."

Oh . . . best Valentine's Day ever.

Chapter Fourteen

Nick paced outside the King Street Metro stop waiting for Eve. He'd checked his watch at least four times already. Of course, he couldn't wait to get started on whatever mission the Lord had for them, but in all honesty, he liked hanging out with her. There was something intriguing about her.

After the fifth watch check, he spotted her navigating her way through the crowd of other passengers. She was bundled in a coat and mittens, and a knitted scarf circled her neck several times. Her curls peeked out from under a matching hat. He grinned.

"Hi!" She hurried toward him.

Her smile warmed his insides. "Hey, Albuquerque." Should he hug her or what? He safely stuffed his hands in his pockets.

She laughed. "Is that my new nickname?"

He shrugged. "Thought I'd try it out. It fits better than Stalker-chick, which is what Jace has dubbed you."

"Oh, geez. Anything would be better than that. So, do you live near here?"

"Not far, but first I want to give you a tour of Old Town Alexandria."

"Great, I love tours. But I must warn you, I only tip if they are both informative and enjoyable."

He saluted. "I'll do my best."

He led her to a trolley car, and they hopped on. The conductor told the passengers that George Washington had lived in Alexandria. He also pointed out a few historic places as they made their way down King Street toward the Potomac River. Nick watched Eve as they rode down the old cobblestone street. Completely immersed in the tour, she paid rapt attention to the stories the guide told them and beamed as she pointed out things to Nick.

Seeing his hometown through her eyes made it fun. He envied her ability to enjoy simple things so much. Why couldn't he be more like that? Probably because he was always worried about who was watching and who knew his identity.

When they reached the waterfront, they hopped off.

"I love these old towns. It's amazing to be surrounded by so much history. Just think, our founding fathers used to walk down these very streets." Eve reminded him of an excited little kid as they strolled past the old buildings.

"If you liked the trolley tour, you've got to do one of the ghost tours. They take you around Old Town, sharing tales of espionage and murder during the Revolutionary days." Maybe they could go together. He pictured her clinging to him during the scary stories. Yep, excellent idea.

"Sounds awesome!"

Nick smiled at her enthusiasm. He could get used to this. Hanging out with her was fun. He hadn't spent much time with friends in a long time, and doing everything with his siblings was getting old.

He pointed to one of the shops. "Let's stop here. I know it's a little cold out, but they have the best ice cream in town."

"Yum. So far, I'm impressed with your tour, Nick Hammond. Informative, entertaining, and a stop for food. Very impressive." She giggled as he held the door open for her.

They ordered their treats then sat at a little table near the front picture window.

After a few bites, he couldn't wait any longer to share what he'd discovered.

"Last night, I asked my dad about Endelbourg. He told me there's some European trade agreement that's in jeopardy because of strained relations between Endelbourg and Germany. He assumed that was the reason he'd been invited to the embassy. As the new senator on the Foreign Affairs Committee, they need his influence against a country as powerful as Germany."

"That sounds promising. But how could we help with that?"

"Not sure." That's what stumped him too. But at least he'd been paired with a great partner in this impossible task. "I thought we could do a little research on it this afternoon."

"Sounds good. Hopefully, our mission will become clear. Shall we head to your house and get to work?"

"All right." Poor girl didn't know what she was in for. "Brace yourself for the madness."

***

One step into the Hammond home and Eve ducked. A remote-control helicopter whizzed past her head.

"Dillon, watch it." Nick's voice competed against the hip hop music blasting through the house.

Eve tiptoed around the army tanks and toy soldiers scattered throughout the foyer. She'd almost made it safely through the battlefield when a dog bounded toward her. The Dalmatian greeted her by pounding its front paws on her chest, nearly knocking her over.

"Lexus! Down!" Nick scolded.

She trailed Nick into the family room, with the dog rubbing against her legs, covering her with little white hairs. She was starting to understand her new friend's reluctance to work at his home.

Dozens of stuffed animals lined the couches of the next room, all with books and pencils in front of them. A young girl stood next to the television. She held a small chalkboard and worked through a math problem, explaining each step to her toy students.

"Excuse me, class. We have visitors." She peered over a pair of glasses too large for her face. "Can I help you?"

"No." Nick winked at Eve. "We're just passing through. Sorry to disturb your math lesson." He turned to Eve. "This is Liv, or as her students call her, Ms. Olivia."

"It's very nice to meet you, Ms. Olivia. Your students are exceptionally well mannered." Eve guessed her to be in about third grade. Memories of all the hours she and Brooke had played school washed over her. For a moment she longed to stay and play with Olivia.

"Dillon and Olivia are twins." Nick explained as they moved on to the kitchen. And there awaited the snarky boy who had been with Nick when they first met. He stood in front of the open fridge, stuffing food into his mouth. A wave of surprise hit her as she realized the beefy guy built like a linebacker was Nick's younger sibling. Wow. Could two brothers be more different?

"You've already met Jace," Nick said by way of introduction.

"Hey Stalker-chick. 'Sup?" Jace smirked at her with a giant grin on his face.

She winced. She'd hoped Nick had been kidding about Jace's nickname for her, but it seemed he'd been all too serious.

Fascinated, she watched as Jace managed to fit an entire bagel into his mouth.

"Oh, I just remembered. I brought brownies." She dug into her bag to pull out a container.

Jace stopped chewing and eyed them hungrily.

She held the container tight to her chest. "Jace, you better not have any. I'm sure you wouldn't want to risk getting poisoned." She was still a bit miffed that he had thrown out the cookies she had lovingly baked for Nick.

"Good point. He doesn't trust your baking. We better keep them for ourselves." Nick slapped his brother on the back.

Jace's protest was interrupted when a thin, middle-school-age girl cartwheeled into the room, her feet mere inches from Eve's face.

"Who's your friend, Nick?"

"It's his stalker I told you about." Jace's words jumbled together as he chewed his bagel. Obviously, he did not possess the same meticulous manners as his brother.

"Why would you bring a crazy girl home?" Nick's sister effortlessly arched backward into a perfect backbend. Her face turned purple from being upside down. Lexus, happy to find a face at dog level, began to lick it.

And somehow Eve was the crazy one?

Nick threw a look her way. She took it to mean "told you we shouldn't have come here." Maybe he had a point.

"This is Eve. She's not a stalker. It was just a misunderstanding. Eve, meet Gabriella, our resident gymnast."

Gabriella scrutinized Eve as she pushed the dog away and flipped upright.

Determined to win his siblings over, Eve smiled. "Okay, let me get this straight. Nick, Jace, Gabriella, Dillon, and Olivia." She counted the names off on her fingers. "So, who's missing?"

"That would be Grace, the baby of the family." Nick reached around Jace and grabbed two waters from the open fridge. "She must be out with my mom running errands. Come on, let's go work in my room where it's somewhat quiet."

Heat rose in her cheeks. She'd never been in a teenage boy's bedroom before. But with a glance around, she realized it was probably the only place they could work. Besides, Nick would be a perfect gentleman. He hadn't shown any interest in her except for working on their mission.

"Is it always this hectic around here?" They sidestepped over Dillon on their way to the stairs. The youngest brother, now sprawled out on the floor, drove a tank toward a tower of blocks. The tank successfully crashed into the structure, sending blocks everywhere, including into Eve's shin.

Nick nodded. "Yep, now you know why I enjoyed working at your place."

"Are you kidding? I love it here! All this activity is fantastic!"

Disbelief showed in his eyes. "You are definitely a glass-half-full kind of person, aren't you?"

Was that a bad thing? "Maybe. I'm still trying to figure you out though."

"What do you mean?" Nick led the way up the stairs.

"Today you've been much more laid back. All the other times I've seen you, you've been very serious. You know, in control."

Nick laughed. "Jace calls it my politician mode. Ever since we've been in the public eye, I've felt this pressure to be responsible when in public. I don't mean to do it; it just comes out."

***

They were deep into their internet search for news about Endelbourg when the bedroom door flew open. A little blond tornado in a purple princess dress hurled herself across the room toward Nick.

"Hey, Grace." He caught her mid-leap, hung her upside down for a moment as her arms and legs flailed around, then set her on her feet.

Eve's heart melted. That was possibly the most adorable thing she'd ever seen.

Nick's mother, whom Eve recognized from her research, leaned against the doorframe.

"Hi, Mrs. Hammond. I'm Eve."

"Nice to meet you. I'm glad you braved the madhouse and decided to work here. Nick told me you have some sort of joint project you're working on?"

"Yes." Nick and his quick thinking!

"Would you like to stay for dinner?" She motioned for Grace to join her.

"I would love that. Let me call my parents and let them know."

Grace squealed and twirled in approval.

After his mother somehow steered the pint-sized princess out of the room, Nick turned to Eve. "Dinner, huh? You are a glutton for punishment."

"No, it'll be fun. Your family is great. Although, I was surprised that Jace is your brother. That day at your school, I figured he was your best friend."

He raked his hand through his dark hair. "Yeah. I don't really have anyone I hang out with anymore."

"Why not?" He was good-looking, smart, athletic, sweet, semi-famous, all the ingredients to be popular.

He paused a moment as if considering his words. "After orchestrating my dad's run for office, things got a little crazy. One of the unforeseen complications was that we all became somewhat famous. People recognized us everywhere we went. It was odd when people we'd never met called us by name. I knew how this town worked and that there were plenty of people who wanted my dad to fail. And some would use any means necessary to take him down. I didn't want to be the cause of his loss, so I felt pressured to act appropriately all the time. I made sure to dress nicely, get good grades, work hard at rowing, and stay away from anything that could possibly cause a scandal. Over time, it became easier to just stop hanging out with people."

He gave a slight shrug of his shoulders like it was no big deal. She was shocked by how much he had sacrificed. Would a hug be appropriate or out of line?

"Wow. That's intense."

"Yeah. Funny thing is, anytime something negative came out about my dad or our family, I felt unbelievably guilty for putting my family in the situation. But once you arrived, I realized it was God's plan and I didn't need to take on that burden. You have no idea how freeing that was."

No one should have to shoulder that much pressure. No wonder she was supposed to come help him.

He grabbed his water bottle and twisted off the cap. "So anyway, did you find anything out about Endelbourg?" He took a long drink.

Guess he was done talking about the past.

Taking the not-so-subtle hint, she turned her laptop toward him. "A little. Apparently, Endelbourg is still a monarchy. The king who ruled for decades recently died, and his son has inherited the crown."

He scanned the article. "I read that too. It sounds like the son is making all sorts of changes, breaking old alliances, and forming new ones. People are worried he's changing their democratic monarchy into a dictatorship."

She nodded, not exactly sure what that even meant. "That trade agreement your dad mentioned must be one of the changes he's implementing. How could *we* possibly help with that?"

"Who knows. At least we have a little background knowledge now. Hopefully our dinner at the embassy will bring some clarity." He shut his laptop. "Speaking of dinner, we should head downstairs before Jace eats all the food."

Mealtime at the Hammond home could only be called an experience. Eve marveled at the massive amounts of food on the table. The large family remained quiet and respectful for the prayer, then the meal turned into a free-for-all. Arms reached for food, rolls were tossed across the table, silverware clattered against the plates. A central lazy Susan, spun by Dillon with a little too much vigor, sent veggies rolling out of a bowl and across the table.

Lexus devoured the items that fell onto the floor. Eve barely had a chance to dish any food for herself since she sat next to Jace, who vigorously scooped several helpings of everything onto his plate.

The tall and handsome Senator Hammond, who had the same dark hair as his son but with graying temples, shared a small amount about his day then focused his attention on each of his children, peppering them with questions. Olivia explained in great detail the experiment she had performed at school, while at the same time Gabriella talked about her upcoming gymnastics event and Dillon sang a song about donkeys. Somewhere along the way, Grace ended up under the table. Eve watched the chaos, mesmerized by every crazy moment.

She caught Nick watching her and smiled. This madness was amazing.

Chapter Fifteen

As the driver pulled up to the Endelbourg Embassy, Nick spotted Eve and her father standing outside the mansion, staring at the grand building. It had been a few days since he'd brought her to his home and introduced her to the chaos that was his life, and it was great to see her again. Tonight, she looked like she'd been transported from the 1950s. Her light green dress flared out from her small waist and hung down to her calves. A matching headband pulled back her straightened hair. He missed the wayward curls.

"Hey, Albuquerque."

She turned and smiled. "Isn't this place amazing?"

"It is. Speaking of amazing, you look fantastic." Most pathetic line ever. Real smooth.

Her eyes widened, then she spun around, her dress fanning out. "Thanks. You don't think it's too much?"

"No, it's perfect. I gotta say I love your unique style."

"Thanks!" Her eyes lit up. "I've gone to Catholic schools my whole life and get so tired of wearing plaid and polos. When I get a chance to wear what I want, I might as well have fun with it."

Who thinks like that? "Makes sense to me."

They followed their fathers, who were deep in conversation, into the impressive embassy. Heavy, luxurious drapes and plush rugs added a touch of color to the dark wood which dominated the enormous entryway. Eve ran her hand along the dark, ornately carved banister of the grand staircase.

The chief of staff, Mr. Stoltz, greeted them with a heavy, German-sounding accent. Nick guessed the talkative, outgoing man to be in his sixties. He gave the guests a quick tour of the main floor, explaining how some of the rooms had been converted to offices, but others, like the dining room and parlor, were left for entertaining.

In the parlor, they were introduced to the ambassador, who spoke only a few words in greeting. His wife stayed glued to his side and simply nodded. Nick assumed she didn't speak much English. Mr. Stoltz motioned someone over to join them.

"Nick, Eve, this is the ambassador's daughter, Natalia."

They turned in unison to greet Natalia. He hoped the shock he felt didn't register on his face. *Don't stare.*

He wasn't sure what he expected an ambassador's daughter to look like, but it certainly wasn't this goth girl, who wore heavy eyeliner and black lipstick. Her unnaturally dark hair matched her all-black outfit which consisted of a tank top, leather miniskirt, fishnet tights, and lace-up boots.

After the introductions, Mr. Stoltz led the adults toward the corner bar for a cocktail. Nick recovered his cool and smiled politely at Natalia. Her scowl turned into a seductive grin as she sidled up to him, uncomfortably close. Heat crept up his neck. He fought the urge to walk away. He was a guest in her home and couldn't embarrass her like that. Just suck it up and deal with it. She slid her arm around his. What was with this girl? He'd been taught over the last year to be polite and diplomatic in every situation. He couldn't believe this diplomat's daughter could so brazenly flirt in front of her father and their guests.

***

Eve felt completely invisible while Natalia clung to Nick's arm and whispered things close to his ear. Who did this goth girl think she was? Sure, she lived here. And sure, Nick was single and looked irresistibly handsome tonight in his suit and tie. And sure, he smelled tantalizingly amazing like spices, leather, and awesomeness. But still. The worst part was he didn't seem at all put off by this girl's attention.

Eve's emotions were all over the place as she watched this uncomfortable public display of affection. Should she embrace the anger and push the European bad girl off him? Or should she acknowledge the rejection and feel sorry for herself?

Stop being a diva. She wasn't here to make friends with Natalia, as if that would ever happen. She wasn't even technically here on a date with Nick, even if she did maybe dress with a little extra care this evening. She had more important things to deal with than teenage drama: things like finding out her mission from God.

Forcing herself to walk away from Nick and Natalia, who didn't even notice her departure (*forget about it, Eve!*), she joined her father, who stood next to the chief of staff, while Senator Hammond and the ambassador were deep in conversation. The ambassador's wife stood awkwardly next to him.

"This building is amazing," Eve told Mr. Stoltz when he nodded at her arrival.

"Yes, it has a rather interesting history as well. It was built for a man named Alexander Stewart, a lumber baron and congressman from the state of Wisconsin."

She had to really concentrate, deciphering his words through his thick accent. "This was someone's home?" What would it be like to live in such a grand estate? Like something out of a fairy tale.

Her father redirected her thoughts. "Many of the embassies were once private homes. At the turn of the twentieth century, Massachusetts Avenue became known as Millionaires' Row. But eventually the homes became too much to handle and began to be sold. They worked well as embassies, and now this area is known as Embassy Row."

Mr. Stoltz took a sip of his drink. "Sadly, Mr. Stewart only lived here a few years before he died. His widow continued on here alone until her death in 1931. But in 1941 during World War II, their daughter sold it to the Grand Duchess of Endelbourg, who lived here in exile due to the German occupation of her beloved country."

"Wow, that's interesting." Dad might be right; history could be fascinating.

"Eventually the Endelbourg government bought the home, and it has served as the embassy ever since."

When an elderly gentleman in a white suit announced dinner, the small group moved on to the lavish spread of food awaiting them in the dining room. The scrumptious aromas made Eve's mouth water, but her appetite was ruined by watching Natalia flirt with Nick. Nick was seated directly across from her, and Natalia insisted on sitting right next to him.

Nick flashed a smile at Eve. Maybe he was trying to convey his apologies for being monopolized by Natalia. She glanced away.

Small talk accompanied the delicious four-course meal until Mr. Stoltz asked her dad a question which quieted the entire table.

"I'm wondering, Professor Donahue, what do you know about the Hamilton, Meyers, and Barrett partnership?"

Senator Hammond chuckled. Dad set his fork down then slowly picked up his wine glass.

"Well, you have been doing a lot of reading and research if you've heard about that."

Something in Dad's tone caught her attention. "Who were Hamilton, Meyers, and whoever he said?"

All eyes turned to Dad. "Well, there has been speculation about these gentlemen for over a century. But I want to make it clear: it is only a rumor. Usually, only treasure hunters and conspiracy theorists are drawn to these baseless rumors. No offense, Mr. Stoltz, but I don't want you to be misled."

Treasure hunters? Her gaze flew to Nick. His eyebrows shot upward.

"How fascinating." Eve hoped to prompt her dad to keep talking.

Mr. Stoltz dabbed the corner of his mouth with his napkin. "Don't worry, Professor Donahue, I only want to understand where such rumors come from. Besides, what better dinner conversation than an intriguing mystery?"

Senator Hammond smirked. "Yes, what is more exciting than Confederate gold?"

A tingle of excitement bubbled up inside Eve.

"Gold?" Even Natalia showed signs of interest now.

Mr. Stoltz reached for his wine glass. "Forgive my ignorance, but why is it a conspiracy? Quite a bit of gold went missing after your Civil War, correct?"

Eve's dad nodded, keeping his eyes on Mr. Stoltz. "That is true. But the theories of what happened to the gold are heavily disputed. Most historians believe any gold would have been divided among the leaders of the Confederates, and those wealthy men would have used it to live happily ever after."

"But is it not true those men were watched for many years because they were suspected of having the gold, and none of them ever had sudden vast amounts of wealth?" Mr. Stoltz held Dad's gaze.

Everyone's eyes went back and forth between the two men, like an intense tennis match. Everyone except for the ambassador's wife who continued to eat in silence.

"True, but they would've known they were being watched so would have been cautious on how they spent the money. Also, many believe if any treasure did exist, it was probably held onto to see how things went after the war. You must understand, it was an extremely fragile time for our country. The war had recently ended, the North and the South were still greatly divided, and the president had just been assassinated. The gold would've needed to stay hidden, in case things in this new united country didn't go well."

Eve could barely breathe as the story unfolded.

Mr. Stoltz tilted his head. "Then what do you believe happened to it?"

"Again, *if* any gold existed, it was probably passed down to the descendants of the men in question."

"Or they buried it." Mr. Stoltz swirled the ruby-colored wine in his glass, creating a dramatic pause.

"So, you think whoever had the gold hid it somewhere?" Skepticism dripped from Dad's question.

"Yes. And I believe they left clues."

The silence in the room was palpable. Eve held her breath. *Clues?*

Her dad spoke first. "You're talking about the symbol."

"What symbol?" Eve's voice came out in a whisper.

Mr. Stoltz grinned like the Cheshire Cat. "This symbol." He set down his glass. Reaching into his breast pocket, he removed a piece of paper, then passed it around the table.

Eve's hand shook as she examined the symbol—a perfect triangle with a star in the center. Was this it? The key to what she and Nick had been called to do? Nick's intense stare prickled her skin. She glanced up and held his penetrating gaze. For a moment it seemed as if they were the only two people in the room.

Senator Hammond's voice broke the surreal moment. "Why do you think this is a clue?"

The overwhelming silence continued another moment while Mr. Stoltz scanned the faces around the table. He clearly relished the attention. "This symbol was found on the graves of Mr. Hamilton, Mr. Meyers, and Mr. Barrett. As you pointed out, treasure hunters and conspiracy theorists have investigated these men for years. This symbol has never appeared on any other Confederate leader's tomb. These men died at different times, but for some reason this symbol followed them to their final resting places."

"What do you think the symbol means?" Senator Hammond shot Eve's dad a look then turned back to the chief of staff.

Mr. Stoltz took a long sip from his glass. "Ah, well now that is the question. If only we could decipher the clue, we might find the gold."

Chapter Sixteen

Nick stared at his phone. Why'd he answer her text so quickly? What happened to his usual pros and cons analysis?

He dropped onto the edge of his bed and buried his head in his hands. What would she think? Should he back out? He wasn't trying to lead her on. Was he? He reread her message.

> Would love to see you again. Why don't you come over tonight, and we'll hang out?
> Natalia

It had been a few days since the dinner party, and he wasn't entirely surprised when he heard from Natalia. But meeting up with her, like he just agreed to do? That probably ranked pretty high on the stupid-move list.

Maybe he should've said no, but sometimes he got a little tired of being cautious and playing the part of the perfect political son every moment of every day. Exhausted, in fact. Everywhere he went, with every person he met, he felt this pressure to be Perfect Nick. But the last few weeks hanging out with Eve had given him a glimpse of life outside the protective cocoon he'd enclosed himself in. He missed being a regular teen.

During the campaign there'd been an incident at a party, and Nick vowed never again to be the guy who gave his dad's opponents ammunition. That close call was the main reason he'd stopped hanging out with friends. He didn't know whom he could trust. So, to get a text from someone like Natalia, someone who pushed the boundaries and didn't care what the world thought of her, made him nervous.

He rubbed his temples. So why had he agreed to meet her?

Because despite everything, this could be an opportunity to find out more about Endelbourg and what he and Eve were being called to accomplish. That was the most important thing.

He glanced at the phone. Who was he kidding? Natalia had a dangerous edge that was exciting. End of story.

***

After dinner, Nick took the Metro to D.C.

He had no trouble finding Natalia. She strode toward him as he approached the embassy, dressed like a heavy metal rock star in a black bomber jacket, black leggings and black lace-up Doc Marten boots. She glanced over her shoulder, then grabbed his arm and pulled him down a side street, away from the glare of the streetlights.

Partway down the street, he stopped walking. "Let me guess. You snuck out?" What had he expected? A night at the embassy playing board games?

Her eyes, lined heavily in black as always, seemed to hold a dare. "So? You aren't that much of a goody two-shoes, are you?"

Nick pictured the headlines. "Ambassador's daughter caught with senator's son." Not good. He looked over his shoulder, half expecting someone to be following them.

"Come on, Nick. Don't you ever do things just because you want to?" She swung around to walk backwards, beckoning him along with one finger.

Why not let loose for one night? He followed.

In silence, she led him up a street backed by a wooded area. They scrambled down a steep embankment and ended up at a bike trail that meandered next to a stream.

"Is this Rock Creek?" Where was she taking them?

"Yep. Come on. I want to show you something."

As they continued down the trail, Nick glanced around, a prickle of discomfort shivering up his spine. If anyone else was in this secluded area, they probably weren't doing anything legal. Somewhere in the dark, a branch snapped. He swung toward the sound as the uneasy prickle escalated, rippling up the back of his neck. *What am I doing?*

Ignoring the model-son part of his brain, he reluctantly followed Natalia across a small bridge then toward a steep hill. A chain-link fence blocked their way.

Nick bit back a relieved sigh. Good. Maybe now they could get out of here.

She turned to face him, her mouth twisting into a mischievous smirk.

He stared at the dark incline in front of them. "What is this place?"

"Oak Hill Cemetery." Natalia's gaze bore into his.

"What're we doing here?" His anxiety increased by the moment.

"Wouldn't you like to know?" Her words seemed more challenge than question.

She walked a few feet along the fence then stopped at a section that had been pulled away from the post. Bending, she shimmied her way through the gap.

Every part of his being wanted to turn around and leave. He ran a hand through his hair. What should he do?

Natalia shot him one last look over her shoulder before traipsing up the hill toward the gravestones.

Now what?

You can't leave her here alone. You're the fool who agreed to meet her. No backing out now. He sighed. *Stupid conscience.* He squeezed himself through the hole and followed her. *This is why I don't hang out with people anymore.*

His long strides soon caught up with her. "I'm guessing this isn't the first time you've come here."

She shrugged. "Living in an embassy surrounded by guards is stifling. I like to come here to get away."

"What do you do here?" The moment the words came out he wished he hadn't asked.

"Whatever my companions want to do." She batted her eyelashes.

Her dangerous allure was losing its charm.

They wandered up the steep hill through a maze of towering trees and meandering paths. Moonlight illuminated a few of the graves. Nick took note of the dates chiseled into the headstones: 1700s and 1800s. Despite his reluctance to be there, the history was fascinating. Still, as his anxiety increased, his interest diminished.

"You said you wanted to show me something. Is this it?"

"Relax. Are you always so uptight?"

Pretty much.

They circled around a mausoleum and went down a darker path. He stumbled once on the uneven walkway. Finally, Natalia stopped.

Trees blocked most of the moonlight there, and Nick silently berated himself. This was insane. He should not be here alone with this girl. He'd put himself in a bad situation. Why? Trying to prove something to himself? *Well, it worked. You proved you're an idiot.*

She turned and lifted onto her tiptoes, pressed herself against him. He took a step back.

"Natalia, if you brought me out here to fool around, then you've wasted your time and mine."

"Well, a girl can hope, can't she?" She sank back down to her flat feet. "But fine. I didn't bring you here for that reason, although it could've been a fun extra benefit."

He took another step back.

She laughed. "One of these days you'll come around, Nick Hammond. I'm kind of irresistible. But this is what I wanted to show you." A beam of light from her phone illuminated a small gravestone.

Beloved Son James Barrett Died in the Battle of Gettysburg 1865.

Underneath the epitaph, a triangle with a star in the center had been carved into the stone, the word Ohio etched below it.

"The symbol." *Whoa.* He bent down and ran his hand across the chiseled stone.

"Yeah, I sneak out here a lot, and this place is the most hidden part of the cemetery, so no one can see me. I've noticed the symbol but never thought anything of it

until the other night when Mr. Stoltz showed us that paper."

Nick pulled out his phone and snapped a picture.

Natalia leaned over him, whispering in his ear. "With
that out of the way, what do you feel like doing now?"

"Going home."

Chapter Seventeen

A huge smile spread across Eve's face when her phone rang. Nick! She hadn't had much time alone with him at the embassy the other night since Natalia had monopolized his time. Juggling to answer the call, she nudged open the apartment door with her shoulder, plopped her backpack on the floor, and kicked the door shut. Home at last.

"Hi! I'm glad you called." Lacking the patience to wait for a reply, she continued. "I'm excited about this Civil War thing. I know a hundred-fifty-year-old mystery about Confederate gold with no ties to Endelbourg seems like a long shot for our 'calling' (and I have no idea why God wants us to find it), but it sounds way more interesting than a boring trade agreement."

"You're right. Guess what I discovered last night."

"Just tell me." Anxious to hear the details, she plopped onto the couch while he told her about the grave at Oak Hill Cemetery. But her excitement about the discovery lost much of its appeal because she couldn't get past one crushing fact. He'd gone to meet *her*.

"You were with Natalia?"

"Yes. Didn't you hear what I said about the grave she showed me?"

"Just so I have a clear picture here. You and Natalia snuck into a cemetery in the middle of the night?" She threw her head backwards against the sofa and almost welcomed the burst of pain when it smacked against the wooden trim.

A slight pause. "Eight-thirty doesn't really count as the middle of the night."

"And she took you to a secluded area to do what?" Eve couldn't get past the unwelcome mental screenplay of Natalia fawning all over him.

He cleared his throat. "To show me the symbol on the grave. She said she sneaks out often and hangs out there in the cemetery. She'd noticed the symbol before but never gave it much thought until Mr. Stoltz showed us that drawing the other night."

"She goes to the cemetery by herself?" She rubbed the tender goose egg on her head. That girl was a menace. *Sorry, God. I know that's not nice, but it's kinda true.*

Another pause. "Maybe she has company sometimes? But you're missing my point."

She sighed. "Fine. I'll focus." *He's right. This is a mission from God, not the time to be jealous of a girl I barely know.* "Mr. Stoltz told us treasure hunters have never found the symbol anywhere except on the graves of those three men. How could they have missed this one for all these years?"

"I bet they were only searching for known Confederate leaders, not their children."

A small twinge of excitement pushed aside her distress. "You said 'Ohio' is written under it. Any idea what that could mean?"

"No idea. But that's not the oddest thing. Without mentioning the symbol, I told my dad about the grave. He didn't think it made any sense."

She sat a little straighter. "What didn't make sense?"

"First of all, the grave indicated James Barrett died in the battle of Gettysburg in 1865. But the battle took place in July of 1863. The war ended in 1865. Also, the casualties at Gettysburg were massive. There were so many bodies, they usually dug mass graves. Dad thought it odd that one soldier would have been brought home. I did a little research and didn't even find a James Barrett who fought in Gettysburg. Then I went on this ancestry site my mom belongs to. Turned out Charles Barrett, who was a builder and designed a lot of the houses around here, did have a son named James, but he died as an infant."

Eve paced the living room. "Weird. Maybe the grave is phony." She gasped at a sudden thought. "I wonder if Barrett's third of the gold is buried there."

"That's exactly what I thought." Excitement edged his voice, like an underlying electric vibration. "At lunchtime, I called the Georgetown Historical Society which keeps the records of Oak Hill Cemetery and found out the grave had first been dug in October of 1865, a few months after the entire war had ended. Then, in 1868, someone dug it up again."

She stopped pacing. "Really? Maybe the gold was hidden there." But the spike of enthusiasm deflated in the next instant. "If the gold was there, it was probably moved, right? Why else would someone dig up a phony grave?"

"I still haven't gotten to the strangest part."

Eve grinned at the eagerness in his tone. "Nick, you're killing me here. What did you find?"

He laughed. "Fine. Are you sitting down?"

She sank back onto the couch. "I am now."

"After it was dug up. *That's* when the family placed the current gravestone there, replacing the old one."

"I don't get it." She stared out the window at the Washington Monument. "Why would Mr. Barrett bother to pay for a new gravestone if the gold was gone?"

"Exactly."

Confidence, not frustration, colored his tone. What was she missing?

Oh.

"You think the symbol is a clue to where they moved the treasure?"

"I think it's an interesting possibility, don't you?"

Eve wanted to share his obvious elation, but someone had to face reality.

"The symbol on the headstone is accompanied by the word 'Ohio.' I hate to be the bearer of bad news, but if they moved the treasure to Ohio, our treasure hunt is over. In case you didn't know, Ohio's a rather large state. Believe me, I know. We drove the whole way across it when we moved."

"If Barrett had a secret place with the symbol, maybe the other two did as well."

Suddenly it didn't seem so hopeless. Why hadn't she thought of that?

"I think we need to find out everything we can about Hamilton and Meyers."

"I think you're right."

***

She wanted to be ecstatic about this new development but couldn't stop thinking about *how* Nick had discovered all the information: from his little rendezvous with

Natalia. Why was he interested in her? She wasn't his type. Though, maybe that was the reason he was into her. *Boys.*

Maybe keeping busy would help erase from her mind the images of those two alone in a secluded graveyard. She made a batch of lemon bars, then did a little online research while the treats cooled. Their newest plan called for her to research Hamilton while Nick looked into Meyers. They'd compare notes in a day or two.

The info she found didn't appear to lead anywhere. She gave up for the moment and carried a plate of the lemon bars across the hall.

Mrs. Grant opened the door a crack in answer to Eve's knock. "What do you want?"

"I'm tired of my own company. Would you like to share these with me?" She held up the plate.

Mrs. Grant eyed the offering. "I suppose you can come in. If you must."

Eve carried the plate in and set it on the coffee table.

"Do you want a sherry to go with them?" Mrs. Grant stood with her hands on her hips.

"Um, I'm not old enough to drink." She sat down. "Do you have any milk?"

"You are rather needy, aren't you?" Mrs. Grant shuffled into the kitchen and brought back one glass of milk and one glass with amber-colored liquid sloshing around in the lower half.

"Thank you."

Mrs. Grant sat in her chair, her intense stare never leaving Eve's face. She would've made a great interrogator. Eve squirmed under the extreme scrutiny, thinking of something to say.

"Have you lived here in D.C. a long time?"

"Why do you want to know?"

Visiting with a neighbor shouldn't be so difficult. "I'm just making conversation."

"I've lived here long enough." Mrs. Grant shifted her gaze to the lemon bars.

"Miss LaVonne told me you worked for the Smithsonian."

"Assistant to the Secretary of the Smithsonian." She reached for one of the treats then glanced at Eve. "For those in the room who don't know, that is the person appointed head of the museum."

Eve sighed at the thought of the Smithsonian and the vision of her and Nick tossing the flying disc in front of the red castle. "The Smithsonian is lovely, isn't it? It would be a great place to go hang out for an afternoon. A perfect place for a date with a boy who liked you."

"Do you always talk this much?" Mrs. Grant broke off a piece of lemon bar and popped it into her mouth.

Did she? Eve thought for a moment. "I guess. I miss my sister who's back at college and my best friend who now lives in South America. I haven't met many people since I moved here."

"You have that boyfriend." Mrs. Grant broke off another piece of the dessert.

She shook her head. "He's only a friend. And I think he's interested in someone else. Which makes total sense. She's pretty, has a cool accent, and is kind of aggressive. Maybe guys like that sort of thing. I don't know why I care . . . it's not like we're soulmates or anything." Completely absorbed in her feelings, Eve didn't pay attention to the usually standoffish gray cat circling her legs. "Sorry, I'm sure you don't care about my problems."

"No, I don't." Mrs. Grant took a swig of her drink.

Eve chose to ignore her neighbor's surliness. "I mean why wouldn't he be interested in me? I try to be nice, and some people think I'm pretty funny, and I don't think I'm horrible to look at or anything. But I guess I can't compete with all that European appeal. I'm not that interesting. New Mexico can't compare to exotic Europe." *He's not your boyfriend, get over it.*

Lizzie jumped on Eve's lap and curled in a ball. Eve absently petted the animal.

"But seriously, why do guys have to like that kind of girl? What's wrong with wholesome ones? I know . . . you're thinking I'm obsessing about this, and I shouldn't. You know what? You're absolutely right! If he's not interested in me, then he's not the one for me. Thanks so much for listening. You helped a lot."

Eve kissed Lizzie on top of her furry head, scooched the cat off her lap, then strode to the door. Turning for a final goodbye, she blinked. Twice. Mrs. Grant's perpetually pursed lips were stretched into a completely out of character smile.

Chapter Eighteen

Nick emerged from the elevator and followed a tantalizing aroma straight to Eve's apartment. The door opened and there she stood, a frilly pink apron tied around her waist. Why did the mere sight of her always make him smile?

"Wow, it smells amazing in here. What're you baking?"

"Cupcakes. I thought we'd need a snack as we worked."

Fantastic. "You are quite the baker, aren't you?"

"Yeah, I guess it's my thing." She shut the door behind him.

She removed the apron and placed a cake plate bearing four frosted cupcakes on the coffee table. Dang, he'd missed her the last few days.

"This is fun, kinda like show and tell." She curled up in a lounge chair. "I'll start. Jonathon Hamilton was a well-known Georgetown lawyer. Because he grew up in the South, a lot of people suspected him of being a Southern sympathizer when the war started. He left his practice and went to Virginia, where he quickly rose through the ranks of the Confederate Army."

Unable to resist the temptation for another moment, he nodded his interest and reached for one of the treats.

She shuffled through her notes. "After the war, he returned to Georgetown, but a lot of people thought he was a traitor. His law practice suffered for years, but eventually he built it back up, along with his reputation. His firm handled two controversial cases at the time. They even defended one of the accused in the assassination plot of President Lincoln and his Cabinet. They also represented Robert E. Lee's family, who wanted to be compensated for the land the Union took from them. Can you believe it?"

"That land is now Arlington Cemetery." Nick tried to refrain from talking with his mouth full, hoping to appear focused on Eve's information instead of how delicious the cupcakes were. "If I remember right, the crux of the lawsuit was that the Union government, upset when General Lee decided to fight with the Confederates, took the Lee family estate. They turned the beautiful land into a burial ground for the Union soldiers to spite Lee. After the war, the family sued and sought compensation for the land."

She pushed a strand of hair behind her ear. "Yes, and they won the lawsuit. The government actually paid the Lee family for the land and gave it back to them. But since there were so many bodies already buried on it, the family sold it back to the government."

He nodded. "Yeah, I always thought the whole thing was kinda twisted. Lee had this beautiful estate overlooking D.C., and to punish him for siding with his native Virginia, they took his land and used it as a cemetery for Union soldiers."

"So many sad things happened during that time." Eve's big eyes misted a little and she shook her head. A couple of soft-looking curls fell forward to rest against her face. "Let's see . . . what else? Hamilton's law practice and home were located off M Street in Georgetown near a canal. He wrote about watching the boats on the canal from his desk."

"Nice presentation, Albuquerque." Nick bounced his crumbled napkin off her forehead and ignored her playful glare. "Okay, my turn. Although I didn't find much on Alexander Meyers. He was under a lot of scrutiny at the end of his life as rumors swirled around him and his ties with the Confederacy. The only noteworthy accomplishment I could find involved his job as curator at the Smithsonian. He worked with the first Secretary of the Smithsonian, a Joseph Henry."

He eyed another one of the cupcakes but restrained himself. "The Henry family actually lived at the castle during the Civil War. Some believe Meyers may have lived there as well. At that time, the Mall and surrounding area were still swampland, making the Smithsonian difficult to get to. But with its close proximity to the Capitol, there was some concern it could be vulnerable to attack. The Secretary of War issued some weapons to Joseph Henry. Neither Henry nor Meyers appear to have supported slavery, but they were opposed to the war and believed the South should be allowed to secede."

Eve's face paled. "Remember my vision about us in front of the Smithsonian Castle?" Like he could forget that. "The Smithsonian must be important. Maybe Meyers left that symbol there as well."

Made sense. "How do we find out? The castle is mostly administrative offices now. It's not like we can just waltz in."

She closed her eyes. "I think I know someone who can help us."

He would've thought she'd be overjoyed by this fact. But instead she started chewing on her thumb nail.

***

Nick stood next to Eve as she delivered a timid knock on her neighbor's door. She wiped her hands on her sweater and took a deep breath. Who was this person she was so nervous to talk to?

The door opened, and a tiny, rail-thin elderly woman stared at them. "You again."

Nick recognized the woman they'd met getting off the elevator a few weeks ago. The one with the groceries. She focused her squinted eyes on him.

"Are we having a party?"

"Sorry to disturb you, Mrs. Grant." While Eve spoke, two cats peered out the door at them. "This is my friend Nick. We'd like to ask you a few questions."

"Why?"

Eve's fake smile reminded him of the ones so often worn by many of his dad's congressional colleagues. Certainly not her usual sincere, joyful smile. A protective impulse shot through him.

"Eve has told me so much about you, Mrs. Grant." Maybe he could win over the older woman and rescue Eve from her obvious distress. "It's a pleasure to meet you. Your cats are beautiful. You must spend a lot of time caring for them."

The woman's eyes softened a bit. "You might as well come in if you're going to yammer away like that." She opened the door for them.

Nick grinned at Eve's bewildered expression.

"Thank you so much. We brought you a cupcake." Eve held the frosted treat out to her neighbor.

"Are you trying to fatten me up?"

"Of course not, I just thought you might like one."

At this rate, they'd never get the information they needed. Nick flashed his most charming smile. "They are delicious. Almost as sweet as you, for letting us barge in like we did."

Mrs. Grant's face brightened. "Oh, aren't you darling. You remind me of my son Robert. He was always such a charmer too."

Eve shot him another look of disbelief then turned to her neighbor. "Mrs. Grant, you told me you worked in the Smithsonian offices. Have you ever seen this symbol?" She held out a drawing of the triangle with the star in the center.

"Sure, I've seen that."

Yes! "Would you mind telling us where you saw it? We've been doing some research for a project and would love to see the original."

"Well, good luck with that. It's in the director's office on a large stone mortared into the wall behind his desk."

That didn't seem so hard to find.

"Do you think we could make an appointment to see it?" Eve stuffed the drawing back in her pocket.

Mrs. Grant lowered herself into a chair that looked old enough to belong in the Smithsonian. "No. I've never met this secretary. He was appointed after I left. But my friend Vera took over my position as the assistant to the secretary, and she still works there. According to Vera, he has no desire to meet with the public. He shows up every day, even Saturdays, for the sake of appearance, but farms out most of his duties to others. He's quite the introvert and doesn't give interviews unless they're required by the board. I hear his staff barely sees him. And Vera is as tough as I was and keeps everyone away. Her nickname is The General."

Eve's hopeful expression disappeared.

Nick reached for the elderly woman's hand. "Mrs. Grant, thank you for the information. You were very kind to let us stop by unannounced and take up so much of your valuable time."

She smiled. "Oh, you weren't disturbing me at all. You should come with Eve when she visits the cats. I could use some stimulating conversation."

He ignored the urge to defend Eve's awesome skills as a conversationalist. "I'll do that. Thanks, Mrs. Grant." He kissed her hand.

Eve's jaw dropped. He responded with a grin and a wink.

Chapter Nineteen

Eve,

I think about you often and wonder how things are going. I believe in you and am always here for you, but I'm worried as well. Remember to pray over every decision so you are certain of what you should do. If God is leading you, that could also make you a target for evil. Be cautious and aware, and don't be fooled by false leads. Please keep me posted.

In Christ,

Father Romero

Hi, Father,

So good to hear from you. Sorry I didn't update you sooner. Darn school and exams got in the way of our investigation. We haven't been able to do anything for the last few weeks, but now we're both on spring break and can focus our attention on the task at hand. Thank you for the words of advice. I will be careful, but honestly, we don't really know what we're supposed to be doing. I'm heading out the door now and hope to have more answers soon. Wouldn't it be easier if God simply sent my guardian angel to tell me exactly what I should do?

Thank you for believing me. This is such a strange situation, and it's comforting to have someone I can talk to. Will keep you updated!

Eve

On her way out of the building, Eve stopped at the front desk.

Ms. LaVonne greeted her with one of her famous smiles. "Where are you headed off to on this fine day?"

Eve leaned her elbows on the counter. "Meeting a friend down on the Mall."

LaVonne arched one eyebrow. "You and the millions of tourists who descend on this city this time of year, not to mention all those school groups that roll into town. Take my word for it, the best times to enjoy all the museums are during the fall and winter."

"Good advice, but there's something we need to take care of."

"Well, better you than me. By the way, I like what you've done with your hair. You've tamed down the wild-banshee look."

"Um. Yeah." Eve's hands flew to her hair, tugging on her curls. "I thought maybe if I grew it out, it wouldn't be quite so insane."

"Honey, you wear it any way you like." She jabbed her long blue fingernail toward Eve's face. "You are an original, and believe me, it's much more fun to be unique than waste time trying to be like everyone else."

"I agree, but sometimes the wild-banshee style is a little too much to handle. Hey, can I ask you a question?"

"Sure, honey."

"It's about Mrs. Grant."

LaVonne leaned back in her chair and held her palm up toward Eve. "Tread carefully."

She nodded in understanding. No one wanted to be on Mrs. Grant's bad side, but she needed to find out more about the woman and what made her so . . . Mrs. Grant-ish.

"One day when I visited her, she mentioned a son. In the past tense. Did something happen to him?"

LaVonne motioned Eve closer and lowered her voice.

"Oh, it's such a sad story. He died unexpectedly from a rare heart condition just a year after she lost her husband. She always had a rough edge to her, but after they both passed away, she pretty much shut herself away from the world."

Eve's hand shot to her mouth. "That's horrible. Thanks for telling me, Miss LaVonne." She waved goodbye then headed out the door.

Before meeting Nick, she had a stop to make. She'd promised her mom she'd come by the Kennedy Center for a tour of where she worked. Even though it was a Saturday and the first day of spring break, her mom still had to work.

As Eve rode the crowded bus to Foggy Bottom, she thought about ways to help Mrs. Grant.

Her mom waited in front of the giant white theater complex. They toured the office areas and the basement. Walking through the building brought back memories, like the thrill of literally bumping into Nick, and then the sting of rejection as he walked away. Funny, she still didn't know how he felt about her. Were boys always so hard to read?

They joined one of the official groups touring the six theaters and enormous hallways. The tour guide pointed out many of the pieces of art located throughout the building.

Apparently, building a theater complex had been President Kennedy's idea. After his death, Congress made it a memorial to honor him. The building's marble, crystal chandeliers, and artwork were all donated by countries from around the world as a tribute to the slain president. Paintings, sculptures, tapestries, and every other imaginable form of art were on display throughout the various theaters. No wonder they wanted someone with museum experience to watch over all the pieces.

Eve leaned toward her mom. "Are there any gifts from Endelbourg?" She had never even heard of the small country before. But after all her research, she was fascinated by it.

"Yes, come on."

They snuck away from the rest of the group. Her mom led the way to the Opera House and up a set of stairs to the Box Tier, where she pointed out a white sculpture of three white teardrops stacked on top of each other. "This piece is called 'Uprising.' Did your visit to the embassy spark this interest in Endelbourg?"

"Something like that. Thanks for the tour, Mom. It was fun seeing where you work."

"I'm glad you could stop by. Would you like to join me for lunch? There's a restaurant on the Terrace Level."

"Thanks, but I'm meeting Nick." She tried without much success to curb her smile.

The edge of her mom's mouth twitched. Not usually a good sign. Now what was wrong?

"Are any of the girls from school around this week? I haven't heard you talk much about them. I'm sure there must be some nice ones."

Eve fought the urge to roll her eyes.

"They're all nice. But most of them are away for spring break. Nick happens to be here this week and offered to show me around."

"Oh. Well, that's nice of him. What're you two doing this afternoon?"

Probably wouldn't go over very well to say, "Sneaking into the offices of the Smithsonian's director."

"We're meeting at the Mall, then I think we'll drop in to one of the museums. Thanks again for the tour. This place is great."

"I'm glad you could come by. You and Nick have fun."

Eve hugged her mom then took the Metro to the Mall. She spotted Nick sitting on a bench in front of the Smithsonian Castle. Her heart flipped when he glanced up.

"Hey, Albuquerque." He stood as she neared. "We've got a little time to waste. I thought we'd look a little conspicuous just standing and staring at the place like we're casing the joint, so I brought something for us to do."

He pulled a flying disc from his backpack and threw it to her. She caught it and threw it back, then glanced to her right. The Washington Monument seemed, in that moment, to fill the whole world, and her head spun. Like déjà vu but not that simple. The vision she had seen so many times during the past six months was happening, right here, right now. Overwhelmed, she sank down into the grass.

Chapter Twenty

Horrified, Nick rushed toward Eve, who'd crumpled to the ground right out of the blue.

"Are you all right?" He knelt beside her. She was nearly as white as the marble monument behind her.

Wide, glazed eyes stared into his. "It happened. Just like this."

What was she talking about?

He helped her sit up. "*What* happened?"

"My vision." Her gaze bounced from one building to the next like she didn't know where she was. "This is exactly what has been swirling around in my head for the past six months. You, in front of the Smithsonian Castle. The Washington Monument to my right. A flying disc. Blue sky. All of it."

"Whoa." He sank down onto the grass next to her. "That's incredible." And a little freaky. "Well, I guess we're on the right track."

She locked eyes with him. "I guess so."

Nick reached for her quavering hand. "Thank you, Lord, for choosing us. Please continue to lead us and guide us to what it is You want us to do. In the name of the Father, the Son, and the Holy Spirit. Amen."

After Eve made the sign of the cross, a small smile slid across her face. "I can't think of anyone else I'd rather be on a mission from God with."

He grinned. "Right back at ya. God's really looking out for me. He paired me with someone with incredible baking skills."

Her laughter brought some color back to her cheeks. "Okay. So, what's our plan?" She rummaged through a drawstring bag and pulled out a water bottle.

"You sure you're up for it?"

She swallowed her sip. "That's why we're here."

"Okay. Well, according to Meredith, every day at precisely twelve o'clock, the director and his office staff leave for a one-hour lunch. No matter what the weather brings, he takes a walk around the entire perimeter of the Mall. His assistant, otherwise known as The General, stays behind to keep an eye on things." He reached out his hand and helped her up.

"One question. Who's Meredith?"

He shot her a sly smile on their way back to the bench where he left his backpack. "She's the lovely lady who answered the phone when I called."

"And she just couldn't wait to give out this information to a stranger?" Her disbelief not only registered in her voice but showed in her eyes as well.

"It's all in the way one asks." He smirked, unable to keep a straight face. How did she bring out the playful side of him that even those closest to him rarely saw?

She shoved his shoulder. "You're unbelievable. So, did this Meredith tell you how to get past The General?"

They sat on the bench, facing the castle.

"No. But I came up with a plan. You're going to distract her while I get a photo of the wall behind the director's desk."

Her eyes shot open. "Me? *I'm* going to distract her?"

"Yep."

Her curls swung back and forth when she shook her head. "Why not you? I'm sure you'd have much better luck with 'The General.' You're the one who could charm a javelina into joining a pack of coyotes."

"What's a ha-va-lena?" *Can't wait to hear this.*

"A wild pig that lives in the desert." She said that like it was something everyone should know.

He laughed. "Well, thanks for the vote of confidence, but you'll have to do the distracting this time. I have to complete the rest of the mission."

Her shoulders fell. "Okay."

The door to the red castle swung open.

"Showtime." Nick nodded toward the tall gentleman who emerged from the building. The man placed a black hat on his head then set off at a steady pace down the path toward the Capitol.

Nick grabbed his loaded backpack, then held out his hand. "Ready?"

She laid her hand on his. "Let's do it."

They made their way into the beautiful building in search of the door Mrs. Grant had told them about that led to the second-floor offices.

After entering the staff area undetected, they made their way up the stairs and down the hall to the director's office in stealth mode. Soon they found themselves in an outer reception area filled with couches and chairs. Beautiful paintings adorned the walls.

His insides jumped around like kids on a trampoline. Time to do this thing.

He sat on a chair near an archway, careful to stay out of sight of The General. On the other side of the open entry, she and her desk stood guard next to a door lead-ing into the director's office.

From his backpack, Nick pulled out several contrap-tions he had made for today's adventure.

First, a baseball cap with an unfolded metal clothes hanger attached to it. A mirror hung from the end. He placed the hat on his head and adjusted the mirror. Now, while sitting at the edge of the archway, he had a perfect view through the open door into the director's office. At her desk, The General tapped away at a computer key-board.

Nick glanced up to find Eve staring at him with wide eyes. He tilted his head toward the archway to indicate it was her turn to shine. She squeezed her eyes shut for a second, took a deep breath, then walked toward the in-timidating-looking woman.

This plan would either succeed or fail spectacularly. Either way, it was time to find out.

"Hi! You must be Vera." Eve approached the woman's tidy desk, devoid of any personal items. On a wall behind the desk, a sketch of the Smithsonian Castle served as the only decoration in the office.

"Can I help you?" Wow. Now that was a voice with about as much warmth as an iceberg. Everything about Vera was stern, from the way her lips pinched together and her eyes peered over her glasses, to the harsh bun on top of her head. No other moniker would fit this woman better than the one she already wore: The General.

"I'm sorry to disturb you." Eve's voice shook a little. "My neighbor, Mrs. Grant, said if I came to the Smith-sonian, I had to stop in and see her friend Vera."

"Iris Grant?"

"Yes, she's my neighbor. I take care of her cats."

Through the mirror, Nick saw Eve peer over her shoulder. He had already started the second contraption he'd brought, a remote-control fire truck with a video camera attached, on its way toward the office. Eve turned back toward Vera and went all chatty, her words running together and her volume excessive.

"I brought you a few of my homemade cinnamon rolls. I hope you like them."

Nick huffed a breath. Eve might not be cut out for spy work.

He focused on the truck, trying not to pay attention to Eve's rambling about New Mexico and her big move to the city. And she'd thought she couldn't distract The General. Turned out she was a natural. Why was he surprised? She'd been distracting him from pretty much everything the last few weeks . . . including now. He winced when the truck nearly ran into her chair leg. *Focus, Nick, focus!*

Eve became so animated when describing her family's drive into town for the first time that he easily guided the device past The General's desk undetected. He had practiced at home, operating the thing while watching in a mirror. But even with practice, figuring out how to make it turn in the right direction took some time. When the truck safely rolled inside the office, he used the remote to raise the little attached ladder. He steadied his hand as he maneuvered the truck in a circle, letting the camera pan the entire room, hopefully capturing everything.

Task complete, he lowered the ladder with the remote and steered the truck back toward his seat in the reception area.

Eve droned on about Mrs. Grant's health and well-being. Vera interjected a few comments but mostly listened while she devoured several cinnamon rolls.

Nick's stomach growled. With any luck Eve had packed extras.

Chapter Twenty-one

Eve concentrated on the reflection of herself and Nick as they sat at the edge of the fountain located in the center of the World War II Memorial. She could stare at his face to her heart's content, and he wouldn't even know. Sneaky. As he reviewed the footage he'd recorded in the director's office, his eyes narrowed and his jaw clenched, completely focused on the task at hand. There were so many different sides to him. Figuring him out was fun.

"Ok, here it is." Nick tilted the small screen of the video camera toward her.

She scooched closer for a better view and found herself transfixed by the tiny, dark stubble on his jawline. Why exactly that was so attractive she didn't have a clue, but she had to force her eyes to shift to the video. Man, it was easy to get distracted around this guy.

"Can you see?"

"Yes . . . yeah, sure." She cleared her throat and focused on the screen.

The remote-control vehicle moved across the carpeted room past Vera's desk and Eve's legs. She grinned a little at the sight of her adorable new saddle shoes. They looked super cute with her rolled-up jeans. Although she could do without the background noise of her incoherent chatter.

The image stopped moving forward and rose up in the air. "Your little contraption is quite ingenious."

"Why, thank you. I figured Dillon wouldn't miss the fire truck from his fleet of remote-controlled vehicles."

"I especially like the doohickey you made to wear on your head. The long wire arm with the attached mirror is a good look on you."

He nudged her with his shoulder. "It's the newest in spyware style. All the great secret agents have them."

She giggled. "Well, I'm glad you were prepared."

"When you're on a mission, you never know what tools might come in handy." He patted his backpack. "I came fully stocked."

"Oh! There it is!" She cringed at her own squeal. Geez! Could she be any more screechy? She pointed at the screen, where a triangular image had become visible behind a large mahogany desk.

"Hold on. Let's zoom in for a better look." He pulled the video camera closer to adjust the image.

The perfect triangle with the star in the center grew larger. Eve leaned in, squinting as she read the single word below the shapes.

"Rose." She turned to look at Nick and her insides spasmed. His face was mere inches from hers. She pulled back in a hurry. "Well, that's less than informative. It could be a woman's name or their favorite flower."

"Yeah." He studied the small screen. "If these symbols are supposed to be clues to where the treasure is, they're not very helpful."

"Of course, we're kind of assuming there even is a treasure and that these symbols actually mean something. Maybe they don't."

Why was this so difficult to figure out?

He turned to face her. "They have to mean something. Why else would your vision have been of us at the museum?"

True. "Something's bothering me. At the dinner party, Mr. Stoltz said no one had ever found more of these symbols besides the ones without words that were on the three gentlemen's graves." She tilted her head toward the video camera. "But this one isn't exactly hidden. Wouldn't someone have known about it?"

Nick stowed the camera away in his backpack. "The people who work at the office aren't exactly the treasure-hunter type. The directors are appointed by Congress, and anyone who works there is all about preserving history. Even if they did hear about the conspiracy theories, I doubt they'd want to risk the castle being torn up, especially since, as you pointed out, there's no proof the treasure actually exists."

"Well, we found Mr. Barrett's extra symbol at the cemetery and now Mr. Meyer's symbol here at the museum. We need to find out if Mr. Hamilton has one as well."

He leaned back, resting on his elbows. "What do we know about him?"

The information she'd researched swirled through her brain. "His offices and home along the canal in Georgetown are long gone. As a lawyer he was involved in dozens of cases, some of which are recorded, but who knows about all the others? His wife died in childbirth during the war, but I couldn't find any record of where he buried her. And he never remarried or had children." She sighed. "For a century, treasure hunters have been trying to figure this out and they've all failed. How are we supposed to do it?"

His grin had a mischievous edge, like he'd just done something naughty. Her eyes narrowed. What was he up to?

"I don't know the answer. But we've used enough brain power for one day. It's our spring break, and we should be having some fun." He stood and held out his hand. "Care to join me?"

Chapter Twenty-two

As they walked along the bustling streets surrounding the Mall toward the Tidal Basin, Nick expertly guided Eve away from all the tourists. They chatted easily about movies and TV shows. He liked how passionate and animated she became when discussing things that interested her. She used her hands and arms as she talked, even her whole body to emphasize points. The tilt of her head, the giggle in her voice, a hunch of her back, walking on her tip toes, it all helped to tell her story. Her effortless joy fascinated him.

As they neared the Jefferson Memorial, she stopped in her tracks. "Oh, wow."

She'd been so engrossed in their conversation, she hadn't noticed the trees surrounding the Tidal Basin. The pink cherry blossoms, in full bloom, created a dazzling pink wonderland circling the water in front of the memorial.

Nick smiled at her awed expression. "Welcome to springtime in D.C."

"I heard about the cherry blossoms, but I didn't realize they would be so spectacular."

She spun in a circle then swept through the pink flowered trees. He snapped a few photos with his phone as she danced around the trees. She gathered a handful of the fallen blossoms and threw them in the air. The pink petals showered down on them. She reminded him of his little sister, full of excitement and wonder, totally oblivious of those around her. Not a trait you usually found in a teenage girl. Just Eve being Eve.

She noticed him taking pictures and stopped twirling. Shoot, he'd ruined the moment. He expected embarrassment to replace her unguarded exuberance. Instead, she reached out her hand.

"Come on. You have to join me."

"Join you?" Don't think so.

She nodded. "Yep, you need to have more fun. You're way too serious."

When he didn't accept her invitation, she grabbed his hand and pulled him along with her, making a figure eight around two trees. She dropped his hand then skipped away. Before she dodged behind a tree, she glanced over her shoulder, a dare in her eyes.

Challenge accepted. He chased after her. She had spun around a large clump of trees, but when he followed, ready to grab her, she wasn't there. Where'd she go? Suddenly, someone jumped on his back.

"I'm pretty stealthy, Hammond."

"I shall never underestimate you again." He held up his phone and snapped a picture.

As she jumped off, she batted a branch, sending blossoms raining down on them. Her face glowed as the pink flowers floated around her. The effect was stunning. On impulse, he grabbed her by the waist and spun her around in circles. Soon they were not only dizzy but laughing hysterically. They collapsed in a heap under one of the trees, ignoring the looks of the tourists who wandered by.

Once Eve caught her breath, she rolled her head to look at him. "Thanks for bringing me here. This place is incredible."

"I thought you'd like it." He picked a stray blossom out of her hair.

"Send me the photos, okay?"

"Of course."

She watched him for a moment then sat up, her brow furrowed.

He leaned on his elbow. "What?"

"I'm trying to figure you out. There are many facets to Nick Hammond. I've seen the sarcastic teenager, the dedicated son and brother, the smooth politician's son, the inventor of gadgets, and now I know there's a goofy side as well."

He reached for a twig with several blossoms still attached. "The goofy side is your fault. I can honestly say I've never danced around the Jefferson Memorial before." He handed the natural little bouquet of flowers to her.

"You've been missing out." She tucked the twig behind her ear then smiled.

Oh, man. Those eyes, that hair, her laugh. Did she have any idea how she made a guy feel?

His phone buzzed, killing the moment. He pulled it out to check the text message.

"It's Natalia." Worst timing ever.

Eve sighed. "What does she want?"

"She invited me over for dinner."

"Oh." Her attention turned to the ducks out on the water of the Tidal Basin. "Are you going?"

He stared at the phone. He had no desire to see Natalia again, but he and Eve were at a dead end in their investigation with no leads to track. "I probably should. This whole thing started at the embassy. Maybe I'll get some more clues somehow."

He watched her stiffen. "Maybe."

Clearly, she wasn't a fan of Natalia. Couldn't blame her. But a golden opportunity to gather more information for their mission couldn't be wasted.

Chapter Twenty-three

Eve schlepped into the apartment building, barely acknowledging LaVonne with an unenthusiastic wave of her hand. Her busy mind might drive her mad. This day had been absolutely wonderful. Right up until Nick received the text from Natalia.

Of course, she and Nick didn't have any kind of special relationship other than an unusual friendship solely based on their belief they shared a mission from God. But it was hard to be logical about it, considering she'd spent months convinced he was her one true love. Now, her feelings for him grew deeper every day. But even if he didn't feel the same way, she worried about him. How could she tell him it would be a huge mistake to get involved with Natalia without coming across as the jealous, wannabe girlfriend she was?

I know, God, I know. Just because I think Nick's totally amazing doesn't mean he's interested in me in a romantic way. I love that You chose us for something incredible, but is there like a rule stating romance can never be part of a bigger plan? Don't get me wrong. Being his friend is great, but it's hard to turn off the feelings that came along with the visions You sent me.

She plodded off the elevator and down the hall to Mrs. Grant's apartment. Her knock was eventually answered by her cantankerous neighbor.

"Oh. You."

"Hi, Mrs. Grant." Eve sulked into the apartment without waiting to be invited.

"Did you bring any goodies today?"

"No. Do you want me to take Tyler on a walk?" Tyler would never leave for a diplomat's daughter who was allergic to color.

Mrs. Grant watched her for a moment then shuffled toward the kitchen. "Just play with him while I make some tea."

Slumping into a chair, Eve found a piece of yarn on the coffee table and slowly moved it around the floor in front of her. The cats stretched and crept closer to the luring temptation. They stared at the swaying yarn, their eyes following the motion. Tyler batted at it half-heartedly. Lizzie was first to run out of patience and pounce. Tyler couldn't hold back any longer either and joined in the game. Even their playfulness couldn't bring Eve out of her funk.

Mrs. Grant carried a silver tray to the coffee table. The teapot matched the cups and saucers, beautifully painted with tiny pink flowers. Eve sighed heavily at the sight, remembering the wonderful afternoon amid the cherry blossoms. So perfect, until . . .

Mrs. Grant poured them each a cup of tea. "Earl Grey cures all that ails you."

"Thank you." She watched Mrs. Grant scoop sugar into the cups. "I saw your friend Vera today. I took her cinnamon rolls."

"You made treats for her but not me?" She handed one of the delicate teacups to Eve.

While Eve recapped her conversation with The General, it became obvious that she had done most of the talking so didn't have much to report about Vera and her life.

"Did you get to see the symbol you were searching for?" Mrs. Grant took a sip of her tea.

"Yes, we did, right where you told us it would be. Thanks." She stared at her tea. Nick had looked so cute in that dorky hat he'd made.

"What's so important about the symbol?" Mrs. Grant's squinty gaze fixed on her.

"It's something from the Civil War that we're researching."

"You and your boyfriend?"

Eve sighed again. If only. "He's not my boyfriend."

Mrs. Grant lifted her cup and peered at Eve over the rim. "But you want him to be."

Eve shut her eyes and pictured them running through the cherry trees, laughing, and taking ridiculous selfies. They were so great together. Why didn't he see that?

"Yes."

Mrs. Grant's gaze seemed glued to Eve's face. "How did you meet a senator's son?"

Eve's eyes snapped open. "You know who he is?"

"I may be old, but I'm not stupid." She tilted her head. "I do watch the news."

"We met at an event at the Kennedy Center." Then she couldn't hold it in a moment longer and blurted out the whole story about her visions and getting her family to move here. Mrs. Grant probably wouldn't believe any of it since she wasn't religious, but Eve couldn't stop herself once she'd begun.

Finished, she held her breath. Why had she gone into all that? Her neighbor's stony silence unnerved her, and she glanced out the window at the fading light of the day. Finally, she braced herself and found the nerve to look at Mrs. Grant again.

Mrs. Grant's gaze went to her fireplace and the photos that lined the mantle. "You really believe God led you here?"

Eve fingered her cross. "Yes."

Mrs. Grant turned to face her. "Why would God use you, of all people?"

The look of total disbelief on her neighbor's sour face tugged at Eve's heart. What to say? Probably nothing would change the woman's mind.

"I don't know. He uses lots of unlikely people." She took a deep breath. "You really don't believe in God, do you?"

Mrs. Grant picked up a small ceramic bird from the side table next to her. Her bony fingers stroked the painted feathers. "I used to."

"What happened to shatter your faith?"

She shouldn't have asked. Mrs. Grant stiffened, and her face hardened. She set the bird down and gathered their teacups.

"Take some advice from someone who has lived a long time. Don't rely on anyone but yourself. Everything and everyone else will fail you."

***

Eve entered the quiet apartment. Her parents were out to dinner, and Nick and Natalia were together. Every time she thought about them it was like a knife to the heart.

She glanced around. Everyone had a life but her. Not bothering to turn on the lights, she trudged down the gloomy hallway to her room to check her email. No new messages. Of course not. Who would be sending any to her besides Father Romero? No one, because she had isolated herself.

Her parents had been bugging her to "make new girl-friends," like that's something you can just put on your to-do list. But maybe they had a point, and she should get involved with something at school, maybe try out for the tennis team. She hadn't played since Mindy left, but what'd she have to lose?

In the meantime, she needed something to occupy her time tonight, but nothing sparked her interest. Not a single movie she wanted to watch, no music she wanted to listen to. She flopped on her bed and picked up one of the books Brooke had given her for Christmas. After reading the same paragraph three times, she conceded defeat. She'd never be able to focus on anything else as long as she kept picturing Nick and Natalia together, her whispering in his ear, him grinning in response.

She flung the book across the room. It smacked against the wall and plummeted to the floor. Eve was so upset she didn't even rush to pick it up and straighten out its crinkled pages. But the sight of the poor innocent novel splayed across the floor eventually pained her booklover self, so she caved in and rescued it. Hey, it wasn't the book's fault that boys were dumb.

After retrieving the book, she slammed it down on her nightstand. Forget him! Forget them both! Who cares what they're doing? No boy was worth moping over. She'd promised herself long ago that she'd never be that girl. She and Nick would finish their mission, then she'd be off to a great college and on her way to an amazing future. That was a good plan. Of course, getting into that great college would require a decent score on her ACT college admittance test which was fast approaching.

With that in mind, she settled in at her desk to study. How pathetic. The first Saturday night of spring break and she was at home alone studying. Didn't matter. Once in college, this night would be a distant memory. She snatched the packet of sample math problems her teacher had given the class and began working on the geometry section with her protractor.

In the middle of figuring out a particular angle, something caught her eye. She stopped, focused on an equilateral triangle she had already plotted on the graph paper. A perfect one, exactly like those in the symbols she and Nick had been tracking. Under the graph paper lay a map of the city, the one they used for their research. Her sample triangle lay on top of several points on the map.

Eve abruptly pushed the math packet and graph paper away. Grabbing the map, she drew a small dot in the middle of Oak Creek Cemetery. She then made a mark on the Smithsonian Castle and, using a ruler, drew a line between the two points. Making the angles sixty degrees from the two locations, she drew another dot on the map and connected the lines.

A perfect triangle.

A chill ran through her body. Holy moly. She knew where the third symbol would be.

Chapter Twenty-four

After Nick walked Eve home from the Metro station, he continued onto Embassy Row toward the Endelbourg Embassy. The afternoon had been awesome. He couldn't even remember the last time he'd had that much fun. At the embassy gate, the guard checked his name off a list and let him enter.

Natalia lounged on the front steps, waiting for him. Her microscopic skirt made it hard to concentrate on anything but her legs. He diverted his attention to the ripped-up t-shirt that completed her outfit—a bodily advertisement of a heavy metal band. As he approached, she slithered up next to him.

He took a step back. "Thanks for inviting me to dinner."

"I would've preferred having you alone, but my father insisted I invite you over for the whole family to enjoy." She batted her eyes.

He smothered a sigh. The upcoming evening promised to be long and exhausting.

This time, dinner was served in a smaller dining room in the private residence section of the enormous home.

Natalia's mother remained mostly silent again, speaking only a few words in German.

Her father, however, talked quite a bit, a striking contrast to his reserved demeanor at the dinner party a few weeks before. As the evening progressed, Nick wondered about the intentions behind this dinner invitation. The ambassador prodded Nick with questions about his father's beliefs, aspirations, and goals. If he intended to be subtle about it, he failed. Was all this a ploy to get close to his father? No doubt having an "in" with the junior senator on the Foreign Relations Committee could be of value to the ambassador.

The onslaught of questions didn't rattle him, though. He easily answered every query in a generic yet diplomatic way. Natalia squirmed in her chair, obviously bored, while her mother calmly ate in silence, seemingly oblivious to any of the conversation.

Eventually, Nick found an opening to change the subject. "I've always been fascinated by the mansions that were turned into embassies. They're spectacular."

"Indeed. This one was built for a lumber baron named Stewart. Sadly, Mr. Stewart didn't live long enough to fully enjoy it. His wife eventually sold it, and it became the embassy. If you're interested, you should talk with Mr. Stoltz, my chief of staff. Both he and his predecessor have also been fascinated with the building's origin and builder. In fact, Mr. Stewart left a diary. I believe it details the construction of his home. He and the builder, a Mr. Barrett, added many unique features."

A frenzied jolt of heightened interest straightened Nick's spine. "Excuse me, did you say Barrett? Charles Barrett built this mansion?" No way.

"Yes."

"So that's how Mr. Stoltz became interested in the Confederate gold."

"Yes, I suppose. I don't know much about it. Who has time for fantasies like that?" The ambassador picked up his steak knife.

A burst of excitement flowed through Nick's veins. "I'd love to see the diary sometime."

The ambassador's eyes narrowed as he scrutinized Nick. "Don't tell me you're one of those treasure hunters who believes the ridiculous theories?"

Nick took a sip of water before answering. "I'm interested in all history. You must admit, this house has an incredibly intriguing past."

Natalia's fork clanged against her plate. "Why don't you tell him about the key, Father?" Her voice dripped acid, disintegrating the pleasant conversation.

"Key?" Nick turned his gaze to Natalia, but her icy stare never left her father's face.

The ambassador didn't seem to notice the daggers his daughter shot at him. He cut his steak into meticulously small pieces as he spoke. "I think the key is a legend. It supposedly was found with the diary, decades ago, by one of my predecessors and his staff. Somewhere around 1970, I believe. But no one knows what happened to it . . . if it ever existed. I'm not one for conspiracy theories. Personally, I don't believe there ever was a key, just like I don't believe there is Confederate gold."

For the first time during the meal, Natalia showed interest in the conversation, leaning forward in her chair. "Nick became intrigued in this so-called 'conspiracy theory' after I showed him a grave with that stupid symbol on it when he and I snuck into a cemetery in the middle of the night."

Nick froze. Natalia's mother looked up sharply, her cover blown. She *did* understand English! Her father stopped eating, his fork frozen in midair. The ticking of the grandfather clock, now the only sound in the room, suddenly seemed as loud as a Sunday morning church bell.

A quick glance at Natalia revealed a self-satisfying smirk on her face. Nick swallowed the lump in his throat and waited to be thrown out of the embassy. What kind of game was she playing?

But the ambassador gained his composure and seemed set on ignoring his daughter's deliberately inflammatory outburst. "You found another symbol?"

"Just kidding." Natalia spat the words as if expelling venom, then pushed her chair back and threw her napkin on the table. "Come on, Nick."

Nick wished he could crawl out of his skin. He looked back and forth between her parents, unsure what to do. They continued to eat, their gazes firmly fixed on their plates. He slowly stood up.

"Thank you, Ambassador and Mrs. Schroeder, for inviting me to dinner. Everything was delicious."

Mrs. Schroeder looked up. "Please come again. You are a delightful young man." The unexpected sound of her quiet voice added to the strangeness of the evening.

The ambassador sawed his knife through the steak on his plate. "Give your father our best."

Nick fled, glad to get away from the uncomfortable gathering. He followed Natalia through the mansion to the back garden. Bright spring blossoms dotted the landscape. She sprawled out on a bench in the garden's gazebo.

"How shall we amuse ourselves now?" She raised an eyebrow flirtatiously.

Enough of this. He leaned against the railing, crossing his arms. "What's going on here?"

"Nothing yet." She grinned. "Unfortunately."

"I don't know what kind of game you're playing, but I don't want any part of it."

"What're you talking about?"

He shoved his hand into his front pocket. "I don't think you're really as bad as you pretend to be. You could easily find someone to be your willing cohort. But instead, you chose me, someone safe. I think this is all an act to get your parents' attention."

Her eyes narrowed, and her face hardened. "You know nothing about me."

He'd struck a nerve. "You're right. I don't. Because you pretend to be something you're not."

"Just leave."

He held her gaze. "Listen, Natalia. I'm happy to be your friend. I'm a great listener if you ever want to talk, but I'm not going to be a puppet in this game between you and your father."

She glared at him with visible hatred then sprang to her feet and stormed into the house, leaving him alone in the garden.

Chapter Twenty-five

Eve paced the apartment, waiting for Nick to arrive. The moment she'd made her discovery, she'd called him. He had just left the embassy and promised to come by before he headed home. The last fifteen minutes had passed in slow motion, her nerves unraveling with each tick of the clock. When the front door opened, she spun, knocking over a lamp from the side table as she hurtled toward the entry. *Criminy!* She lunged to catch it just as her parents walked in accompanied by Nick.

Three curious sets of eyes watched as she clumsily averted disaster and set the lamp back on the table.

"Oh, hi!" She adjusted the skewed lamp shade then dropped her hands to her sides. Nothing unusual happening here.

Mom tilted her head in confusion but thankfully didn't ask any questions. "Look who we ran into in the lobby."

"Nick told us you are working on a joint project?" Dad shut the door behind them.

"Yep. A joint project." She grabbed Nick's arm to pull him toward her room.

But Mom didn't seem to understand the urgency she felt. "What kind of project?"

She froze, her mind blank. No idea what to say. But as usual, Nick had it covered. Good thing someone around here was capable of quick thinking.

"We'd been searching for a topic to research and, after the dinner at the embassy, we thought it might be fun to check into the theories surrounding the missing Confederate gold."

Eve stared at him. Telling the truth, at least mostly, had not occurred to her.

"It's an interesting topic." Dad moved to his recliner. "But I'm afraid there's not much information. You may find yourselves struggling to come up with enough content for your paper. If you do have any questions, though, feel free to ask. I'd be happy to help."

Nick smiled. "Thanks, Mr. Donahue. We appreciate it."

"Yeah, sure. Thanks, Dad. But right now, I want to show Nick what I found." She pulled him down the hall.

"Please keep your door open."

Oh, help. Really, Mom? What did she think they were going to do while in the very next room? Could the evening get any more embarrassing?

As Nick settled into the desk chair, Eve plopped on her bed. She could barely contain her excitement. In fact, she didn't even care how his dinner with Natalia had been. Who cared about the European femme fatale? He was here with her now.

That adorable grin of his graced his face. "Okay, what is this earth-shattering news?"

She took a deep breath. "I've figured out where the third symbol is."

His jaw dropped. "Really?"

She bobbed her head.

"Where?"

Drawing out the suspense might be fun, but she couldn't hold it in a moment longer. "Arlington Cemetery."

His eyebrows raised. "Arlington Cemetery?"

"Yes. Look." She grabbed the map with the equilateral triangle drawn on it, connecting the Smithsonian Castle to the two cemeteries. "I was sitting right where you are, working on some geometry problems. The map was underneath my papers. I kept staring at the two locations we've already found. Then I started to think about the shape of the symbol and wondered if it could be more than just a decoration. Maybe it was some sort of a map. And voila, the final point of the triangle lands in Arlington Cemetery."

Nick studied the map. "Hmm. Hamilton was the lawyer for General Lee's family when they sued about the land. I guess it could be there."

Eve started to focus on the next step. *Oh, no.* Her shoulders slumped.

"What's wrong? You may have figured out where the third symbol is."

She flopped back on her bed. "Even if I'm right, there's no way we can find the symbol. Arlington is massive. And it's a military cemetery: we can't very well go digging it up."

"Well, let's think this through." Nick stood and began pacing. "Even at the time of the lawsuit, the family probably knew they didn't want the land anymore after so many soldiers had been buried there."

She sat up, continuing the thought process. "As the lawyer, Mr. Hamilton would have known their intentions were to be fairly compensated, then hand the land back to the government."

Nick rubbed the back of his neck. "And Hamilton would have known that if it remained a cemetery, the land would be dug up."

"So, if he did bury his portion there, he would have to put it somewhere that wouldn't be disturbed." Eve smiled, enjoying how well they worked together.

They stared at each other for a moment. Holy moly, his eyes were stunning. She felt the telltale signs of a blush creep along her jaw and looked away before her cheeks turned their annoying shade of red. She focused on smoothing out the crinkles on her bedspread. *Way to play it cool, Eve.*

Better to just stay on topic. "But why on earth would he leave a portion of the treasure or even a clue to its location on a Union-controlled site?"

He sat back down. "Hiding the Confederate gold right under the Union's nose would have been extremely risky but probably kinda satisfying."

"Okay. So, if there is another symbol there, where is it? What part of the land wouldn't have been disturbed in over one hundred years?"

He thought for a moment. His eyes snapped to hers. "Arlington House."

A tingle shot up her spine. "You mean that building on top of the hill overlooking the cemetery, the river, and the rest of the city?"

"The very one. It was actually General Lee's home, but now it's called Arlington House and is a popular tourist attraction. Part of the deal with the government might have been that they had to make the house a museum to the Civil War and General Lee. Mr. Hamilton

would have been assured the home wouldn't be disturbed, making it the perfect place to hide his gold."

She clapped her hands together. "Guess what we're
touring tomorrow!"

Chapter Twenty-six

Nick leaned against the railing, watching passengers disembark the Metro train. A Sunday afternoon in the spring basically meant everyone departing was a tourist, cameras around their necks, maps in their hands, backpacks and bags full of items they might need for their day in the nation's capital. When he spotted Eve, he couldn't help but chuckle.

Did she get up each morning and think, "How can I be unique today?" Or did it just happen? Either way, he found her irresistible.

Eve waved and hurried over to him. "Hi!"

"Hey, Albuquerque, I see you dressed the part." He jutted his chin toward her "I Love DC" t-shirt.

"Today, I *am* a tourist. I've never been here before."

"I especially like the Hello Kitty tennis shoes."

She glanced at her feet. "I figured we'd be doing a lot of walking today." Like that explained the unusual choice of footwear. "You look a bit touristy yourself, with your baseball hat." She tapped his brim.

"My lame attempt at a disguise, hoping no one will recognize me."

"Stalker-chick!" The voice burst into their conversation without warning.

Eve flinched, then turned to face Nick's brother.

"Oh. Hi, Jace. I didn't know you were coming along." She glanced at Nick.

He grinned. "Surprise."

She didn't seem amused.

"Hey, Jace, maybe you could come up with a different nickname." Behind Eve's back, Nick gave Jace a "help-me-out-already" look.

"Sure, how about Red?" Jace batted one of her curls.

She pushed his hand away. "How about Eve?"

"Nah."

"Eve!" In moments, the rest of his siblings surrounded her.

"Wow. Everyone came." She shot another look his way. Annoyance? Confusion? He couldn't tell. But her smile seemed genuine when Liv hugged her, and Grace skipped around them in a circle. Even Gabriella, who usually only concentrated on her gymnastics routines or fiddled with her phone, acted happy to see her. "I'm surprised you didn't bring Lexus, too."

"Oh, Grace tried to. I brought the whole crew along because I thought we might need a distraction. And no one's better at causing commotion than my family."

"Did you bring any food this time?" Dillon pushed his way to the front of the crowd.

She bit her lip. "No. Sorry. I would have if Nick had told me you all were joining us."

"Way to go, Nick." Jace punched his arm.

He ignored his brother and handed Eve a ticket. "Ready to board the tour bus?"

"Let's go." Eve took Grace's outstretched hand and walked with her toward the blue and white open-air tour bus.

As they drove into the cemetery, a guide recited the history of the land.

Nick was double-checking the map when Eve tapped him on the shoulder and motioned with her finger for him to lean closer. She was in the process of having her hair braided by Liv.

"What's the plan?" Her floral scent reminded him of the cherry blossoms from the day before. Too bad they weren't alone again. Maybe they could ditch his siblings later.

He spoke quietly so the rest of his clan wouldn't overhear. "I called this morning and spoke with the head tour guide of Arlington House. She told me about the cellar and the storage area that's down there. I think that's the most likely place to search."

"How are we going to get into it?"

He glanced around to make sure no one was listening. "We'll be sneaking off and exploring on our own."

"There's a flaw to your plan. I've been on lots of tours around this city in the last few months, and I know they keep a close eye on tourists."

"That's why we brought along our own distractions."

Eve, her newly braided hair trailing down her neck, glanced at his siblings squirming in their seats.

The first stop on the tour happened to be their destination: Robert E. Lee's home, otherwise known as Arlington House. They played the part of tourist and exited the bus with everyone else. Grace clasped onto Eve's hand again. As they walked into the old mansion, they were placed into a smaller tour group.

"Good morning! I'm Tatiana and I'll be your tour guide. Please follow me." The exuberant guide appeared to be in her mid-forties. Her eyes darted around, not missing a thing.

Tatiana led the group of about fifteen people to the main parlor and started talking about the home and the furnishings. Nick loved the way Eve took in every detail with great interest, completely immersed in the experience. The group obediently followed their leader through the home, listening to her speech.

An elderly gentleman kept asking questions while his wife snapped photos of everything. Would they ever look at all those photos? Grace, thrilled with her new full skirt, twirled around in every room, making the entire group nervous. Dillon inundated poor Tatiana with a litany of questions about what life at the home would have been like prior to the Civil War. Nick grinned. His distractions worked magnificently.

The tour continued throughout the historic home then finally down to the damp and musty cellar. The brick walls were painted white which helped brighten up the space. A hard-packed dirt floor was a rustic change after the splendor of the home. Nick noted the few old items strategically placed around the space to add authenticity. Tatiana pointed out the wine room, but a half gate blocked entrance. Nick scanned the room and spotted a door at the back of the cellar. Bingo.

Tatiana was in the middle of her spiel when she was interrupted by a soft moan.

"What *is* that?" Gabriella looked over her shoulder.

"I'm not sure." Tatiana glanced around the cellar.

The moaning grew louder, accompanied by a strange rustling sound.

Jace smirked. "Sounds like a ghost."

"Jace, stop it," Olivia pleaded.

"Hey, it's not me." He raised his hands. "I warned you this place is haunted."

Tatiana raised a hand, trying to calm the kids. "I don't know what that sound is, but I can assure you this home is not haunted."

Suddenly a light flickered in the shadows. Grace clung to Eve's side. She in turn edged closer to Nick.

"Whoa." Dillon gasped while everyone's eyes darted around nervously.

"Nothing like this has ever happened before." The wide-eyed tour guide tried to soothe the nervous tourists. "It's an old building, and the electricity is probably a little faulty down here."

A metal milk can slid across the floor, knocking into Nick. Eve gasped and jumped away. He grabbed her arm. Olivia and Grace screamed and ran out of the cellar. The rest of the group looked to Tatiana for guidance, but she seemed transfixed by the milk can.

Finally, the guide caught a breath and composed herself. "I think we'd better end our time here and find the girls." She scurried up the stairs with the rest of the group close behind.

Nick held onto Eve's arm to keep her from fleeing the cellar too. "Told you they were good at distractions."

Her eyes grew wide. "You did all that? How?"

He grinned. "My original plan involved claiming to see a rat, which would have caused plenty of mayhem. But Jace kept teasing the girls about ghosts living in the house, so I thought I'd play off that theme."

"Well, it was quite convincing." Her hand covered her heart. "My pulse is still racing."

He held up his phone. "Just needed a strobe effect on my phone and some eerie music."

"And how'd you make the milk can move?"

He shook his head. "That wasn't me."

Her face paled. Nick couldn't contain his amusement and started to laugh.

She punched his arm.

"Sorry, you should've seen your face." He pulled the powerful magnet that was connected to a switch out of his pocket. "I adjusted one of my science fair projects and flipped the switch to activate the magnet. I didn't know if there'd be anything metal down here, so the milk can was quite the bonus."

She shook her head. "Ingenious, but I think you may have permanently scarred your siblings."

"Nah, I'll fess up, show them how I did it, and they'll be fine. You should be feeling bad for the poor, unsuspecting souls they'll inevitably pull the same prank on."

She covered her mouth to suppress a giggle. "Poor Tatiana. She may never want to lead another tour."

He pulled out a note from his pocket. "I don't want to start any rumors, so I'll leave an anonymous note of explanation behind." Too bad he couldn't explain to the elderly couple. But at least they'd have a good story to go along with their hundreds of photos.

"You've thought of everything. Won't she miss us though?"

He led her toward the wine cellar door. "No. She'll have her hands full calming everyone down. The final stop of the tour is outside, so she'll assume we started wandering the grounds. And she'll be thrilled to be done with our rowdy group."

Nick helped Eve climb over the gate to the wine room then easily leapt over it himself.

"Be careful not to disturb anything." Eve pulled out a few bottles to check the wall behind them. "I feel bad enough about sneaking in here."

"We only have about ten minutes before the next tour group comes down. I think we should start looking behind that door." He pointed across the room. "It leads to a storage area."

"Let me guess. Your friendly informant told you that?"

She sounded so surprised.

"Like I've said, people are willing to talk if you ask the right questions."

Nick turned the knob on the old door and pushed it open. Eve located a switch, and light illuminated the space. Old furniture and stacks of tables and chairs filled the dusty room. They slowly made their way around the perimeter, searching for the symbol.

Eve scanned the walls. "Did you tell Jace what we were up to?"

With his shoulder, he pushed a huge armoire to the side.

"I told him if we disappeared for a few minutes not to worry and we'd meet up with them outside. He probably assumes we snuck off together because you wanted me all to yourself." He watched in amusement as her cheeks turned a deep pink. "You're awfully fun to tease."

Her hands covered her cheeks. "I know. My dad always says my cheeks turn the same shade as the Sandia Mountains at sunset."

He smiled at her description as he shoved a filing cabinet away from the wall. "Those must be some really colorful mountains."

"Yeah, at sunset they turn this beautiful shade of red. In fact, *sandia* means watermelon in Spanish." She knelt to peer under a rug.

"Hey, I was just kidding. I didn't tell Jace anything, but I did have to promise to take them all to the Nationals baseball opening game on Saturday."

"Seems like a small price to pay."

She helped him carefully pull an old piano forward. He glanced behind it. Nothing.

"You would think so, but anything with that crew is a challenge. And don't think you're getting out of the fun. Grace and Liv agreed to go only if you go too."

"Sounds great." She moved to a stack of paintings and carefully leaned them forward to check behind them.

"That's what you say now. Get back to me after a day of screaming crowds, sticky baseball foods, and umpteen bathroom breaks."

Eve laughed at his description, probably thinking he was exaggerating. Just wait till she found out how accurate it was.

Her hands went to her hips. "I don't see the symbol anywhere."

"I know. Here, help me move these barrels. It's the only place we haven't checked yet."

They shoved several heavy wine barrels out of the way and found themselves staring at a triangle carved into the stone wall.

She clamped onto his hand. "I can't believe we actually found it."

"Thanks to your brilliant deduction about Arlington being the third location."

He turned to look at her. Their eyes locked, and for a moment, neither of them moved. His insides jumbled into a giant knot. When her cheeks colored again, he resisted the urge to reach out and touch them. She glanced away, breaking the connection. Again.

"Ok, let's see what it says." She fiddled with her phone. Soon her flashlight app illuminated the triangle.

Nick snapped a photo. "Chesapeake."

She traced the symbol with her fingers. "What's Chesapeake?"

"I'm not sure. There's the Chesapeake Bay not far from here."

"So, the three words on the symbols are Ohio, Rose, and Chesapeake." She raised her hand in defeat. "Those are the worst clues ever."

Couldn't disagree with that. "Come on. Let's get out of here before we're caught."

They shoved the barrels back in place then snuck out of the storage room and back through the wine cellar. He offered his hand to help her over the gate, surprised by her slight hesitation before she accepted his help. Shoot. That moment in the back room must've made her un-comfortable.

As soon as they stepped out of the building, his siblings surrounded them. Grace predictably clamped onto Eve's hand.

"Did you see the ghost?"

"No. Luckily, we did not." Eve shot a quick smile at him. "Okay, now for the rest of the tour."

Chapter Twenty-seven

Eve listened as Liv enthusiastically described her favorite book while they walked down the path from President Kennedy's grave back to the tour bus. After her initial disappointment that Nick had brought all his siblings along on their adventure, she had to admit she enjoyed every moment with the Hammond kids. After so much time either spent alone or in a small group, she loved all the noise and chaos that came with this large family.

Dillon and Gabriella led the way while Nick, with Grace perched on his shoulders, walked next to Eve. As hard as she tried to concentrate on Liv's description of her book, she kept thinking about being alone with Nick in the cellar . . . how they'd looked at each other. Her heart somersaulted. She could still feel the warmth of his hand when he'd helped her over the door. Did he feel the same connection she did?

Jace squeezed in between them, interrupting her thoughts. "So, you can tell me, did you guys steal something back at Arlington House when you snuck off?"

Eve gasped. "Of course not!" How could he think such a thing?

"You're an idiot." Nick gave his brother a playful shove.

Jace held up his hands. "Hey, just trying to figure out why we're being followed."

"What?" Eve spun her head toward him.

"Don't look now, but two dudes in suits—obviously not tourists—are watching you two."

Eve turned to look up at Grace, riding on Nick's shoulders. "Hey, how's the view up there?" She used the natural change of position to glance at the two men in dark suits a few yards back. One guy's wavy blond hair was pulled back in a ponytail. The other sported a buzz cut. How had she missed them? They didn't blend in at all amid the tourists, kind of like one of those "Which item doesn't belong?" picture puzzles.

"Who are they?" Unease swept through her.

Jace cocked his head. "How would I know? They're not following me. I noticed them at the Memorial Amphitheater stop. While everyone else snapped photos and read all the signs about the site, these guys just watched you two."

She looked at Nick. The only clue to his reaction was a slight twitch of his jaw.

Jace draped his arms around their shoulders. "Hey, you know me. I'm always up for an adventure. But the least you could do, since I'm now an accomplice, is to tell me what's going on."

Nick knocked his brother's arm away. "I'll explain later. Just get everyone back home."

The bus stop swirled with chaotic throngs of people as one tour bus emptied its passengers at the same time another began to load. Nick lifted Grace off his shoulders and passed her off to Jace then clamped onto Eve's hand. This time his touch didn't make her insides all gooey. Instead, his tense grip intensified the situation. Were they really being followed?

She clung to his hand, struggling to keep up as he pulled her through a large group of Japanese tourists. Why would anyone be following them? From the midst of the Asian tour group, they turned to watch as the waiting crowd, including Nick's siblings, pushed their way onto the empty vehicle. She didn't spot the guys in suits and hoped they had boarded.

On the other side of the road, a bus faced the opposite direction, its doors open to loading passengers. Nick jerked his chin toward it, and the two of them sprinted across the road. As they climbed on, the crowded bus carrying Nick's siblings pulled away. Eve scanned the dozens of faces and spotted the men in suits walking down the aisle searching the rows of passengers.

Nick leaned back in his seat. "Looks like Jace was right. Those two won't be happy to find out we ditched them."

"Why would anyone be following us?" She wiped her clammy hands on her jeans.

"They weren't security guards, so it has nothing to do with our sneaking away from the tour. It must be related to this treasure hunt we're on." Nick's knee bounced up and down, belying his otherwise calm demeanor.

"What're we going to do?" She searched his eyes, a little crease between her own.

He turned toward her. "Find out who they are."

"How?" She nibbled on a fingernail. Did he have any kind of plan?

"Well, the only people who know we're interested in these symbols are your neighbor and Natalia. Mrs. Grant doesn't strike me as the obvious choice to have us followed, so we're going to talk to Natalia." He pulled out his phone and began to text.

Fabulous. She hated the thought of seeing Natalia again, watching that girl throw herself at Nick. But she had to admit his plan made sense.

An hour later they were sitting at a coffee shop in Dupont Circle when Natalia entered. Natalia didn't even acknowledge Eve's presence. Not a huge surprise, but the icy greeting she gave Nick was. The girl folded her arms across her chest and jutted her chin out when she saw him. He stood to greet her, but his chivalrous act was met with an acid-dripping glare. What on earth had happened?

"Thanks for meeting us." Nick politely pulled out a chair for her.

Natalia ignored the gesture and sat in the other open seat. "What do you want, Nick? You aren't finished telling me what a horrible person I am?"

Eve's mouth dropped open. Wow! When did all that happen? Hadn't Nick been falling for all that goth charm?

He sighed. "I never said you were a horrible person. But I think you've been using me to get your father's attention."

With a roll of her eyes, Natalia slumped in her chair. "Whatever."

Eve's faith in this teenage boy's judgment was restored. *Hallelujah!*

Nick calmly continued. "I told you I'd like to be friends, and I meant it. Deny it all you want, but I don't think this whole teenage rebel thing you've got going on is who you really are."

"You don't know anything about me. You think you're so smart and have everything figured out. Well, you don't. I'm not trying to get attention from my father."

Natalia spewed the words with such venom that Eve felt like cowering in a corner. But Nick didn't flinch. How was he not affected in the least?

"Then what's going on? Like I said before, if you wanted someone to party with, you wouldn't have chosen me."

A thought suddenly occurred to Eve as she watched this uncomfortable exchange. "Natalia, did your father tell you to get close to Nick?" Maybe the ambassador had sent those men to follow them.

She cringed when Natalia's evil-eyed gaze snapped her way and sent a thousand darts flying across the table. Yeesh.

"Natalia, please." Nick's voice remained steady. "I'm sorry for the way things went the other night. I didn't handle it well, but something is going on with you." He glanced at Eve, then back to Natalia. "We want to be your friends. Please? Talk to us."

Who said she wanted to be Natalia's friend? Still, she said nothing and let Nick steer the conversation.

Natalia looked back and forth between the two of them. Finally, her face softened a bit. "Fine. After my dad became an ambassador, my parents sent me off to boarding school in Switzerland." She picked at her nail polish as she spoke. "I loved every moment of it, had a ton of friends, and met this awesome guy. My parents didn't approve and made me come live with them. I want to go back, and I figured if I made them nervous enough with my behavior, they would change their minds and realize they made a mistake."

An astonishing change overcame Natalia. The rebellious edge evaporated. She suddenly seemed like a girl dressed in ridiculous clothes for Halloween.

"Thank you for telling us the truth," Nick responded.

"Sorry for using you." Natalia concentrated on the black flecks chipping off her nails.

Wow. Who would've guessed all that goth stuff was just a role the girl was playing?

Nick did, somehow.

Guilt washed over Eve for being so wrapped up in her own feelings that she hadn't noticed Natalia's cry for help. Some Christian servant she was. *Sorry, God.*

But maybe they could still help somehow. "We could brainstorm with you for a way to talk to your parents."

Natalia shrugged. "Thanks, but I don't think it's possible."

"Anything's possible." Like the seemingly impossible task of moving her family halfway across the country.

Nick laid his hand on top of Natalia's and prayed aloud. "Dear Lord, please help Natalia as she deals with the stress of her situation. Give her the confidence to talk with her parents and lead her to whatever is best for her. Amen."

Natalia stared at him like he was some kind of freak.

He ignored her reaction. "Listen, we need to ask you something. Did you say anything more to your dad or anyone else about the symbol on the tombstone?"

She squirmed in her chair. "Yeah. After you left last night, my father came to my room. He demanded to know about the gravesite and the symbol we'd discovered." She rolled her eyes. "Can you believe that? He didn't get upset that I had snuck out of the house and broken into a cemetery with a boy I barely knew. He only wanted to know about the stupid symbol." Her sheepish look gave Eve another shock. "It made me so mad. I told him you had tracked down several symbols and thought you knew where to find the Confederate gold."

Chapter Twenty-eight

Nick walked into the kitchen for breakfast and found his dad at the counter preparing a travel mug of coffee.

"Well hello, stranger." Dad smiled as he stirred cream into the hot brew. "Feels like I haven't seen you in ages. Thanks for taking the kids out yesterday. Sounds like they had a blast."

"Yeah, we had fun." Nick sat on a stool at the kitchen counter.

Dad pushed a lid onto his travel mug. "Sorry we couldn't do anything special for spring break. Maybe this summer we can get away."

"It's okay. I think the week might end up being pretty special after all." His mind jumped to Eve.

"Really? Does that have anything to do with a certain young lady?"

"Maybe." Discussing feelings with his dad did not rank high on his to-do list. Ever. Time to change the subject. "You've been working a lot lately."

"Yeah, we're dealing with a lot on the Foreign Relations Committee. Working with all the ambassadors and diplomats is exhausting."

"Still involved with the Endelbourg trade agreement?"

"Yes, that's the stickiest situation at the moment. Ever since the new king took charge, they've been threatening a trade embargo, making life difficult not only for the people of his own country, but also all the other countries involved. Not sure what's going on there. But I'm sure it'll all work out. What're your plans for the day? Mom mentioned the zoo?"

"I had to pass on that. Practice this afternoon." Nick was thankful for the excuse to get out of the excursion. He liked their family outings, but another tourist attraction with massive mobs of spring break tourists sounded painful.

"I've noticed some boats out on the water already. I'm glad you'll be getting back out there with the team. You haven't hung out with friends much lately."

"It's hard to know who to trust." He noticed the slight grimace on his dad's face and regretted his honest answer.

"I didn't realize my election would affect you so much. I'm sorry it's been hard on you."

"Don't be. I'm glad you became a senator, Dad. It's great that you can make a difference. I honestly just haven't cared about hanging out with kids from school lately. But I'm looking forward to practice starting up."

"Glad to hear it." He patted Nick on the back. "Well, have a good day."

Nick noticed a slight slump in his father's shoulders as he headed for the door.

"Hey, Dad, don't worry. It'll all work out. The committee's lucky to have you." Maybe it was a little unusual for a teen to offer such encouragement, but even if it was

God's will, he felt the pangs of responsibility for his dad being elected and all the stress he now faced.

After breakfast, Nick headed outside for a run and a chance to think. He still couldn't believe someone had followed them yesterday. Of course, Confederate gold would be worth a fortune, but he hadn't appreciated how serious some people still were about finding it. Would Natalia's father really have him followed to see what he knew? The ambassador's chief of staff was the one who'd seemed obsessed with the whole notion of the treasure. Maybe they were working together. How could he find out?

Despite the long run, his thoughts remained a jumbled mess. Maybe a hot shower would do the trick. He rounded the corner to his street and slowed to a walk. A black sedan was parked in front of his house. As he neared, a man and woman exited the car. An uneasy prickle crawled up his spine, putting his senses on high alert.

The pair stood and waited for him to approach. The unusually tan middle-aged gentleman with immaculately coiffed silver hair seemed familiar. He wore designer jeans, dress shoes, and an untucked button-down shirt. The thin, exotic-looking woman wore a tailored suit and extremely high heels.

"Hi, are you Nick Hammond?" The man flashed a dazzling ultra-white smile.

He could deny it, but why bother? They already knew his identity. "Yes."

"Great." The woman reached out to shake his hand. "I'm Ms. Selco, and this, as you may already know, is Jeff Normandy."

He scoured his brain. Where had he heard that name before?

"You may have seen one of his television specials," the woman prompted.

Ah, yes. Jeff Normandy was a treasure hunter of sorts. Who knew if he'd actually ever found any, but he produced several TV specials each year, trying to solve famous mysteries. He and his crew had searched for ancient Aztec temples and Czar Nicolas's supposedly hidden fortune. His last case had centered around some priceless paintings stolen by the Nazis.

Nick braced himself for what was coming.

"Is there someplace we can talk?" Ms. Selco glanced at his house.

Her emotionless voice and dark sunglasses made it impossible for him to get any sense of her intentions.

Time for politician mode.

"It's nice to meet you both. Mr. Normandy, I've always found your specials intriguing. Now, may I ask what this is all about?"

"Confederate gold." Jeff Normandy stated it with such enthusiasm, Nick wondered if there were hidden cameras on them.

"I assume you're getting your information from the ambassador's office, but I'm afraid I don't have anything to tell you." Nick chose his words with care. He didn't like to lie, but if God really wanted them to solve this mystery, Mr. Normandy's propensity to profit from and sensationalize his adventures wouldn't be a good path to take.

"I think you'll be quite interested in our offer. Why don't you have your parents give me a call." Ms. Selco held out a business card. Nick glanced at it but made no move to accept it.

"A mystery right here in America about Confederate treasure would be ratings gold." Mr. Normandy's eyes lit up.

Nick grimaced at the pun. Was this guy for real?

Ms. Selco studied his face. "If it's all right with your parents, we could have you take part in the special. You could work closely with Jeff on and off the camera. Think of the resources and influence we can offer you."

He took a deep breath. "I'm sure it would be very exciting, but I can't help you. Someone from the embassy showed me the symbol at Oak Hill Cemetery. Like everyone else, I thought it fascinating but couldn't tell you if other symbols exist."

"We were led to believe you could help in this century-old mystery." Mr. Normandy's friendly demeanor began to slip away.

"I can honestly say that I am not able to help you. Now, if you'll excuse me, I need to go."

The pair seemed skeptical but didn't press the subject.

Ms. Selco pushed the business card toward him again. "If you do uncover anything new, please give us a call. We can make it worth your while."

Reluctantly, he took the card.

He watched the car pull away. Whether this whole thing was a mission from God or simply an exciting adventure with a fascinating girl, one thing was for sure. Things were getting complicated.

Chapter Twenty-nine

You won't believe who else knows about our extra-curricular activities. If you can get away, meet me at the row club around 5.

Well, he'd certainly piqued her interest.

The message had come as a welcome surprise. In fact, Eve hadn't expected to hear from Nick today. She'd still been processing their odd interaction with Natalia as well as their excursion at Arlington Cemetery, from the excitement of their moment in the cellar to the startling realization they had been followed. But then this morning she'd received Nick's text.

She'd wasted most of the day in the kitchen distractedly playing with Mrs. Grant's cats but couldn't get that cryptic message out of her head. Unable to concentrate on anything else, she finally made her way over to the row club a little before five.

Now, sitting along the river with the water lapping against the wall, Eve realized she hadn't been following Father Romero's advice very well. Doing so was important, especially now, with creepy guys following them.

Besides, Father had told her that visions were usually used to draw people to God. That probably required some extra direction. So, she prayed for guidance and understanding.

Dear God, thank You for everything You've done for me. Thank You for leading me to this amazing place. Please continue to guide me and help me to know what it is You want us to do. And please keep us safe. It still seems a bit strange that You want us to find gold but hey, whatever. Oh yeah, thanks for choosing me. Amen.

Sitting there with her legs dangling down toward the water of the Potomac, she contemplated how much things had changed in the last few months. Her life now was so different from what she'd always known. As she watched the long, sleek boats pass under the massive arches of the Key Bridge, she had the oddest feeling, like she now lived in a dream world.

Eve watched the boats with their eight rowers quickly and smoothly skim across the river. The front person, who sat backwards, barked orders as the others pushed and pulled the oars in exact precision. Several teams dotted the massive river, but she couldn't make out any of the individuals, so it was impossible to locate Nick.

One of the long boats pulled up alongside the dock, and she spotted him, looking oh-so-cute in his workout clothes. He waved and motioned for her to come down. She jumped off her perch and made her way through the Boat Club building down to the dock.

He smiled when she approached. "Hey, there, thanks for coming."

"Sure, although you did disturb my very exciting day of cat-sitting. Oh, and I did a little baking. Gingersnaps." She held up her bag.

He stretched. "Perfect. I'm starving."

"I also packed a picnic." She smiled sheepishly. "We should eat while you tell me about your mysterious message. Curiosity is eating me alive."

"Sounds great. I'll text my mom and let her know I won't be home for a while." He pulled out his phone.

"Where should we go? Are there any parks nearby? I guess we could head up to the university."

He grinned at her. "I've got the perfect spot. Just give me a minute." He disappeared into the building, leaving her on the slanted dock which angled right into the Potomac.

He returned a few minutes later holding two life jackets.

"What are those for?"

"I'm taking you on a boat ride."

"Really?" Eve swallowed hard. She couldn't think of anything more romantic.

He handed the smaller vest to her. "Sure. You told me I need to have more fun. So, let's go have fun."

After a few minutes, they were on the water in a boat for two with Nick controlling both oars.

As they passed under the towering Key Bridge, she marveled at the huge structure. "I can't believe how big that is. I feel so tiny." *Wait till I tell Brooke.*

He grinned as he controlled the little boat.

"I'm glad you don't need my help. If you were relying on me, we'd probably just make a giant circle." She pulled out her phone to snap a few pictures. "Everything looks so different from this angle."

He looked around. "Yeah, I guess I've gotten used to it, but the views are pretty cool."

Her gaze drifted from his cute face to his flexing muscles as he moved the oars back and forth through the water. This particular view was pretty nice as well.

She glanced up to see him watching her. *Busted.*

Maybe a change of subject would keep him from noticing her fire-red cheeks. "Why did everyone on your team only control one oar? Don't people usually use two?"

"That's a sweep boat. This one's a sculling boat. I'm glad you finally got to see them. Now you can stop picturing me in a little wooden dinghy." A teasing twinkle lit his eye.

"I do still like the image of you rowing a tiny little wooden boat." He wasn't the only one who could tease.

Nick guided them toward an island in the center of the river and glided up to a dock. After securing the boat, he offered his hand to help her out.

"We have arrived at our destination, Mademoiselle." He bowed slightly.

"Thank you, kind sir," she answered with a curtsy. "Where are we?"

"Roosevelt Island. It's a national park to honor Theodore Roosevelt. It can only be reached by boat or footbridge."

"Very cool. And here I thought I wouldn't be doing any sightseeing today."

"You never run out of things to tour around here."

He led her toward a picnic area overlooking the water with a spectacular view of the monuments across the river as a backdrop.

"Okay." She'd been patient long enough. "Now tell me about your mysterious text."

As she pulled out their picnic, he told her about his encounter with Jeff Normandy and Ms. Selco.

"Whoa. How did they find out?"

He unwrapped one of the sandwiches. "It had to be someone at the embassy. I just hope they believed me and will leave us alone."

She pulled open a bag of chips. "Why is the ambassador or his chief of staff so interested in all this anyway? I know it's intriguing, but they seem a little obsessed."

"Oh, I forgot to tell you. Turns out the builder of the embassy was none other than our Mr. Barrett."

"You're kidding."

He finished chewing a bite of his sandwich and swallowed. "When I was there for dinner the other night, the ambassador told me that back in 1970, someone from the embassy discovered the diary of the original owner, Mr. Stewart. He wrote about how close he had grown to the elderly Mr. Barrett. The embassy staff became interested in Mr. Barrett and discovered his link to the Confederate gold legend."

"Do you think those guys who followed us yesterday work for Mr. Normandy?"

"I don't know. Maybe Ms. Selco hired them to track me down." He took a swig of his soda.

"What's our next step?"

"Continue our search, hopefully without their interference."

"Do you really think the gold used to be buried in those three locations we found?"

She reached for another chip. His hand also moved toward the bag at the same time. Their fingers touched. She drew her hand back, a giggle bubbling out. Super smooth.

He cleared his throat and withdrew his hand from the chips as well.

"Maybe originally. I think as time went on the three men realized they were going to be watched and observed for a much longer time than they had originally thought, making it impossible for any of them to use the gold. They would have realized it couldn't stay there. With the city growing, the treasure wouldn't be safe in the Smithsonian or the Arlington House. Whether the gold was once kept in those locations or not, those three symbols have to be the clues to where it is now."

"But those clues are impossible." Why was this so difficult? "Rose could be someone's name, and Chesapeake and Ohio don't help much."

"Yes, but . . . wait." His eyes widened. "What did you say?"

"Umm. Chesapeake and Ohio don't help much?" Why was that interesting?

He lowered his sandwich and stared into space. "Could that be it? It would make sense but . . . I don't know. Is it possible?"

"Um, Nick, I'm not a mind reader. You need to speak complete sentences for me to follow."

"What?" He seemed surprised to find her sitting there. "Oh, sorry. I think I may have figured it out." He rose and started pacing. "Chesapeake and Ohio. Yes, that's the key! Eve, you're brilliant. I could kiss you."

Her insides did a strange little flip at those words, but Nick continued to walk back and forth, oblivious to what he'd said. She pushed her food away, mesmerized. She could practically see his brain churning.

"You know the canal that runs through Georgetown?" He raked his fingers through his hair. "It's called the C&O Canal." He stopped moving and placed his hands on the picnic table, leaning in toward her. "The *Chesapeake and Ohio* Canal."

A shiver ran down her spine.

He sat back on the bench. "It makes sense. Mr. Hamilton's law office and home overlooked the canal. I can picture him staring out his window, trying to figure out where and how to move the gold, with the answer right there in front of him." Nick's eyes lit up with excitement.

"Where does the canal go?"

He gestured up the river. "It basically runs alongside the Potomac up into Maryland. It created a way to transport goods between here and there. I'm pretty sure it's only a tourist attraction now, but back then it had several stops through Maryland."

"How do you know all this?" He continually surprised her.

"When we have school breaks, my mom likes to take us on little field trips. She doesn't want us to grow up here and not visit the sites. During fall break we toured the C&O Canal." He picked up the remainder of his sandwich and took a bite.

"The third symbol said Rose." How could he eat at a time like this? Her surging excitement curbed her appetite. Maybe this wasn't so impossible after all. "Could that be a clue to where along the canal they moved the treasure?"

"All right, I guess we've got more research to do and only have a few days left before we're back in school. Maybe we can find a connection to the three men at one of the stops along the canal."

"Good plan." Eve began to gather up their trash.

He reached out and touched her arm. "Come to think of it, research can wait a little while. Right now, let's just enjoy those cookies you made and watch the sunset."

She smiled. Excellent plan.

They sat next to each other on the bench, the river flowing in front of them, munching on gingersnaps. As they chatted about favorite trips they'd gone on and waited for the sun to set, she wondered if she'd ever been this content before. If only this moment could last forever.

Chapter Thirty

Nick studied Eve's face. She had this intriguing, positive vibe that just seemed to radiate around her. What was it about her that fascinated him?

She sat next to him on a bench along the C&O Canal, her forehead crinkled as she watched the tourist attraction in front of her.

Two National Park Service employees dressed in early nineteenth century work clothes ushered tourists onto a long wooden boat. Once everyone boarded, they brought out two mules, hooked them to a rope attached to the front of the boat, and began walking them on a path next to the canal. The mules pulled the boat along the waterway.

"This is amazing." Eve's mass of curls swept across her shoulders when she turned toward him. "Is that actually how the boats made their way along the canal? By mules?"

"Yep." He could look at those wide, curious eyes of hers all day long. "They obviously didn't have motorboats back then, and mules were cheaper than horses." He stood up. "Come on, you haven't seen the most interesting part yet." They walked along a path on the opposite side of the canal from the mules.

"Well, I can tell this was not a real speedy mode of transportation." They strolled along beside the slow-moving boat. "You said the canal runs parallel to the Potomac. Why didn't they just use the river?"

"Well, for starters about fifteen miles upstream on the Potomac, there's a rocky waterfall that makes boat travel impossible. That's why canals were designed, to transport lumber, coal, and other materials. But there's another reason which I'll explain soon."

Her face scrunched in confusion.

"It's just easier to show you than try to describe it."

Their hands brushed against each other as they walked, making his heart race. How would she react if he took her hand?

"Oh!" She slapped his shoulder. "I almost forgot to tell you!"

Moment lost.

She clapped her hands together. "I think I found something useful. Turns out that Mr. Barrett originated from Virginia, making him a southerner, but his wife grew up in Cumberland, Maryland. Does the canal go there?"

"Nice work, Albuquerque. I also pulled up some information on the canal and found out it ended at Cumberland. It's a small town in the mountains of western Maryland, about two and a half hours from here."

Her eyes lit up. "Time for a road trip?"

Sounded like the perfect way to spend a day.

"Hey, did Barrett's wife's name happen to be Rose?"

"No. Annabelle."

Right. That would've been too easy.

The mule stopped as the boat came to a wooden gate in the water.

"How are they going to get past that?" Eve sat down on the hillside overlooking the canal.

"Just watch."

A second gate closed behind the boat.

She pulled out her phone to take a photo. "What's happening?"

"It's a lock."

Eve frowned, clearly confused.

"It's a way to get boats to move upstream. The water is displaced, and the boat rises." He pointed. The boat in the lock slowly rose. "Several locks along the route lift the boat up. The tour guide describes the lock as a water elevator."

Eve sighed. "Sometimes living here feels like I'm in another country or something."

"I'm sure there's stuff in New Mexico that I've never heard of, like that wild pig you mentioned."

Her smile returned. "The javelina."

"Exactly. Anyway, you've probably heard of the Panama Canal. They use the same lock concept to get the ships across."

"Oh, okay." She watched the boat rise to its new level. "You think Barrett and the others moved the gold this way?"

"Well, that's what the clues imply. Besides, it probably would have been less risky to move it this way than traveling through the countryside with a horse and wagon. There were trains back then, but they might have been more closely monitored." The front wooden gate opened, and the mule continued to walk, pulling the boat along. "I wonder if they had help from one of the captains or somehow disguised the gold to get it on the boat.

Who knows exactly how it happened, but I'm sure they were nervous with people always watching them and were anxious to get the gold away from D.C."

He felt a sudden connection with those men because, unless he was mistaken, he and Eve were being watched.

Chapter Thirty-one

Eve waited at her neighbor's door. When it opened a crack, Mrs. Grant took one look at her and sighed. Eve smiled at the not-so-welcoming greeting.

"I wasn't expecting you."

"No, I thought I'd surprise you. I brought Chinese food." She held up a bag.

The door didn't open.

"What if I don't like Chinese food?"

"You can at least read your fortune."

"What if I already ate?"

"Then you can keep me company while I eat."

"Why don't you go home and eat with your parents?"

"They are away at a dinner party. Besides, I want to eat with you."

"Fine."

The door finally swung open.

While Eve spread the food onto the dining room table, Mrs. Grant went in the kitchen to get drinks.

The cats rubbed against Eve's legs as she worked. "I didn't know what you liked so I got a bunch of different things."

"You've been coming and going at different hours this week." Mrs. Grant shuffled back into the dining room, carrying a tray with glasses of water, plates, and silverware.

Eve smiled. So, the woman was paying attention to her schedule. Surely that meant she was making progress with her.

"It's my spring break, and I've been busy taking in some of the sights. You know about Saturday's trip to the Smithsonian, but we've also been to Arlington Cemetery, Roosevelt Island, and today we explored the C&O Canal."

"We?" Mrs. Grant handed her a plate.

"Nick and I." She didn't even try to hide her smile.

Mrs. Grant scooched her chair closer to the table. "I thought he had a new exotic girl that interested him."

Aha! Mrs. Grant actually did listen and pay attention to what she said. She looked up from her plate, excited to have a friend to share her thoughts with.

"Well, get this. I told you how Natalia kept throwing herself at him, and he seemed flattered? I mean, I didn't blame him. What guy wouldn't like attention from a beautiful European girl who doesn't wear much in the way of clothes? But we met with her the other day and from the moment she saw Nick, she got all angry and cold, obviously not thrilled to see him. I was completely shocked. Well, it turns out, he hadn't been fooled by her tough-girl act and had called her out on it. He knew she was only acting like that to get her parents' attention. How he knew all that, I don't know."

"I suppose you're going to tell me how she reacted?" Mrs. Grant peered into the carton of kung pao chicken then scooped some onto her plate.

"She tried to deny it but then relaxed a bit. Maybe she was happy she could stop pretending to be something she really wasn't. Then Nick surprised her and prayed that things would work."

"You honestly think praying solves problems?" Mrs. Grant reached for the rice container.

Eve watched the older woman. "Absolutely."

Mrs. Grant's bony right shoulder lifted in a slight shrug. "I've been around a lot longer than you have and, in my experience, God doesn't care about what I wish for."

Please, God, how do I reach her?

"Mrs. Grant, did you grow up believing in Jesus?"

"My family didn't go to church much. My husband grew up a believer though, and we raised our son in the Church. But God turned His back on us."

She'd never heard anyone say such a thing. How could Mrs. Grant think that? Then she remembered what LaVonne had told her, that the woman's husband and son had both died, and only a short time apart.

Eve set down the cheap chopsticks that came with the food. "I don't know all the answers, but I believe God does have a plan for our lives. Sometimes horrible things just happen. God hears all our prayers—and answers them—but sometimes His answers aren't what we want. Because He has a different plan. We may not understand the larger picture; we just have to trust Him."

Mrs. Grant's face hardened. *Darn it. I pushed too hard.* Would Mrs. Grant make her leave? She didn't want to blow this opportunity to reach the woman she'd grown to care for, so she started rambling.

"For instance, I believed God called me to move here so I started to pray about it. And someone offered my dad a job at Georgetown, making it happen. I call that a miracle. The reason I thought I was supposed to come here had nothing to do with you, but maybe part of my purpose in moving was to become part of your life."

Mrs. Grant still looked skeptical but not as angry.

Who knew Eve's ability to ramble could be used for good?

"See what I mean? God works in mysterious ways. A few months ago, you probably never would have imagined a teenager becoming part of your life. And now look at us, becoming such great friends."

"Well, I don't know that we're *such* great friends. Sometimes you're more of an irritation."

Eve laughed and saw Mrs. Grant's mouth turn up in a small smile.

"Mrs. Grant, I can honestly say I've never met anyone like you before."

"Right back at ya."

She laughed even louder. Then she got up, walked around the table, and gave the woman a hug. Mrs. Grant didn't return the gesture, making it a rather awkward moment, but Eve didn't care. She'd reached her neighbor in an important way.

Thanks, God.

A brilliant idea popped into her head as she returned to her chair. "Easter is coming up soon. Would you like to join my parents and me for Mass and Easter dinner?"

Mrs. Grant's mouth pursed in irritation. "You really are a persistent thing, aren't you?"

Eve suppressed her glee. She had pushed hard enough for one evening.

"I think it's one of my gifts." She reached for one of the take-out boxes. "So, what should we do after dinner? Do you like to play games?"

Mrs. Grant groaned and shook her head.

Chapter Thirty-two

Nick pulled up in front of Eve's apartment early in the morning, ready for their drive to Cumberland. She pushed open the glass door just as he arrived, and he grinned. She wore an oversized Georgetown sweatshirt and shorts, with her thick hair piled on top of her head. A good look. The best.

"Good morning." She slid into the passenger seat.

"Good morning to you, Albuquerque." He smiled. "You must be a morning person."

"Of course! Each day is filled with new possibilities."

This road trip promised to be a blast.

"Did you bring any baked goods for the trip?" He negotiated his way through the Georgetown traffic.

She patted her bag. "Banana chocolate chip muffins."

"Excellent choice." The thought of her in that pink frilly apron filled his mind. What was new? She'd been on his mind a lot lately.

"Any idea where we're going to search in Cumberland?"

He checked over his shoulder as he switched lanes. "We could check out Mrs. Barrett's family home if it's still there. But I have another lead too. Since two of the symbols were at cemeteries, I decided to look into the Cumberland Cemetery. Guess what its name is?"

"What?"

"That's not a guess."

"Fine. The Cumberland Cemetery."

He laughed. "Really? That's your guess? You think I'm excited about it being named The Cumberland Cemetery?"

"Hey." She held up her bag. "Do you want me to share these muffins with you or not?"

"Don't even threaten such a thing."

"Then tell me." She was cute when she acted tough.

"Fine. Rose Hill."

"You're kidding! Rose was the third clue. That has to be where the treasure is."

"My thoughts exactly."

"Oh. I almost forgot, do you mind making a little detour along the way?" She batted her eyes at him.

This should be interesting. "What did you have in mind?"

"Well, when my family drove across the country during our move, we stopped at as many covered bridges as we could find. They're adorable, like a step back in time. Anyway, there's one not too far off the highway, on our way to Cumberland."

"Covered bridges, huh? Sounds very Americana; let's do it." Like he could say no to her even if he wanted to.

She beamed at him. "Thanks. I love the city but, it's fun to get outside the Beltway for the day."

"Yep." He handed her his phone. "Why don't you pick the music for the road trip."

"I made us our very own playlist. I call it 'Nick and Eve's Adventure.' Hopefully, you'll like the songs since I don't know what kind of music you listen to."

Half a dozen notes into the first song, he grinned.

"What's this?" Old school country music, twang and all. Would not have expected that.

Her hand flew to her chest and her mouth dropped open, feigning shock. "Are you serious? You don't know Willie Nelson? You can't have a road trip without the classic, 'On the Road Again.' Geez, what kind of life have you been living?"

He laughed. "Apparently, an uninformed one. I think I'm going to learn a lot about you through this playlist."

"Don't worry, there are plenty of new songs as well. But I wanted to represent most decades and genres."

He smirked and shook his head. "Great. Can't wait to hear them all. So, what's your favorite music era?"

"I love current music, but I must say I have a bit of an affinity for '50s songs."

"Somehow, that doesn't surprise me."

As her eclectic playlist continued, they chatted and played car games, like locating the letters of the alphabet in the signs they passed and inventing stories about where the other cars were headed.

Using her phone's GPS, Eve directed him through a few narrow country roads to the covered bridge. She gasped when she saw it.

"Oh, look! It's so pretty."

He pulled the car off the road, and they climbed out. The long bridge hovered over a small stream. The white wooden structure, a relic from another era, made him feel like they had gone back in time, a time when a nasally twang was new and modern in music. Curious about its construction, Nick studied the structure while Eve snapped a bunch of photos. She insisted he join her in a series of selfies with the bridge in the background. Smiling, serious, goofy, contemplative, scared: all moods had to be covered.

As fun as it was to take ridiculous pictures together, he was anxious to see what they could find in Cumberland. "To quote Willie Nelson, shall we get 'on the road again?'"

"Sure. Thanks for bringing me to see the bridge."

An '80s tune provided the background music on their way back to the highway.

She shifted in her seat to face him. "Can I ask you a question? I've been curious about something."

"Let me guess. You want to know what actor I think should play me when my life story becomes a movie?"

She laughed. "No, that wasn't the question, but it's a good one. We'll have to discuss it later."

"Okay, so what's your question?"

"Why don't you have a girlfriend?"

Wasn't expecting that one.

"I mean, not to give you a big head, but you seem like quite the catch. You're smart, and clever, and a senator's son."

Nick glanced over at her. Was she being serious? "Hmm. I don't know. I guess I never found anyone intriguing enough to spend a lot of time with." As soon as the words left his mouth, he realized they weren't true. He found her completely intriguing and always looked forward to spending time with her.

She leaned her head against the back of her seat. "Does that mean you've left a trail of broken hearts along the way?"

"Hardly." He peered over at her, suddenly wanting to open up. "I used to be much more social before I convinced my dad to run for office. But then something happened, and I kinda backed away from my social life."

"What happened?"

He focused on the road. "Well, it was during a heated part of the campaign. My dad's opponents were trying to smear his name. Anyway, I went to this party with some friends from school. It was actually pretty low-key, just friends hanging out, with soda and pizza. But someone took some photos of me acting like an idiot, with a red plastic cup in my hand. The next day I got a text from some number I didn't know, threatening to send the pictures to the press and claim I had been drinking and driving, which would completely obliterate the clean-cut image of my family the media had created."

"Oh, my gosh. That's horrible." She placed her hand on his arm. The gesture was comforting, but just as quickly as she had put it there, she moved it away.

He shrugged. "Yeah. After that I didn't know who to trust anymore, so I stopped hanging out with anyone. You know, I never told anyone about that." It felt good to confide in someone.

"Thanks for trusting me."

"What about you? Any serious boyfriends in the past?"

"No. I mostly spent all my time with my best friend, Mindy. We did everything together and kinda isolated ourselves away from all the other kids at school. But then everything changed. Her family moved away, my sister went off to college, and all of a sudden I was alone. But then one day I had my vision of you and thought you might be my boyfriend."

With Nick unsure what to say, silence reigned, except for the electric guitar solo coming from the radio. The discomfort grew by the moment.

"Totally stupid, huh? That's what happens when a lonely girl gets a message from God: she turns it into some silly romance." She turned to stare out the side window.

He didn't know how to read the situation. Was she into him still or was she embarrassed that she'd ever thought of them as a couple? Were girls always this hard to figure out? Say something. *Anything.*

"Well, it is understandable, since I am so devastatingly handsome."

She threw a muffin at him.

Phew! It worked.

"Thanks." He reached for the sweet treat that landed on his lap. "I wondered when you were going to share those. But seriously, speaking of your vision. I've never told you how amazing it is that you had the faith to convince your whole family to pick up their lives and move here for something you didn't even really know existed. That's incredible. God chose the right person when He picked you."

She turned toward him. Oh, man. How could one smile stir up so many emotions?

Chapter Thirty-three

"This place is stunning." Eve knew she was not being of much help. In fact, she had pretty much given up on the task at hand. The Rose Hill Cemetery was breathtaking. She couldn't concentrate on anything except its majestic trees towering like protective guardians over the stone statues, marble benches, and intricately carved tombs. Sunlight dappled down through the tree branches and fluttered across the graves, creating a dazzling effect.

Nick glanced her way, probably wishing she'd spend more time checking out the names on the tombs and less time marveling at the spellbinding beauty.

Her hand grazed across a moss-covered headstone. "I want to be buried somewhere as lovely as this."

He bent to examine a stone in desperate need of restoration before it crumbled into oblivion. "You know, your spirit will be somewhere infinitely more beautiful, and your dead, decaying body won't care where it's buried."

She shoved his shoulder as she walked past. "Don't ruin my daydreams with your logic."

He shook his head. "We can't all be romantics; nothing would ever get done."

She meandered through the lush green grass. "I've never seen a cemetery like this. Look at the dates on the headstones, they're all *so* old."

"New Mexico doesn't have old cemeteries?"

"Not like this. They're more like the Old West ones you see in the movies, simple headstones, more rustic. These are just so . . . elegant."

He moved past her, continuing his thorough search. "If you like this one, you should go check out Oak Hill, it's really scenic."

Her face twitched. "Oh, that's the site of your midnight rendezvous, right?" Even knowing the truth about Natalia's act, she was still a little salty about that night.

His eyes flicked her way. "First of all, it wasn't midnight and secondly, I wouldn't call it a rendezvous. You really don't like Natalia much, do you?"

She wandered down another row, trying to focus on the names. This sure would've been easier if they could've checked the burial records.

"Well, I think I like the Natalia we saw the other night. I didn't like seeing her throw herself at you." Too forward? "I mean, at anyone. And wearing those provocative clothes. I'm glad it was all an act."

"A dangerous one. She assumed I was harmless, but she took a huge risk."

"Think she'll follow your advice and open up to her parents?"

He circled around a large tomb with a human-size stone angel standing on top. "I hope so. Plan A certainly hasn't worked for her."

Eve scanned the large cemetery. This was going to take forever. Which wasn't such a bad thing–more time with Nick.

"Natalia told you she found Barrett's grave when she snuck off with other guys. Do you think that was true?"

"I think she probably snuck out by herself, at least I hope so. I guess it's a good thing she did, or we never would've known about the symbols and clues."

"I didn't realize they would still have such detailed records from the time of the Civil War." Before they arrived at the cemetery they'd stopped at the hall of records. "Of course, a mere mortal like myself wouldn't have found the information. Who knew we'd need your special power of charm to find out there were no Barretts living here at that time."

He grinned. "I helped my dad trace some of our ancestors. That's how I learned the old records weren't as thorough as the newer ones are. You just have to know how to ask."

"Well, I feel much better snooping around here knowing if we do find a Barrett gravestone, it's probably not a family burial site." They'd searched for information on Mrs. Barrett's family the Worthingtons and discovered her father had been the town's mayor. After being designated a historic building, their home had been converted into a bed and breakfast on the edge of town.

Eve wandered toward a large, grassy mound. "If we do find the missing gold, what're we going to do with it?"

"I've been wondering about the end game too. We'll just have to keep praying and wait for the answer. My guess is, most of the people who've searched for it over the years had less than pure motives. Maybe that's why we're supposed to find it, to protect it."

And if Father Romero was right, somehow lead people to God.

The front of the knoll revealed a burial vault that had been dug into the side of a hill. A massive iron gate protected the tomb. Above the gate, a white stone protruded from the natural formation.

"Nick!" She could barely breathe. Carved into the stone were the words:

To My Beloved Virginia Barrett—1870.

He came up beside her. "There was no mention of a Virginia Barrett in the town's records or anywhere in our research. Virginia could refer to Charles Barrett's beloved state. Maybe the gold's buried here."

They looked at each other. A charge of electricity passed between them.

Nick pulled on the thick metal gate, rattling the locked structure. He fished a flashlight from his backpack and pointed its beam into the dark space. The light revealed a large rectangle of white stone, about the size of a dining room table, in the center of the vault.

Eve swiped away a cobweb from between the bars of the gate. "How do we know this is the right one?"

"We need to get to that stone and check for the symbol."

Oh, super easy. "And how do we do that? Do you know how to pick locks?"

He shook his head. "No need for that." He turned off the flashlight and slid it in his pocket. "Help me find some long branches. The straighter the better."

"What exactly is the plan here?"

"Oh, Albuquerque, when will you learn to trust me?"

She crossed her arms. "I don't think you understand how this partnership thing works. You're supposed to share your ideas, and then I can help improve them."

He shot her a mischievous smirk. "That could work, but isn't the element of surprise more exciting?"

She rolled her eyes but helped him search the area until they found two long branches lying near some bushes.

He pulled a roll of duct tape from his handy back-pack. While Eve had brought muffins, he, as usual, came much more prepared for unforeseen circumstances. He secured the branches together, end to end, then attached a mirror and the flashlight to the tip. Watching him work was fascinating. The contraption reminded her of the extension pole her dad used to hang Christmas lights.

When Nick finished his device, she helped him maneuver the branch through the iron bars of the gate. Slowly, they angled it toward the stone coffin in the middle of the locked crypt. The flashlight illuminated the stone, and the tilted mirror let them see any possible engravings. They moved the mirror carefully around, until finally some words appeared.

Nick slowly guided the contraption while she read the words:

May the remains of my beloved Virginia rest in peace until we meet again.

"So, if Virginia refers to the state and not a person, then the 'remains' may refer to the gold. Maybe it means letting it rest in peace here, until he could use it to rebuild his state again."

Oh, wow. "Do you see the symbol?" Her voice quavered.

She tried to help steady the makeshift pole to scan all sides of the stone, but her hands shook so much she became more of a hindrance. Instead, she focused on the mirror but saw only smooth white marble. Then a small dark sliver appeared and slowly widened. Her breath caught as the perfect triangle finally came into view.

"We found it!" Her arms flew around Nick in celebration. "This is so exciting!"

He was unable to return the hug, even if he'd wanted to, since his arms still steadied the branch.

"Are there any words below it?" She unwrapped her arms and leaned into him, trying to get a better view of the mirror's image. The muscles of his arms flexed against her side as he adjusted the cumbersome branch. For a moment she forgot to concentrate on their finding.

"No, but there's something inside the triangle besides the star. It's hard to tell, but kind of looks like three pitchforks."

Hmm. "Or three tridents? Maybe they liked mythology, and it represented the three of them being the guardians of the treasure."

"Maybe. Who knows?" He pulled the branch back toward them.

"Now what? How do we get through this gate? We need to move that massive stone cover off the creepy coffin thing and check for the gold."

"I have no idea."

She examined the heavy metal gate while Nick knelt to disassemble the items from the branches. The keyhole was designed for one of the old-fashioned metal keys. "Somewhere, there's got to be a key to this."

Nick stopped working, his eyes large. He leapt up, grabbed onto both her arms, and pulled her to him. "You are brilliant."

Oh my!

Chapter Thirty-four

After holding her close in that quick hug, Nick really wanted to hold her hand on the way back to the car. But what if she didn't want him to? That would be really uncomfortable, and it was a long ride home.

"The Endelbourg Embassy has a key that belonged to Barrett?" Eve's question pulled him from this inner battle.

He had blurted it out too fast to explain very well. "Not exactly. Remember, I told you there was a diary that belonged to Mr. Stewart, the original owner of the mansion? It was found at the embassy in 1970, and it detailed the close relationship between Mr. Stewart and Mr. Barrett, the home's builder. The two men apparently became quite close. Mr. Barrett thought of Mr. Stewart as the son he never had. Well, supposedly, a key was found with the diary, but no one at the embassy knew what it belonged to."

"Where's the key now?"

He hitched his backpack higher on his shoulder. "That's the problem. No one knows. The key disappeared soon after that. Only the diary remains."

She stooped to pick up a flower that lay in the middle of the path. "Do you think the ambassador is searching for the gold?"

"I don't know if it's him or someone on his staff, but those men only started following us after Natalia told her father that I was onto something."

She lifted the flower to her nose. "Then maybe he has the key and is waiting for you to lead him to the treasure."

"Could be. But why bother telling me about it?" It didn't add up.

"If we can't find the key, how will we see if the gold is in there?"

There was one way. But was it worth it? "Jeff Normandy could probably arrange it."

Her head snapped his way. "I hope you're joking. That guy is about as trustworthy as a hungry mama scorpion with her babies."

He laughed. "I take it that's not very trustworthy."

The flower twirled between her fingers. "She's not exactly mother of the year when she's hungry and will eat the babies if she can't find any other food."

As they reached the parking lot, they both stopped in their tracks. A tremor of fear shot through Nick. Eve's flower fluttered to the ground.

Two men leaned against Nick's car—the guys who had followed them around Arlington. Today, they wore jeans and leather jackets. Nick quickly sized them up. They were younger and more fit than they'd appeared the other day. Not good.

"Oh, no," Eve whispered.

"Come on, let's see what they want." He acted braver than he felt.

"Well, Nick Hammond. What a joy to finally catch up with you." The tall one with the buzz cut crossed his ankles as they approached. "What've you been up to?"

"I don't know what you're talking about. Now, if you'll please move away from my car, we'll be on our way." How was he going to keep Eve safe?

"I think we need to have a little chat first." The man stood to confront Nick. His blond accomplice cracked his knuckles.

Play it cool.

Eve shifted to stand slightly behind him, clutching his shirt.

"Maybe I should call the police. I believe there are laws against harassment."

The man's nostrils flared. "Believe me, when we harass you, you'll know it. We only want to know about the gold and what you've discovered."

He fought the urge to clench his fists. *Keep calm.* "You've been misinformed. I don't know where the gold is." Technically that was true. He didn't know its location for sure.

The man took a step forward. "You've been quite busy running around in search of something."

Nick held the guy's stare. "We've been sightseeing. Eve is new to D.C."

Okay, God, a guardian angel swooping in to help would be great right about now.

The man's eyes flicked to Eve. "Look, Nick, I'm trying to make your life, and the lives of your loved ones, easier. This could get messy, which I'm trying to avoid. One way or the other, you *will* tell me what you know. You can do it now and make this little encounter a pleasant one, or I can use a few of my various techniques to make you talk."

Some internal prod made Nick move. He put his arm around Eve and pushed past the guy to the passenger door. "I wish I could help you, but I don't know anything." He pulled the door open for Eve then walked around to the driver's side.

The man didn't try to stop him. "Wrong answer. Well, young Mr. Hammond, we'll be seeing you soon."

Nick slammed the door shut and pulled away with a squeal of his tires.

Thank You, God, for protecting us.

A glimpse in the rear-view mirror showed the two thugs watching them drive away. He couldn't shake the chill that ran through his veins.

"I've never been so scared in my life." Eve's voice came out as a whisper. "Do you think they'll actually try something?"

His jaw twitched. "I don't know, but what can we do? We can't let people like that get a hold of a national treasure."

"We should probably tell someone about all this. It's getting dangerous."

"You're right. I'll talk to my dad, he'll know what to do. But first we have a stop to make. Would you text Natalia, please? Ask her to meet us at the coffee shop and see if she can bring the diary."

She nodded and pulled out her phone. Her fingers trembled as she typed in the message. Nick gripped the steering wheel more tightly. The ugly confrontation had shaken them both.

Chapter Thirty-five

Conversation on the drive back to D.C. was almost non-existent. Eve spent much of the journey home in prayer. Whenever her mind drifted to those men and their threats, a chill ran down her spine. How had their mission spun so out of control? When did it become so dangerous? Father Romero had warned her that evil always tried to stop good. She should have been prepared for something like this, but she wasn't.

When they hit the Capital Beltway, the frenzy of the city shocked her back to reality.

She sneaked a peek at Nick's rigid jaw. Guess she wasn't the only one who couldn't shake the sense of doom. "Do you think Natalia can get the diary?"

His eyes remained focused on the road. "If anyone can, Natalia will."

Another shiver passed through her. "You know, it's been a stressful day. Maybe we should meet her tomorrow." She just wanted to go home and climb under a pile of blankets.

He glanced at her. "Someone at the embassy has to be behind all this. This may be our only chance to see the diary. Hopefully, she got to it before those guys checked in with whoever they're working for." How could he be so logical at a time like this?

Nick eased the car into a parking spot a block from the coffee shop. His parallel parking skills were impressive, especially with his fried nerves. But he'd grown up in a city; he'd probably had to learn that skill quickly.

While he ordered three lattes, Eve settled in at a table by the window.

"She's late." Nick set the drinks on the table.

"I don't think punctuality is necessarily one of her strong suits."

"True." He sat next to her. The continuous tap of his fingers on the table did nothing to soothe her nerves.

She hunched over her drink, her frigid hands wrapped around the warm cup. Why was she so cold?

"You're in shock."

She looked up at his watchful eyes. "What?"

"The reason you're so cold. It's the scare from earlier." He sipped at his drink.

Reading minds must also be part of his skill set. Or maybe she was just that transparent.

His eyes shifted back to the door. The tapping continued.

"I made sure she knew the request to meet came from you. I didn't think she'd be all that thrilled to hear from me."

He glanced at his phone. "I still think most of her tough-girl attitude was an act. Don't give up on her. I think she could use a friend like you."

Yeah, right. "I highly doubt she wants to be my friend."

"I'm serious. She could use an example of someone with strong beliefs, who knows herself well, and doesn't pretend she's something she's not, just to get her way."

Eve shook her head. "You're sweet, but even though we know she was putting on a show, I'm pretty sure she still has no interest in being my friend."

"Maybe God wanted her to meet you, to give her a positive role model."

"I'm not sure I'm anyone's role model."

He scanned her face. Those intense brown eyes held hers. Okay, maybe she was starting to heat up after all. "Of course, you are. I've never met anyone with such strong beliefs before."

Yep. Her temperature was definitely rising. "I could say the same about you."

"Well, then I guess we make the perfect pair."

A little heart spasm made her twitch. What did that mean? Was he suggesting they were good buddies or that they'd make a great couple? He was just so amazing! Smart, funny, good-looking, with a deep faith. Her feelings for him grew stronger each time they were together, but how did he feel about her?

A moment later, Natalia entered the coffee shop. When her gaze landed on Eve, she peered over her shoulder like she might bolt. Instead, she sighed and walked to their table. Although the girl still wore her usual black attire, she'd toned down the heavy makeup.

"I didn't know it would be both of you."

"Hi, Natalia. Thanks for meeting us." Eve tried to give the other girl a warm smile but was pretty sure it came out as fake as Natalia's goth-girl act, only less believable.

"Did you have trouble getting the diary?" Nick slid the third cup toward the girl.

"No. Stoltz and my father are at a dinner meeting. But it can't be gone long. Stoltz keeps it right on his desk and will notice if it's missing."

"He's obsessed with the treasure, isn't he?"

She pulled a brown leather journal from her purse. "He and my father both. I don't know why, but they keep talking about it. Ever since my dad found out you were interested in it as well, he's showered me with attention. Last time he gave me this much notice, I had gone on a joy ride in the embassy limo."

"Thanks for helping us." Nick took the diary from her.

She shrugged. "Well, you've been nice to me. I figured I could repay your kindness with this. Then we're even."

He tipped his head back, frustration spreading across his face. "Natalia, don't you know how friendship is supposed to work? You don't owe me anything."

She crossed her arms. "I have plenty of friends back at the boarding school. I don't need any here."

He opened the diary. "Too bad. Eve and I are your friends whether you know it or not."

Eve kept quiet during the exchange. Anything she said might upset Natalia, and that was the last thing she wanted. While Nick snapped photos of the diary pages with his cell phone, Natalia pulled her phone out too. She probably wasn't checking on anything, just using it as an excuse to not make small talk. But hey, that was fine. It had been a difficult enough day without adding more unpleasantness.

Eve sipped her coffee and glanced around the shop at the other patrons. A cute couple on a date, holding hands across the table. A mother and her young child sharing a muffin. An elderly gentleman reading the newspaper. Then her eyes landed on a man in the back corner. He slouched down in his chair, a baseball cap pulled low over dark sunglasses. No coffee, food, or newspaper on his table. As she observed him, he shifted uncomfortably then gazed out the window.

Maybe he was an accomplice to those guys at the cemetery.

"Um, Nick." She nudged him, not taking her eyes off the guy.

He looked up at her then followed her gaze.

"Man, we can't catch a break," he muttered. He took one last pic of the diary and handed it back to Natalia.

Then he called out to the suspicious-looking man. "Mr. Normandy, what a small world."

That was Jeff Normandy?

The man looked startled, then faked recognition. "Oh, hi. Nick Hammond, right?"

Eve had seen a few of Mr. Normandy's TV specials but never would have recognized this man as the cheesy treasure hunter. As he walked to their table, she noticed the designer jeans and expensive shoes he wore.

"What a surprise, seeing you again." He flashed a blinding smile as he approached their table. His abnormally white teeth practically glowed in contrast to his unusually tan face.

Nick nodded. "Yes, quite a surprise."

"I don't believe we've met." Mr. Normandy held out his hand to Natalia.

Natalia looked at him with zero interest, rejecting the handshake. Nick made the introductions.

"This is Natalia Schroeder. And this is Eve Donahue." At least he included her in the conversation.

"A pleasure to meet you." Mr. Normandy directed his attention to Natalia.

Eve resisted the urge to yell, "Hello? I'm here too!" Apparently, she was invisible or not worthy enough for the famous treasure hunter. This charlatan probably knew Natalia's identity and was playing some angle to find the treasure. Question was, how did everyone know about it?

"What do you have here?" Mr. Normandy's fingers brushed the old diary. "Looks valuable."

Natalia jerked it away and shoved it in her purse.

Nick took a sip from his drink. "No. Just an old book Natalia found."

"I noticed you taking photos of it. It must be interesting." This guy was nothing if not persistent.

Nick leaned back. "I'm helping her translate a few lines."

The two stared each other down. Eve found the battle of gazes excruciating.

Mr. Normandy was the first to flinch in the testosterone-filled standoff. "Ah. I see."

"So, what brings you here Mr. Normandy?"

"I love the chai tea."

"Looks like you forgot to order it. We'll let you go do that." Nick stood. The simple act dismissed Mr. Normandy and signaled to Eve and Natalia to gather their things.

The man gave him a smug smile. "Right. I hope we'll see each other soon."

"I'm sure we will."

Outside, they said their goodbyes to Natalia, then walked to Nick's car.

"How did he know we were there?" Eve asked as they drove the few blocks to her apartment.

"My guess is, he's following Natalia. Someone at the embassy must have tipped him off that she was coming to the coffee shop."

Eve pulled her hands inside her sleeves. Her chill had returned. "Our treasure hunt has gotten crowded."

His left hand lifted off the steering wheel and pinched the bridge of his nose. "It has. I wish I knew what everyone's motives were. I mean, obviously, Normandy wants the fame, but who's he working with? And who hired the thugs to follow us? The ambassador and Mr. Stoltz are obviously both up to something." He let out a long exhale. "I'm worried this could get dangerous."

He'd read her mind again.

Chapter Thirty-six

Nick stopped in the doorway of his father's office and observed for a moment before entering. His dad sat with his elbows on the desk and his head in his hands. This was not the strong and confident John Hammond that Nick had grown up admiring. The old guilt of starting this stressful trajectory flooded over him.

"Hey, Dad." After he'd dropped Eve off at her apartment, he'd admitted to himself that he needed some advice. Dad was still at work, so Nick headed over to the Senate office building next to the Capitol.

His father waved him in.

"You okay?" He sat in a chair in front of the desk. When had those dark circles appeared under his dad's eyes? And those creases . . . were they new? Nick hadn't noticed them before.

Dad lifted one hand and squeezed his temples. "It's been a long day. Quite frankly, they are all long. And tiring." His smile looked forced. "I'm glad you stopped by. Been enjoying your week off from school?"

"Yeah, it's been good. I've been showing Eve some of the sites around town." Was he always going to grin uncontrollably when he thought of her?

Dad's eyebrow arched. "Ah. Well, she's nice. I'm glad you've found someone to hang out with. I hated seeing you withdraw from your friends."

He shrugged. "After seeing the importance of elections and the future of our country, the stuff my old friends were interested in felt kind of trivial, that's all." No way would he divulge the real reason.

Dad chuckled. "You've always been like an elder statesman living in the body of a kid."

"I only wish I had that kind of wisdom."

His dad's eyes narrowed. "What's on your mind, son?"

Nick wanted to unload about the guys who had threatened him and about the treasure hunter who lurked in the shadows. But how to explain it all? The search for the Confederate gold, the way he and Eve had really met, the real reason he had wanted his dad to run for congress. It all tied together in a complicated way that would sound totally insane to most people.

Before he could think of where to begin, someone knocked on the office door.

Dad shot him an apologetic look. "Come in."

An older gentleman stormed into the office. An air of authority surrounded him. "John, we need to talk." He visibly reigned in his fury when he noticed Nick. "Oh, excuse me, I didn't realize you had another appointment."

"Bob, this is my son Nick."

Nick stood and shook the man's hand.

"Nick, meet Senator Abrams. He's the chair of the Foreign Relations Committee."

"It's an honor to meet you, sir."

Senator Abrams' smile lacked any warmth. "It's a pleasure to meet you, son. I watched some of the local coverage during your dad's campaign. I was impressed with the way you handled yourself. You may have a real future in politics."

Hopefully not. "Thank you, sir, that's kind of you to say."

The senior senator turned back to Nick's father, his face hardening once again. "John, we need to speak. There's been a development."

His dad gave a curt nod. "Sure, Bob, I'll be right over. Let me walk Nick out."

Nick noticed the slight stare-down between the two men. Senator Abrams nodded to Nick and walked out.

"Geez, that was intense."

"Tell me about it. I knew being in the Senate would be tough, but . . . dealing with so many strong personalities, all of them used to getting what they demand, is exhausting." He sighed.

"Is this about the European trade agreement?"

"Yeah, the treaty is in jeopardy, and the relations are failing quickly. I get the feeling there's more going on than meets the eye. Something doesn't feel right."

"That's why you're the man for the job. You're able to see through the politics and bring a new perspective."

Dad gave him an exhausted nod of appreciation. "Thanks, I hope I'm up to it."

Old words of wisdom came to mind. "I'm pretty sure you once told me that fighting the good fight is not always easy."

Dad chuckled. "I hate when my words come back to haunt me. Wasn't there something you were about to tell me?"

Now was not the time.

"I don't think Senator Abrams likes to be kept waiting. We'll talk later, Dad. See you at home."

"Hopefully. I find myself spending more time here than at home these days." He glanced at the door. "I'd better go find out what the crisis is."

Nick hated seeing his dad's shoulders sag. He just couldn't burden him with any more problems.

Chapter Thirty-seven

Eve tossed and turned most of the night, her mind on the events of the previous day. When she did manage to doze off, she was plagued by nightmares about being chased by those two incredibly scary men.

Morning finally rolled around, and she trudged into the kitchen for a caffeine boost. Her parents sat at the table drinking coffee and reading the newspaper. They had been out again when she got home last night. Their social life had certainly improved since they moved to D.C.

"Hey kiddo, you're up early." Dad set down his mug.

"I couldn't sleep."

Part of her wanted to fill them in on all that had been happening, but what if she told them and they put her under lock and key, not allowing her to investigate any more? That was probably the responsible thing to do, but if she and Nick were on a mission from God, they couldn't stop now.

"Want some breakfast?" Mom pushed her chair away from the table.

"More like, do *you* want some breakfast? I'm craving pancakes. Want some?"

Mom's eyes lit up. "That sounds delicious. I have some fresh strawberries for the top." She joined Eve at the kitchen counter.

Dad patted his stomach. "Oh, you girls spoil me. Eve, you truly are an exceptional baker. I just don't know where you got your skills."

"Hey!" Mom threw a dish towel at him before opening the fridge. She pulled out the container of strawberries and slanted a look at Eve. "You certainly have spent a lot of time with Nick this week."

Super smooth, Mom.

Dad looked up from the editorials. "Where did you tour yesterday?"

"We drove out of town to Cumberland, Maryland, and saw this cool covered bridge along the way."

"Cumberland? I just read something about a farm out there." Dad flipped through the newspaper. "Here it is. A young couple is trying to convert their family farm to a rehabilitation facility for wounded veterans. They're working on raising funds for the project."

"What a great place for something like that! It's incredibly peaceful out there." At least it would be if thugs weren't lurking around the local cemetery. She shook off her thoughts and concentrated on dumping ingredients in a large bowl.

Mom started slicing berries into small pieces. "Are there any girls from school you'd want to have over tonight when we get back from our tour?"

This again? She kept her voice light. "Most everyone went somewhere for spring break." She whisked the batter, displacing her annoyance.

Mom pulled a bowl out of the cupboard. "I just don't want you to fall into the same pattern and isolate yourself."

"Don't stress, Mom. I have plenty of friends at school but I'm only here another year then off to college. I want to enjoy the city and soak up as much history as I can." She scooped batter onto the heated pan. "Most of the kids who live here don't have any interest in tourist stuff, since they've grown up around it. Nick happens to enjoy it all as much as I do."

Time to change the subject.

"Hey, speaking of hanging out with people, would it be okay if Mrs. Grant joins us next week for Easter Mass?" She flipped the pancakes.

Mom carried the bowl of berries to the table. "Really? Did she say she'd come?"

"She didn't say she wouldn't come. I'm still working on it. I think she's a sad person and I'm trying to reach out to her."

"That's wonderful. I think she desperately needs someone to care for her. Of course she can come with us. I'm proud of you for helping her out."

Eve placed a stack of fluffy pancakes on the table.

Dad finally put down his section of the paper. "Those look fantastic. So, are you ready for our grand adventure?"

It was Thursday, and she'd promised to spend the day with her parents. They probably felt guilty they hadn't taken her somewhere for spring break, but she just wanted to spend the day with Nick. Of course, she always wanted to hang out with him, but it stressed her out that they hadn't uncovered more during their week off. Come Monday, they'd be back at school with limited time to investigate. She had no idea what their next move should be. Hopefully, Nick would come up with a plan.

Still, she didn't want to disappoint the folks. She put on a smile and feigned enthusiasm.

"Yep! Where are we going?"

"Manassas." Dad emphatically stated the answer.

"Let me guess, a Civil War battlefield?" What else could it be?

Mom laughed. "She knows you well, dear."

Eve grinned and reached for the bottle of syrup. "As long as we don't have to dress up and participate in a re-enactment, I'm in."

***

Touring the battlefield proved to be way more interesting than she ever would have thought. Between the museum's impressive displays and the knowledgeable tour guides who described the battles and stories in amazing detail, she could visualize so clearly the events in her mind. It was fascinating and tragic at the same time. Dad's interest in the Civil War must be contagious.

She'd honestly never thought a lot about the war, but as they walked through the battlefield, a new understanding washed over her. The tragedy of all that had happened on this field was horrifying: hundreds of young men brutally fighting, their dying bodies scattered over the field. Her heart broke just thinking about the deadly reality.

"Dad, we tend to think of the South as being on the wrong side of the war, but hearing the stories here in Virginia, I get a different sense of it now."

He nodded. "The American Civil War is often simplified when it's taught. Most people think it was all about slavery, but there were also other issues that led to the division, things like economics and states' rights."

"While Nick and I researched the rumors of the Confederate gold, we found out Hamilton and the others were against slavery but sided with the South because they didn't want the government involved so much with their states."

"Yes, and there is a point to be made for that. Each state is unique; maybe they should have more say in what goes on with their people."

"But then others would argue that we're not very united," Mom chimed in.

"Exactly!" Dad beamed. "Aren't these discussions fun?"

Eve rolled her eyes. *'Fun* wouldn't really be the word I would use, but thought-provoking for sure. Speaking of Hamilton and the gang, if there was hidden Confederate gold, what do you think they were saving it for?"

Uh oh. She knew by her dad's smile that she'd awakened the beast. He'd spotted her intrigue and would now constantly be sharing stories and theories that he found interesting.

Hmm. Maybe that wasn't actually *so* bad.

He patted her shoulder. "Another great topic to ponder. I've thought about that a lot. Those three men, who supposedly were the ones in charge of the safekeeping of the gold, were all very honorable. None of them had ever owned slaves but, like you said, they were concerned about the government taking all the power from the states. As I told you before, it was an uneasy time. Lincoln had been assassinated, making the country even more unstable as it tried to unify after the bitter war. I believe Hamilton, Barrett, and Meyers were waiting to see if things would unify or further separate. Since they never used the gold, it seems to me they really wanted unity, not war, and were trying to figure out what was best for the country. Of course, that's speculation, assuming the gold ever existed. It's interesting to think about the possibilities."

If he only knew how real the possibilities were. "What would you do with all that gold if you found it?"

"Wow. What a huge responsibility. You'd want to make sure it went to good use and didn't fall into the hands of people with bad intentions."

"Exactly." But how do they figure that out?

"I'd like it to help people who need assistance. Jesus tells us to care for the poor and the crippled, so I think that would be the right thing to do." He leaned closer. "Don't ask Mom though. She'd probably want to use it for the repairs at the Kennedy Center."

Mom smacked his arm.

Seeing her parents' playful side always made Eve smile. "I didn't realize the Ken Cen needed repairs."

"Just a bit of TLC. We're starting a fundraising drive to earn the necessary money to fix a few things."

"I guess it is really old. Wasn't it built in like 1963?"

Her mom laughed. "I don't think things are 'really old' if they're from the 1960s."

"Great job with your history though," Dad added. "The assassination of President Kennedy happened in 1963. But it was over a decade before they built the memorial."

Eve's phone buzzed. Nick! She quickly read his text.

Can you get together tonight?

Eve's mouth turned up in a smile. When she glanced up, her parents were watching her.

Mom linked arms with Dad. "I'm guessing that was a message from Nick."

Dad steered them toward the parking lot. "Well, at least we got her for a little while today."

Mom nodded and heaved a fake sigh. "It's hard to compete with the cute son of a senator."

Chapter Thirty-eight

The moment Eve climbed in the car, Nick handed his phone to her, unable to stop the slight tremor in his hand.

"I got a text this afternoon, from Natalia."

Eve's brow furrowed as she took the phone from him. She read the message, and her face went white.

"Is this real?" Her eyes shot to his.

He took back the phone and stared, for the hundredth time, at the picture on the screen. Natalia sitting in a chair, her arms behind her back, and tape across her mouth. The message read:

I told you we were serious. Don't contact the police unless you want to make things worse for your friend. We will be in touch.

"Oh, my gosh," Eve whispered. "What have we done?"

***

"Yes, Mr. Ambassador." Nick glanced at Eve as he spoke on the phone. "I understand. Sorry to disturb you. We wanted to make sure everything was all right."

He hung up and leaned his head against the steering wheel. Before his call to the ambassador, they had driven to the Lincoln Memorial. They were now parked along Constitution Avenue.

Why was everything so complicated?

Eve touched his shoulder. "What did he say? Doesn't sound like he's very concerned about his daughter being kidnapped."

"He said she has gone on 'holiday' with a friend and that this was probably one of her 'shenanigans.' He apologized that she involved me and implied this kind of thing is not unusual."

"What do you think?" She dropped her hand.

"I'm not sure. I know she used to make up stories and pretend to be something she wasn't, but she promised she was through with all that. And I can't stop thinking about those guys who followed us. Maybe they grabbed her."

"She did know we were nervous about them. Could she be pranking us?"

He sat back. "Maybe, but I'm worried she might be in real trouble. Besides, I don't think she has many friends around to be on 'holiday' with."

"True. But what can we do if her parents don't think anything's wrong?" She bit her lip.

"I have no idea, but we're the ones who got her into this mess, so we're the ones who have to save her." How to pull that off was a mystery.

"Do we just sit and wait to hear from them?"

"I don't know what else to do. Maybe when she doesn't come home, the ambassador will realize something's up and take this seriously." He glanced out his window. "Come on, let's go for a walk and clear our heads."

The moon and stars shone brightly in the clear night sky. It was a perfect night to check out the monuments. He enjoyed taking Eve to the sites in town. Her reactions were always priceless. Everyone else he knew was so used to seeing the monuments and museums every day that they never paid them any real attention.

As they walked along the reflecting pool, the long, rectangular-shaped pool of water situated between the Lincoln and Washington Memorials, a magnetic pull seemed to draw his hand toward hers. It would be so simple to reach over and link their fingers together. But a nagging worry held him back. Eve was amazing—fun to be around and undeniably cute—but he was nervous about starting anything. What if it didn't work out? He didn't want to lose her friendship.

"Well, tell me about your day with the family?" Her question broke into his thoughts.

He shoved his hands into his pockets. "Fine, I guess, if you think going on a hike up to Great Falls with my family sounds fun."

"Umm, I think you're expecting a different answer but that actually does sound fun."

He grinned. "It may seem like a great way to spend the day, but this is *my* family we're talking about. Even the easiest of outings always gets a little crazy. Grace kept whining and begging Jace and me to give her piggy-back rides. Olivia was convinced some wild animal would jump out at her and kept squealing at every sound and rustle of leaves. We sort of lost Dillon twice because he kept wandering away from the group. Gabriella wasn't watching the trail (too busy texting her friends) so she tripped on a rock and twisted her ankle. And my dad was completely distracted the whole time."

Eve's eyes sparkled at his description. "Sounds like an adventure. Why was your dad distracted? Senator stuff?"

He kicked a stone out of the way. "Oh yeah, I meant to tell you about that but forgot with the whole Natalia thing. It was pretty obvious Dad's mind was elsewhere. Whenever we asked him something, he kept answering with weird statements that made no sense. I finally had a chance to walk next to him and asked him what was up. He told me it had to do with the Endelbourg trade agreement."

"Really?"

"You can't say anything to anyone."

She shook her head. "Of course not."

He glanced over his shoulder, making sure no one could overhear. "As soon as he said it, he tried to backtrack a bit. I'm sure he's not supposed to talk about any of this outside of the Senate. But he told me there are rumors that the new king of Endelbourg and some of the neighboring countries want to break away from the European Union and join a rebel group from Russia."

"But why?"

"The king claims they're being absorbed by Germany and need to break free."

"That doesn't sound good, but what does it mean?"

He veered through the park toward the monuments. "I'm not sure. But he mumbled something about overturning governments and disrupting the peace in the area, which doesn't seem like it will turn out well."

"Hmm." Eve frowned. "Somehow our mission must be related."

"I agree. I bet a stack of Confederate gold would be quite helpful for their cause."

"If tensions in that region were to escalate, it could turn into a war."

"Yeah."

"Do you think that's what we're supposed to stop?"

"Maybe." Stopping a war? Not overwhelming at all.

They climbed halfway up the steps to the Lincoln Memorial, then Nick stopped and turned back toward the Washington Monument. He watched Eve, anxious to see her expression.

She didn't disappoint.

Her mouth fell open in a gasp as she took in the sight of the beautiful white obelisk lit against the dark night sky. Her eyes sparkled like the mirror image of the tall monument, shimmering in the reflecting pool below.

"It's so pretty!"

With her gaze on the view in front of her, she lowered herself to sit on the steps. "Did you ever get a chance to examine the pictures you took of the diary?"

Nick sat next to her, careful not to be too close. He rested his arms on his knees. "Yeah, reading the letters kept me up half the night. Mr. Stewart wrote about the great friendship between him and Mr. Barrett, and how one day Mr. Barrett shared an incredible story about the Confederate gold that he and two colleagues had become the guardians of. At first, Mr. Stewart was skeptical and thought the elder gentleman enjoyed telling tall tales, but over time he believed him.

"The other two men (Hamilton and Meyers) had already died, and Barrett didn't know what to do with the treasure. With his health declining, he worried he'd also die, leaving no one alive who knew about the gold. So, he shared the location with Mr. Stewart before he passed away. In the diary, Mr. Stewart said that he now possessed the key and didn't know what to do with it. That was the last entry. I searched online and found that he died in a train accident. He probably never had a chance to do anything with the treasure either."

He expected some reply so glanced her way when she remained silent. She sat staring at him, her mouth and eyes wide. "You didn't think to tell me this?"

Oops. "Sorry, I've been a bit distracted."

"So, sometime in the last fifty years, someone at the embassy came across this diary and the key." Her voice rose a bit, and she turned toward him.

"But no one knew where the treasure could be found." Pieces were starting to fit together.

"But now they need the money and are desperate to find it." She continued the thought process.

"So, they looked for experts who might be able to help them." He edged forward, getting caught up in their back-and-forth exchange.

"That's why they invited my dad to the dinner party, to get more information regarding these three men." Eve leaned closer, her eyes shining.

"And somehow, we started to figure it out." He joined her enthusiasm as they puzzled it out.

"That's why they're following us! They're hoping we'll lead them to the treasure."

In their excitement over figuring things out, they'd inched closer to each other with each revelation. They were so close now that Nick could see the tiny freckles across the bridge of her nose. Embarrassed, he cleared his throat and backed away. Eve's cheeks reddened and the glimmer in her eyes faded.

Perfect moment broken.

She turned her attention back to the reflecting pool. "So where do we find the key?"

"I doubt it's in the house or they would've found it."

"So where is it? And who hid it?"

As Eve pondered the dilemma, Nick spotted the two guys who had harassed them the day before at the cemetery. Fear and adrenaline spiked through him. The men pretended to be tourists but, as usual, stuck out in the crowd. Suddenly, he was more mad than afraid. Enough of playing defense.

"I think it's time for a selfie." He pulled Eve up and spun them around so the guys were behind them. Eve leaned into him. But instead of taking a photo of them, he zoomed in to get a shot of the two men instead.

"Um, Nick, you're not very good at this. That's not us."

"No, it's our two friends. We're being followed again."

Chapter Thirty-nine

Drop everything, Albuquerque. I think I know where Natalia may be.

Eve had woken up to Nick's adrenaline-inducing message. As she anxiously waited out front of her building for him to arrive, a cab pulled up with Mrs. Grant inside. Eve opened the door for her while the elderly woman paid the fare.

"Where've you been? Anywhere fun?" She offered her arm to Mrs. Grant as her neighbor slid out of the taxi. Surprisingly, the help was accepted without protest.

"Vera, my friend at the Smithsonian, took me out for brunch."

"How nice." Eve led her over to a bench. It would be fun to visit while she waited for Nick.

Mrs. Grant didn't seem quite as responsive to the idea. She clutched her purse like she expected Eve to snatch it and run off. "You made quite an impression on her. I knew just who she was talking about when she said a girl who never quit talking came to see her. Your visit made her realize we hadn't seen each other in a while, and she wanted to catch up. So, I guess it's your fault I had to get all dressed up and go out to a restaurant which couldn't even offer a decent Bloody Mary."

"Next time you should invite her to your place, and I'll bake you a coffee cake or something. Then you can make the Bloody Marys the way you like them."

Mrs. Grant pursed her lips.

Wow, no argument. That was practically an agreement.

"Oh, good news. My parents said they'd love for you to join us for Easter Mass next weekend, and then you can come over to our place for brunch."

"Oh, what good news," Mrs. Grant said dryly. "What do people wear to this church service of yours?"

Basically, another yes. Eve was on a roll.

"Most people dress up a bit more on Easter. A nice dress, like you're wearing, would be perfect."

Mrs. Grant crinkled her nose. "Do I need an Easter bonnet?"

Eve beamed. "See? We think alike. Sadly, not many people wear Easter hats anymore, but I always do. I love the old tradition. Maybe we could go shop for some, together." She tried to picture herself and Mrs. Grant at the mall. The image never got better than blurry.

"I don't need to go shopping. I have a whole closet full of hats."

Better yet. "Perfect! May I borrow one? It would be fun to see your collection."

The edges of Mrs. Grant's mouth turned slightly up, making Eve smile even bigger. Together they watched as Nick pulled into the circle driveway at the apartment building and came to a stop in front of them.

He climbed out and walked around the car.

"Hi, Mrs. Grant." He took her hand in his, being as smooth as a piece of petrified wood. "Nice to see you again. Thank you for your help with the Smithsonian. The information you gave us turned out to be incredibly useful."

Color rose in Mrs. Grant's cheeks. Yet another heart won over by Nick's charm and warmth. "Eve said you've been showing her around town."

"Yes, we Washingtonians need to show her the ropes, don't we?" He gave her a conspiratorial wink.

Mrs. Grant nodded. "The big city can be a bit over-whelming for someone from the *West*." Eve tried not to be offended. The woman said "west" like it was a conta-gious disease or something. "Have you taken her to Mount Vernon yet?"

"No, I haven't. That's a fabulous idea though. Mount Vernon has always been one of my family's favorite places to visit."

"We'll culture her up before she knows it." Mrs. Grant gave Nick the kind of smile that made them seem like accomplices. Eve's jaw nearly came unhinged. *Who is this woman?*

"Where are you going today?" The nice lady in Mrs. Grant's body seemed genuinely interested.

"Nothing too exciting, just a tour around Foggy Bot-tom."

Okay. These two were getting a little too chummy. Time to go.

She stood up. "Can we help you inside before we leave?"

Mrs. Grant reached out for Nick's hand to help her stand. "I've been walking into buildings since before you arrived in town."

Eve wrapped her arms around the elderly woman in a good-bye hug. Mrs. Grant huffed but tapped her back a few times anyway before she shuffled her way into the apartment building.

Eve turned to Nick. "What's in Foggy Bottom? That's where the Kennedy Center is, right?"

Nick sat on the bench and tugged her down beside him. "Right, but look at this. I received another text from the kidnappers." He angled the screen of his phone towards her. Along with the same photo of Natalia tied up were the words:

If you want to see your friend again, meet us at your coffee shop at noon and tell us everything you know about the treasure.

"But the coffee shop's not in Foggy Bottom." What was she missing?

He handed his phone to her. "No, but I think Natalia is. Look closely at the photo. Notice anything in the background?"

She concentrated on the photo. "Well, there's an open window and some building in the background."

"Exactly! Do you know what that building is?"

"Um, no. Should I?"

Nick pulled the phone from her hands. "It's the Watergate Hotel. I don't know why I didn't notice it before. Those circular buildings are pretty distinctive."

"But there's got to be a ton of buildings with views of the Watergate. How do we narrow it down?" Still not quite ready to rejoice with him.

He grinned, looking like a little kid ready to blurt out a secret. Irresistible. "The Watergate sits on the edge of the Potomac, next to the Kennedy Center. Which means, there are buildings only on the north and east sides of the complex. Most of those are apartments and office buildings." He pointed at the picture again. "Look, you can see long drapes at the edge of the window, part of a bed on one side of her, and a desk on the other."

"A hotel room."

"Yes!" He paused for a moment. Whether on purpose or not, it created a dramatic effect. "Only one of the two hotels in the area faces the right direction to have a view of the Watergate. A simple process of elimination."

Eve threw her arms around his neck. "Are you the most brilliant person or what?" She pulled away when he flinched. Did he not like hugs? Or just not hers? "Okay. How do we find out what room she's in and get her out?"

"I'm so glad you asked."

Oh, that grin of his—just too cute for words! Maybe she could forgive him for treating her spontaneous hug with such blatant aversion.

Chapter Forty

Nick strode into the hotel with as much confidence as he could muster. Guests milled around the lobby. Some dragged luggage behind them. A few, drinks in hand, chatted in the lounge chairs. A group of swimsuit-clad children followed their mother like a family of ducklings.

He took a moment to check out the two workers at the front desk, then motioned for Eve to approach the middle-aged gentleman behind the counter.

After a deep breath, she pulled a ridiculously large map from her bag and moved into line behind the clerk's single customer.

A few moments later Nick approached the front desk but joined the line in front of a young woman whom he guessed to be somewhere in her twenties. He bit back laughter at Eve's loud descriptions of all the hotels her family stayed in during their move from New Mexico. The gentleman clerk patiently listened to every word, never losing his smile. He had to hand it to Eve— she was almost as good of a distraction as his siblings.

"May I help you?"

"Hi. I hope you can." He read the female clerk's name tag. "Anika?"

She smiled brightly. "Yes, and you pronounced it right too. What can I do for you, sir?"

He glanced around the lobby then lowered his voice. "I'm kind of in a bind." He hated lying, but they needed to save Natalia, and this was the best plan he could come up with.

Her pencil-thin eyebrows furrowed. "What's wrong?"

"My dad and his business partner are at a business meeting." Which was probably true, but it had nothing to do with him being at this hotel. Or with his dad. "I went out to get a little fresh air, and now I can't find my key. I guess I must've left it in the room. So, I'm locked out. To make matters worse, I didn't even notice the room number." He paused to huff out a breath and pull his eyebrows together in a frown he hoped looked genuine. "He already thinks I'm totally unreliable and . . . well, I wasn't supposed to leave the hotel." He probably shouldn't even be at the hotel, but she didn't need to know that. "I don't suppose you can help me?"

Anika smiled. "What's your dad's name?"

Hopefully, his acting skills could pull this off. He shot her a sheepish look. "Well, the room is registered in his partner's name, and I can't for the life of me remember it. I'd never met him until this trip. What should I do?" He tried to look just a little bit afraid, so she'd put her own interpretation on that statement.

She tapped her chin with a polished fingernail. "Do you happen to have a photo of your dad? Maybe I'll recognize him."

Time for his relief expression. "Yes, I do! Here's a photo of him and his partner when we were at the Lincoln Memorial last night."

While she studied the photo he had snapped of the two men who'd been following them, Nick sneaked a look at the next window.

Eve unfolded her map, spread it across the counter, and started plying the overwhelmed hotel clerk with questions about Ford's Theater. Nick listened, totally impressed. Why had she been so unsure of this plan? She was a natural.

The female clerk started nodding. She lowered her voice. "I know exactly who you mean. I remember these men. I was here when they checked in, and they were—well, rather rude."

Agreement face. "Now you know what I'm dealing with."

"I think I saw them leave a little while ago."

"Was anyone else with them?"

She shook her head. "No, just the two of them."

Worry. "I don't suppose I could get a key to the room?"

Her smile seemed truly sympathetic. "Sorry, I wish I could give you one, but since you're not listed as a guest . . ." She shook her head.

Not surprising.

Begging. "Could you at least tell me the room number? Then I can wait for them in the hallway and pretend I got locked out when I went to get ice or something."

She pondered this for a moment, glanced at her colleague who was now intently listening to Eve's thoughts on the weird similarities between President Lincoln's and President Kennedy's assassinations, then leaned closer to Nick.

A few minutes later he and Eve were riding the elevator up to the fourth floor. He nudged her with his elbow. "Great job distracting the other clerk, Albuquerque."

"Thanks." She nudged him back. "Congratulations to you for sweet-talking yet another helpless female."

He shot her a give-me-a-break look. "Seriously, I think we make a rather good team." That might be the most truthful thing he'd uttered all day.

"I agree, but at the moment I feel more like Bonnie and Clyde. I can't believe she gave you the room key."

"Oh, she didn't."

Her head tipped. "How do we get in then?"

"We'll knock."

"Knock?"

Why did she always question his brilliance? Granted, this probably wasn't one of his better ideas, but it didn't need to be genius. It just needed to work.

"Anika said they left a little while ago, alone. Which means Natalia is not with them. Maybe she's still here. We're assuming there are no other men watching her, but if there are, they'll answer the door. If not, we'll confide in the cleaning crew that someone might be in trouble and have them check in the room."

When they reached the room, they found a "Do Not Disturb" sign hanging on the door handle. Nick ignored it and knocked sharply on the door. "Room Service."

They heard the security bar being moved. Nick prepared himself to either ram his shoulder into the door and catch the kidnapper off guard or throw a punch to the guy's face.

He did neither. When the door opened, he just stood and stared. Unbelievable. "You're looking well today, Natalia."

Chapter Forty-one

Eve held her breath, her gaze fixed on the spasmodic twitch in Nick's clenched jaw. He had given Natalia the benefit of the doubt, and here she stood, obviously *not* being held captive. Natalia tried to shut the door, but Nick jammed it with his foot. She then flounced across the room and onto the bed, where she grabbed the remote and started flipping through channels, like she had no cares in the world.

What a piece of work!

Eve followed Nick into the room and shut the door.

"What is wrong with you?" Nick's voice had an edge to it that Eve hadn't heard before.

"Nice to see you too, Nick." Natalia sassed back.

He strode to the TV and pushed the power button, ignoring the girl's nasty look. "I thought we were friends. Why would you try to convince us you were kidnapped?"

She glared at him. "I don't have any friends."

Nick stormed toward the window.

Eve stifled the urge to shake Natalia like a little goth rag doll.

Maybe she should have a go at the girl. A little reverse psychology came to mind. "For the record, I'm not surprised. I wasn't so sure about this whole hostage thing, but Nick believed in you and was really worried."

"That's his problem."

"What changed? You trusted us enough to bring us the diary the other day. Why would you suddenly team up with the guys who've been chasing us? Are you working with them?"

Natalia leaned her head against the headboard. "I may have been gullible for a while but I'm smart enough to look out for myself."

"What're you talking about? Nick's done nothing but try to be your friend."

"I don't need friends who use me."

Nick strode back toward the bed. "What's that supposed to mean?"

"Mr. Stoltz told me, Nick. You're working with some TV treasure hunter to find the gold and you've been using me to get information." Her chin jutted out.

Nick's shoulders relaxed a bit. "I admit we've been interested in the treasure, but we're not working with Normandy. I probably shouldn't have asked you to get the diary for us. But everything else we've ever talked about is the truth. And I still think you should stop being someone you're not and talk to your dad about what you want."

Eve watched as Natalia stared at Nick. She seemed to be questioning his sincerity.

Time to break the uncomfortable silence. "Natalia, did you tell Mr. Stoltz we were curious about the diary?"

Natalia sighed. "He caught me returning it to his desk the other night. I thought he'd start screaming but he calmly asked what I most desired. So, I told him about my boyfriend, Sergei, and how I wanted to return to Switzerland. He promised he would make it happen if I helped him. I agreed, and he hatched this kidnapping plan, so you'd have to tell what you know about the stupid treasure."

Nick ran his hand through his hair. "Look, I'm sorry you felt used by us. I did think you could help us, but I haven't been using you for information. I was asking you as a friend."

Wow. For once he didn't have the perfect words for a situation but instead seemed unsure of himself. But at the moment, Eve worried more about the men returning. Sooner or later, they would realize Nick was a no-show for their meeting and make their way back here. Being here when they returned probably wouldn't be such a great idea.

Time to get this show on the road. "Natalia, do you trust Mr. Stoltz?"

"What do you mean?"

"We believe someone wants this treasure for reasons that could possibly lead to a war involving Endelbourg. Do you think Mr. Stoltz has honorable intentions? Or could he be behind something more sinister?" She didn't want to bring up the fact that if Stoltz was innocent, then the ambassador himself might be the one with evil plans.

"Are you serious?" Natalia sat up straight. "That would mean I'd never get to go back to school. I have no idea why he wants to know what you guys know. I assumed he just wanted to find the treasure first." Her eyes travelled between the two of them. "I think my dad trusts him, but I've never liked him."

Nick sat on the edge of the bed. "We need some kind of plan. Those guys will be back soon. You should leave with us. We'll take you back to the embassy."

Natalia bit her thumbnail. "Maybe I should stay and try to get some information for you."

"No," Nick stated emphatically. "Who knows what they might try, to get our attention. The best thing to do is get you safely back to the embassy. You can tell Mr. Stoltz that you were scared, that you changed your mind and don't want his help anymore. Eve and I will help you talk to your dad and make him understand your feelings."

Natalia frowned. "You'd do that for me?"

Nick nodded. "How many times do I have to tell you, I'm your friend? I've meant it every time I've said it. Now come on, let's get out of here before they come back."

His patience was astounding.

Natalia bit her lip. "Wait. There were some letters with the diary, but I didn't take them to the coffee shop since you only asked about the diary. I think they're in the adjoining room." She nodded to the door connecting the two rooms.

Nick eyed the door. "I thought Mr. Stoltz kept the diary at his office in the embassy."

"He did, but I guess he decided it was safer away from the embassy, especially after I took it."

A possible new lead? "Maybe the letters will give us more information."

Nick sighed. "Okay, but we've got to hurry. They'll be back soon."

Natalia crawled off the bed, went into the bathroom, and turned on the shower. When she came out, she shut the door behind her. "That might keep them from realizing I'm gone, for a little while."

Nick turned the doorknob to the connecting room. The door opened only partway. A privacy chain, hooked on the other side of the door, kept them from going any further.

"Oh, great." Eve's shoulders sagged. "Now what?"

Nick turned toward them. "Do either of you have a rubber band?"

Chapter Forty-two

Nick took the hair tie Eve offered him, along with the skeptical look that accompanied it. He made a loop in the rubber band then squeezed his hand through the partially opened door. He eased the loop around the end of the chain which hung in the sliding lock. Then he lowered his hand and looped the other end of the band onto the door handle. He slid his hand out of the door then closed it.

"What was that about?" Natalia shared Eve's not-impressed look.

"Voila." He turned the knob and opened the door, the chain no longer attached. He raised one eyebrow, basking in their astonished expressions.

Eve grabbed his arm. "Where'd you learn to do that?"

He held the door open for them to enter. "Once, on vacation, Dillon locked the door to our adjoining rooms, then fell asleep with the TV on. The kid can sleep through anything and didn't hear us calling, so we had to get creative."

"Well, nicely done."

He scanned the room. "Let's hope they didn't put the diary in the safe, because that I can't break into."

Luckily, he didn't need to try. The diary lay on the desk with some letters placed inside the front cover. Nick unfolded them and snapped photos with his phone.

Eve tugged on his shirt. "Come on, let's get out of here."

She was right; time was ticking.

After making sure the diary, letters, and door were left the way they had found them, they exited the room into the hallway. They were almost to the adjoining corridor when one of the elevators dinged. The trio froze in their tracks.

"No, he didn't show," gruffed a man's voice. *Blondie!*

Nick nodded toward the exit sign. They scurried into the stairwell just as the man rounded the corner into the corridor. Nick pressed his ear against the crack in the door.

"Taggert stayed behind, in case they eventually make an appearance. I came back to the hotel to check on the girl."

It wouldn't take long for him to realize Natalia wasn't there. Her little diversion might buy a few extra minutes, but they needed to escape the hotel. Now. They sprinted down the stairs, slowing only when they reached the lobby to avoid any unwanted attention. Once outside, they hustled to Nick's car and piled in.

He'd barely pulled onto the busy street when Natalia leaned forward from the back seat. "Where are we going?"

"Somewhere safe, where we can read these letters and figure out a plan."

They rode in silence as he made his way to Wisconsin Avenue and continued up to the National Cathedral. The farther they got from Foggy Bottom and the embassy, the better. He figured they'd be safe at the crowded tourist attraction, and besides, being there always gave him a sense of protection and security.

He led the girls through the towering building, prodding them along as they both kept gaping at the exquisite stained-glass windows soaring above them. They followed him through a side door and out to an enclosed garden. He breathed easier once they were surrounded by the beds of blooming flowers, religious statues, and flowing fountains. No one should look for them here in this peaceful outdoor sanctuary.

He located two secluded benches underneath a tree bursting with fragrant white blooms. Thoughts of their recent escapade amid the cherry blossoms filled his mind. But there'd be no light-hearted moments today. The intensity of their mission had ratcheted up since then.

Eve settled in next to him on one of the benches while Natalia sprawled across the opposite one. He handed Natalia his phone, and she read the letters out loud, interpreting from German to English.

When Natalia finished, Eve turned to face him. "Let's go through this slowly. These letters were written by someone named Mr. Adelmann and addressed to a Mr. Hartzler, who was the Endelbourg Ambassador in the 1970s."

He nodded. "Right. We only have this one-way communication, but it sounds like these two men were part of a growing resistance to the Endelbourg government." This had to be related to the issues Dad was worried about now, the royal grandson hoping to finish his grandfather's plans. He glanced at Natalia. Where did her father's loyalty lie?

"The embassy was remodeled a few years before these letters were written and the diary and key were found by this Mr. Hartzler," Eve continued.

"Yes, and it sure sounded like the men were extremely excited to learn of the hidden Confederate gold. They probably considered it an opportunity to get the money their movement would require." Things were starting to add up.

"But Hartzler couldn't figure out where the gold was hidden." Eve somehow anticipated his thoughts.

He leaned toward her. "So, the two of them came up with a plan to hide the key until they discovered the location of the gold."

"Do you two always do this?" Natalia grumbled. "Continue each other's sentences? It's annoying."

He glanced at Eve, who turned away, trying to hide her blush. He bit back a smile.

Natalia crossed her arms. "Why would they hide the key but then never go back for it?"

Nick slowed his spiraling thoughts to explain. "The tyrannical king died soon after that. Next in line for the crown was his son, who believed in peace and wanted to take the country in a new direction, unifying with the other European countries."

Eve turned back toward them, her cheeks a more natural shade again. "Which means, those in the old king's inner circle could no longer advance the plan."

He continued the theory. "Fast forward to present day. The peace-loving king has died, and his son, the new leader, wants to follow in his grandfather's footsteps and pull out of the European Union. The disruptive plans have been re-enacted, and the treasure is suddenly important again. Which leaves us with the strange note signed by Hartzler, presumably stating where the key is located."

Eve leaned forward, resting her elbows on her knees. "Can you read that part again?"

Natalia looked at Nick's phone.

Great change takes time. It is a slow process, but true power comes in the uprising.

"That part is written in English for some reason."

Nick looked up at the towering spires of the cathedral. "My guess is that they didn't want the meaning to be lost in translation." *But what does it mean?* The granite gargoyle perched high above jeered down at him for being so slow and unable to decipher the riddle.

Natalia handed the phone back to him. "True power comes in the uprising? I don't get it."

"Uprising means a resistance or revolt." He glared at the gloating gargoyle.

Eve gasped.

His head snapped her way. "What?"

Her brows burrow in concentration. "What year did Hartzler live at the embassy?"

"From 1970 to 1978."

Her eyes widened. "Oh, my gosh, so he was around then." Her hand shot to her mouth. "And he would have been the one to give the gift. Oh wow. It's literally *in* the Uprising."

A surge of energy ricocheted through him. He shot the gargoyle a look. *Ha! We figured it out!* Then he directed his attention back to Eve.

"What're you thinking?"

Her eyes met his and he could almost see the pieces of the puzzle clicking together. But then she glanced at Natalia, and her excitement diminished.

"Oh, um, never mind." She fiddled with the cross around her neck. "I thought I might be onto something, but forget it. It doesn't make sense."

He watched her for a moment. She was purposely keeping something from them. Not hard to figure out why. She didn't trust Natalia. Time to shift gears.

"Well, let's keep brainstorming. Maybe something will come to us. Natalia, have you thought about what you're going to say to Mr. Stoltz, about why you suddenly left the hotel? He's going to be furious. I'm worried about you."

She shrugged. "I can fend for myself. I'll tell him I got bored and wanted to head back home. Don't worry, I won't tell him you rescued me."

"Thanks. I promised you I would help you talk to your parents. Do you want to do that now?"

"No. I don't think you should show your face at the embassy for a while. Besides, I'm a big girl, Nick. I can talk to my parents by myself."

Why was she always so difficult? It was exhausting.

"I know you can, but you don't have to. We're your friends. Sometimes a little moral support and an outsider to diffuse a tense situation is helpful."

She rolled her eyes. "You don't always have to be the knight in shining armor, you know—riding in to rescue the fair maiden."

***

After they dropped Natalia off near the embassy, he drove Eve home. He parked in the circle drive of her building and turned to face her.

"Okay. Spill the beans."

Her eyes shifted to the right. "What're you talking about?" She was not a good liar.

"You figured it out, didn't you? Where's the key?"

She bit her lip and glanced at her hands then back at him. "Well, I'm not positive but I kept thinking about where, in 1970, the Ambassador of Endelbourg would hide something small. And that 'uprising' statement rang a bell in my head: it sounded familiar. Then I remembered. The gift Endelbourg gave to the Kennedy Center was a small ceramic statue. And guess what its name is."

"The Uprising?" The air suddenly rushed from his lungs.

She nodded. "Yep."

Oh, man. "So, you think the key to the gold is inside a one-of-a-kind art piece, dedicated to the memory of President Kennedy?" He rubbed his hand along his stubbly jaw. Yet another complicated turn of events.

She shut her eyes for a moment. "Sounds crazy, doesn't it? That's why I didn't say it in front of Natalia."

"I assumed it was because you don't trust her."

"Well, there's that too." She grinned. "So, what do we do with this bit of information?"

He shook his head. "I have no idea. Let me think about it. The key's safe at the moment, and we have some time to decide what to do. In the meantime, tomorrow is the home opener for the Washington Nationals. Remember, I promised my siblings I'd take them to the game in exchange for helping us out at Arlington Cemetery? And having you go with us was kind of what sealed the deal."

She clapped her hands. "Great! I've never been to a pro baseball game. Play ball!"

Chapter Forty-three

The tantalizing aroma of bacon pulled Eve out of her dream world and into reality. Curious, she made her way down the hall to the kitchen to find her dad busy at the stove.

"Is there a special occasion I should know about?" Stifling a yawn, she plunked down at the counter.

"No. I just thought I'd treat my ladies to breakfast, for once." He placed a plate of crisp bacon in front of her.

She took one of the hot strips and nibbled on it.

"Hmm. Delicious."

He flipped opened the egg carton. "Now, what kind of eggs do you want with it?"

"Definitely over easy, kind sir."

"Your wish is my command." He cracked a few eggs into a pan. "What are you and Nick up to on this beautiful Saturday?"

She reached for another slice of bacon. "He's taking me to my very first major league baseball game."

"Ah, the great American pastime."

"I hope they sell peanuts and Cracker Jacks. I want an authentic experience."

Dad seemed focused on the eggs.

"Are you happy we moved here?" she asked.

He glanced up, concern washing over his face. "Why? Are you missing home?"

She shook her head. "No. I love it here. I just want to make sure things are going well for you."

He flipped the eggs. "I'm glad you like it, because I honestly couldn't be happier. Teaching these courses on the Civil War is my dream come true. I often find myself wondering why I didn't jump at the opportunity sooner. I guess I worried about uprooting you."

She slid off the stool to grab a napkin and fork. "Mom seems happy too."

"Are you kidding? With all these museums and galleries, she's in heaven. Hey, Brooke called yesterday. She'll be home next weekend for Easter." He slid the spatula under an egg, transferred it to a plate, and set it in front of her.

"That's good. I missed seeing her over her spring break."

"I guess a chance to go to New York City with friends sounded more exciting than a week with her family."

"Hard to believe." She cut into the egg, and yellow goo flowed across her plate.

Dad carried his plate around the counter and sat next to her. "I've been meaning to tell you how proud I am of you for inviting Mrs. Grant with us to Easter Mass."

"She's gruff on the outside but she's actually quite sad and lonely. She's turned off from religion, but I think if she'd give it a try, it could help her find peace."

He reached for the bacon. "You know, she's been good for you, too. It's like you were meant to meet and become friends."

She stopped chewing to ponder that thought.

***

Eve exited the train at Metro Station and was instantly swarmed by Nick's siblings. Grace plowed into her for a hug. Olivia and Dillon started rambling on about the team and players. Gabriella even looked up from her phone long enough to say hi.

Nick had instructed her to meet them there and then together they'd take the green line over to the Navy Yard stop and walk to the stadium together.

"Hey, Red, love the hair." Jace tugged on one of the ponytails flowing out from under her baseball cap.

Nick smiled. "You do look ready for the game."

She hoped her red, white and blue ensemble wasn't too over the top. But like her dad had said, baseball was the great American pastime. And with a team named the Nationals, how could you not be patriotic?

"Have you really never been to a ballgame?" Olivia asked incredulously as they boarded the green line and found seats.

Grace scrambled onto her lap.

"Well, I've been to some college games but never to a professional baseball game. There aren't any major league teams in New Mexico."

Dillon peered over the back of his seat. "You're gonna love it."

"Do you play baseball?"

"Nah. I tried once but I'd rather keep track of the ball speed and player stats. Jace plays though."

Jace winked at her. "That's right, I'm your man if you have any questions."

Eve rolled her eyes at his macho-esque attitude.

"But there is one important rule." Grace spun around in her lap to look directly into Eve's eyes. Her expression turned very serious. "If the kiss-cam shows your face on the big screen, you *have* to kiss."

Nick leaned in. "Grace is a bit obsessed with the kiss-cam."

"It's called a kiss-cam for a reason. It's not a smile-and-look-embarrassed cam," Dillon explained.

Eve tried not to crack a smile while mirroring Grace's matter-of-fact expression. "You have a point there."

The three younger kids spent the rest of the ride describing what they had been doing all week while they were out of school. She tried to catch everything they said but found it nearly impossible as they all spoke at the same time.

***

The ballgame was fabulous. Eve loved the excitement in the stands, the music that played when the batters walked up to the plate, the cheering and jeering from the crowd. And, of course, being with Nick's family.

Could there be a more perfect day for baseball? The sky was a brilliant blue, the Nationals were playing well, and their seats were fantastic at only a few rows behind the visitors' dugout. Then during the fifth inning, Grace squealed in delight. Eve looked up at the big screen above the scoreboard and watched as the camera zoomed in on couples. Time for the infamous kiss-cam.

The crowd clapped and cheered when couples who noticed they were onscreen obliged the crowd with a quick kiss. One couple just leaned together in an awkward hug, which prompted a round of boos, and another didn't even notice they were on display for the whole stadium to see.

Even as she watched, the camera focused on another couple. Grace started screaming. With a jolt, Eve realized she and Nick were on the giant screen.

Oh, boy. She looked at him. He arched one eyebrow as if to say, "What do you think?" She started to shake her head no but then she glanced at Grace. They couldn't let her down, so Eve shrugged in agreement and leaned in for a quick peck.

But the moment her lips touched his, she lost all sense of where she was. Electricity surged through her body as emotion overwhelmed her. Nick pulled her closer, and she vaguely heard the roar of the crowd beyond the pulsing of her heart.

Chapter Forty-four

Nick wasn't sure how he made it through the rest of the game. Things had been great until the kiss-cam ruined it. Why'd the stupid camera have to focus on them?

He couldn't stop thinking about kissing Eve. Honestly, he wished he could do it again, but she hadn't looked him in the eye since it happened. He was crazy about her but had no idea how she felt. When they first met, she'd thought they'd be a couple, but he wasn't sure she felt that way now. Maybe, after all this time of hanging out together, she just wanted to be friends.

Now things were super awkward, and it didn't help that no one would stop discussing it. The couple behind them had bought them sodas for "the great show." Jace and Dillon kept nudging him and chuckling. Grace and Olivia chattered on and on about how "awesome" it had been. Gabriella complained that they had totally humiliated her. Eve still asked questions about the game but wouldn't make eye contact.

What had happened, anyway? It had been like a magnetic pull, and they just couldn't part. Not exactly how he would have planned their first kiss—in front of forty thousand people. And he certainly wouldn't have wanted to embarrass her like that. Grace and her stupid kiss-cam rules.

Somehow, they made it through the rest of the game. He debated whether he should head back to Alexandria with his family or take the metro to Dupont Circle with Eve and try to talk to her about the incident. He had no idea what he'd say, but he didn't like this strange silence between them. What a disaster.

When the game ended, they didn't leave the stadium right away. Afraid they might lose Grace in the throngs of baseball fans exiting the stadium, Nick suggested they stay in their seats while the crowd thinned out. As it began to clear, Grace, Olivia, and Dillon created some new game and started running up and down the aisles and rows in front of them. Eve pulled a Gabriella and began fiddling with her phone, something she rarely did. He had to fix this.

His phone vibrated, and he grabbed it, glad for the distraction.

"It's Natalia." He announced then answered the call. "Hey, what's up?"

He could hardly understand her. Her words blurred together, her accent heavier than usual. It sounded like she'd been crying. Concern washed over him. Clearly something was wrong.

"Natalia, you've got to slow down."

He glanced at Eve. Questions filled her eyes.

"Eve's here with me. I'm putting you on speaker. Okay, go ahead."

Natalia's strained voice came over the phone. "I'm sorry. I really am, I don't know what comes over me sometimes. I don't mean to be an awful person but sometimes I just can't help it. I'm sorry."

He tensed. "Natalia, what are you talking about? What happened?"

"I tried to talk to my father when I got back home yesterday. I tried to explain that I was only acting out because I wanted to go back to the boarding school. But he wouldn't listen. I've never seen him so mad."

"About what?" Nick glanced at Eve, who stared at the ground in concentration.

The story came out between sobs. "He said you had called and were worried I had been kidnapped. He kept yelling at me that I had humiliated him because I had played one of my tricks on a senator's son and was furious that I might have jeopardized his relationship with your father. He kept saying I was a disgrace as a daughter."

Nick groaned. He should've helped her talk to her dad. Now things were worse than ever. "Natalia, I'm sorry. We were worried about you and called your dad to see if you were okay. Let me come over and talk with your dad. I know I can smooth things over."

Eve nodded her agreement.

Natalia sniffed. "You'll never want to help me when I tell you the rest."

"What 'rest'?" He gripped the phone tighter, unease creeping through him.

"I was so hurt by what he said." Her voice quieted. He had to strain to hear her. "When I ran out of his office, I bumped into Mr. Stoltz. I thought he'd start yelling at me too, since I had ditched his guys in the hotel, but instead he comforted me. He took me to his office and calmed me down." She gulped. "Nick, I'm sorry. I was upset at my father."

Nick and Eve exchanged a look. "Natalia, what are you trying to say?"

"I know I shouldn't have, but I wanted to somehow hurt my father, so I blurted out that you had actually rescued me from the hotel. That you took photos of the letters, and that Eve said something about the key being in the uprising."

Eve gasped and sank back in her seat. Nick's stomach clenched as if he'd been kicked in the midriff. Natalia sobbed again.

"Nick, I'm sorry. You asked me to keep it all a secret, so you probably hate me now. You and Eve have been nice to me, and I went and ruined everything."

Nick shut his eyes. Blowing up at her, like he wanted to, wouldn't help anything. "It's okay. I'm sorry I put you in that position. I told you I would help you with your dad, and I will, but right now I have to take care of some things. Natalia, thank you for telling us what happened."

He hung up and stared at Eve. "Do you think he'll know what the 'uprising' is?"

She took a deep breath. "He can probably figure it out."

He stood. "Come on, let's get out of here."

"What're we going to do?"

"Let's go talk to your mom. We need to convince her to protect that sculpture."

Chapter Forty-five

Exhaustion hit Eve like a tsunami as she and Nick trudged back to her apartment from the Metro. It had been a long day. A confusing, awkwardly emotional, *very* long day. The game had been fantastic, then the kiss happened. *Oh, that kiss!* Her heart still pounded when she thought about it, but that moment had changed everything. Nick went all weird, and she suddenly lost the ability to act normal. Then, to top it off, came the phone call from Natalia. How could that girl have been so reckless? Ever since they left the stadium their conversation had been all but nonexistent, both of them lost in their thoughts, trying to figure out the next move.

Mom greeted them from the couch when they entered the apartment. "Hi, Nick, good to see you again."

Dad turned from the TV and peered over his shoulder at them. "How was the game?"

That was the last thing she wanted to discuss. Luckily Nick answered the question for her.

"Fantastic. The Nationals won 8-5."

"What a beautiful day for baseball." Apparently, Mom couldn't see the distress that her youngest daughter was in. Instead, she happily chatted like nothing was wrong. How could she not notice? All that museum bonding time had clearly done nothing to strengthen her mom's thought-reading ability.

"Well, you're just in time for sports. Let's hear about the highlights of the game." Dad turned up the volume as the sportscaster showed clips of the best plays.

The perky female newscaster joined in the conversation. "I heard it was a sold-out game, Mitch."

"Yes, Andrea, and there were several local celebrities in attendance. One observant fan even spotted Senator Hammond's adorable kids in the crowd."

A still shot of Eve and the Hammond crew filled the screen.

"Wow, there you are," Mom exclaimed.

Ms. Perky continued. "And I hear one lucky girl enjoyed more than the game this afternoon."

And just like that, the video from the kiss-cam filled the screen. Horrified, Eve watched as she and Nick turned toward each other, shrugged, then leaned in to kiss. But instead of parting quickly like normal people, they kept kissing. Her cheeks burned, and her stomach flipped as she remembered how that moment felt. But now she got a look at what had happened around them as they were lost in the moment. The crowd erupted in cheers, but Nick's siblings were the real highlight of the video. Jace and Dillon started fist pumping and high fiving. Olivia and Grace gaped at the giant screen above the scoreboard with their mouths hanging open until Gabriella reached over and covered Grace's eyes.

The sportscaster moved on to analyzing other games around the country while Nick, Eve and her parents kept staring at the TV.

"Um, yeah . . . that happened," Eve muttered, humiliation oozing from every pore.

Mom covered her mouth too late to hide the smile that was forming.

The usually smooth and polished Nick started stammering. "Oh, um . . . wow. I'm sorry you had to see that. We just, um, got caught up in the, um, excitement."

"You certainly did." How did Dad even speak through such tightly gritted teeth?

Nick turned to him. "I would never disrespect your daughter, sir. I honestly don't know what happened."

She couldn't read her dad's expression but thought it was probably a good time to change the subject.

"Hey, Nick actually walked me home to discuss something else with you."

"Do we want to know?" Dad grumbled.

Best to ignore dear old dad for the moment.

"Mom, I know this is going to sound totally insane, but we have a suspicion that someone might break into the Kennedy Center and steal the Uprising sculpture, the one Endelbourg gifted to the center."

Mom's face bunched up in confusion. "Why on earth would someone want to steal that?"

"We were chatting with Natalia, the ambassador's daughter, and she has reason to believe someone might take it. We were thinking, to be on the safe side, you could maybe go get it and lock it in your office."

"You're right, Eve, that is insane. Even if you had credible proof that someone wanted to take it, I can't remove it. There's a whole set of security protocols in place. If anyone—including me—tried to move it without the proper procedures, the sensors would be set off."

Dad shook his head, finally coming out of his shock. "Natalia doesn't seem like the most reliable person in the world. Do you think she might be making it up?"

This wasn't going as planned. "We don't know, but we can't just ignore it. What if she's right and someone takes it?"

Mom shrugged. "I can check into moving it on Monday, but until then the best I can do is ask the weekend security detail to watch it more closely."

Out of ideas, Eve turned toward Nick. He always seemed to know what to say.

"Thanks, Mrs. Donahue, that would be great if you could warn the security guard. There was one other thing I wanted to ask you both. Tonight is the Back on the River spring event at my rowing club, and I wanted to see if it would be all right if I took Eve."

Eve stared at him, confused. He was giving up that easily?

He stuffed his hands in his pockets. "It's at the row club, right below Georgetown, along the river. There will be live bands, food, races on the river, and fireworks at midnight. I hoped to introduce Eve to some of my friends. It would be a great way to meet some more people in town."

Her parents shared a whole conversation through a glance. Their mind meld was always fascinating to watch.

"I guess." Mom answered tentatively. "It would be nice for her to meet some new friends."

"As long as she's home by midnight," Dad bristled.

"Dad, the fireworks start at midnight." She knew how Nick's mind worked. He was up to something.

He pulled a paper from his pocket, unfolded it and handed it to her dad. "Here's the information. The main band also starts at midnight. But I could have her home between one and one-thirty. I promise to keep her safe."

Dad studied the flyer but didn't answer.

Nick cleared his throat. "I know you're worried about my intentions after seeing the video from the game, but I have incredible respect for Eve. She's an amazing person. One of the smartest, kindest people I've ever met. I got caught up in the moment at the stadium but I'm a gentleman when we're together. I promise you, sir."

Oh. Her heart did a little leap to her throat. Mom seemed to melt at his words, and even Dad softened a bit.

"All right, but home as soon as it's over."

"Thank you, sir." Nick reached out to shake her dad's hand. "I should head home to change." He turned to her. "I'll be back to pick you up around nine o'clock."

She searched his eyes for an explanation but came up blank. "Great. Let me walk you out."

When they were alone in the hallway, she pounced.

"Okay. What's going on?"

He pushed the button of the elevator. "There is an event tonight. I wasn't planning on going, but now it seems like a good idea."

"We're going to a party?" This made no sense. "What about the sculpture?"

He looked her in the eyes. "The party is our cover. Tonight, we're breaking into the Kennedy Center."

Chapter Forty-six

Finding a parking spot along the crowded Georgetown streets took some patience. Nick finally found one several blocks away from the row club. He parked, then walked around the car to open the door for Eve. Should he offer his hand or not? How could he get things back to normal?

She stepped out of the car before he had a chance to decide. "I'm confused. If we're breaking into the Kennedy Center, what're we doing here?"

"Well, I couldn't completely lie to your parents about our evening plans." He grabbed his backpack from the back seat, once again loaded with anything he could think of that might come in handy for their task. "And actually, for the first time in a long time, I do feel like going to a party—with you."

Her face lit up with the first genuine smile since before the kiss-cam fiasco. "I wish I'd known we were actually coming here. I have this really cute sailor outfit that would've been perfect for a party at a boat house."

He grinned. Of course she did. He shut the door and started walking toward the row club. "We won't be here long. I told you, we will be sneaking into the Kennedy

Center." He took in her outfit, black pants and shirt with a shiny silver sweater. "Is your disco theme the perfect outfit for that?"

She flicked her finger into his shoulder. "No. I didn't really know if you were serious but thought if we did go to the Ken Cen, we needed to look like we belonged there. The sweater is meant to dress the ensemble up a bit."

"Ahh."

"You know, if you'd tell me the plans instead of leaving me in the dark, I could dress more appropriately."

"What's the fun in that?" Nice to have their usual vibe back.

She rolled her eyes. "Anyway, why are you so sure we need to get to the Kennedy Center? Maybe Mr. Stoltz hasn't figured out what the 'uprising' means. My mom said she'd have the security guards check the sculpture. Surely, it'll be safe for the weekend."

"These guys have been thinking about this revolution for decades. The gold has been tantalizingly close to them for all these years. Believe me, Stoltz will figure it out."

"But they're the Endelbourg officials. Couldn't they simply make up an excuse and get the sculpture back in their hands for a short time?"

He shifted the heavy backpack to his other shoulder. "Exactly. Hopefully your mom will be able to secure it on Monday. I'll tell my dad about our theory, then they can have the piece examined for the key. But if Mr. Stoltz figures it out, he'll also know we think the key is in the sculpture, and he'll need to get to it before we do. They're desperate, Eve. A security guard and alarm system aren't likely to stop them."

"Yeah, I guess that makes sense. So, what's your plan then? Camp out in the Opera House for the rest of the weekend?"

"No. I want to set up a security camera. My dad bought a few portable, motion-activated ones during the election for around the house. I just need to set one up near the sculpture and link it into the Wi-Fi. If something activates it, the app will send an alert to my phone. If the security guard or cleaning crew sets it off, I'll ignore it. But if someone does try to steal the sculpture, I'll call the police. I checked. There's a performance tonight, and then the Opera House will be dark tomorrow." He stopped walking and turned to face her. "We'll sneak in, set it up, then sneak back out. No harm, no foul." It was a solid plan.

A small smile slid onto her face. "You certainly bring excitement into my life."

"That's funny, I was thinking the same thing about you."

"Nick!" Someone called from across the street.

He turned to see his friend Drew approaching.

"I didn't expect to see you." Drew's eyes shifted to Nick's side.

"Hey, Drew. This is Eve."

"Nice to meet you." His tall, blond teammate shook her hand then turned back to him. "We haven't seen you on dry land in months. You never seem to be able to make it when we get together. Some of us were starting to think you were too good for us now."

A joke or a slam?

"I had a lot going on during the off-season. But you'll be seeing me more often now."

"Glad to hear it, man." Drew slugged his shoulder.

***

For the next hour they chatted with his friends, danced to the bands, and devoured mouth-watering barbeque. Eve charmed everyone with her bubbly self. She even convinced him to participate in one of the races on the river. But it was hard to concentrate on maneuvering the boat around the buoys, with her jumping up and down and screaming for him to hurry.

It felt good to be back, socializing with his teammates. He hadn't realized how much he'd missed hanging out with friends. At the moment, he had a hard time remembering why he'd stayed away.

After the awards ceremony where he received a plastic medal for winning the race, he led Eve to a small two-person boat. He helped her get on, handed her his backpack, then began to paddle them down the river.

"That was so much fun." She hugged her sparkly sweater tight around her to block the breeze. "I loved watching you in action."

"Thanks." He pulled the oars through the smooth, dark water. "I don't think I've ever had such an enthusiastic cheering section before."

"I don't know why you weren't planning on coming. Everyone's really nice."

"Yeah, I guess they are." Maybe it was time to start trusting again.

"You know, you can't hide away from people just because one person tried to hurt you. There are some bad eggs out there, but if you avoid everyone, you'll miss the good ones too." It was like she'd read his mind. She had a point, but he wasn't going to let her off the proverbial hook.

"You know, advice goes both ways. I haven't seen you meeting any new people either."

She pulled back her shoulders. "I've met you and Mrs. Grant."

He gave her a sideways look.

She frowned. "Oh, okay. Point taken. When spring break's over, I'll try to meet more people."

Hopefully, those new people wouldn't keep her too busy. "Good, and I'll try not to rush back home after school and practice."

"Deal." She turned toward the dark river. "Isn't it beautiful how the city lights reflect off the water?"

He watched her sitting there, the moonlight lighting up her face. "Yep, the view is incredibly beautiful tonight."

She turned back and noticed him watching her. He expected her to turn away, embarrassed, but instead she graced him with one of her stunning smiles.

***

After securing the boat in a small cove outside the Watergate Hotel, they walked the short distance to the huge theater complex. They slid inside while the patrons were leaving after their shows.

He leaned close. "Where do you think is safe to hide out? I'm sure security checks all the offices and bathrooms before locking up for the night."

"I think I have the perfect spot." She led him to a plain wooden door near the main entrance and pulled out her mom's keys. Good thing he'd remembered to have her bring them along. They climbed a few flights of stairs in the dark, illuminated only by glowing exit signs. When they reached the third floor, he followed her down a maze of corridors.

"Is this where your mom's office is?" They passed odd-shaped rooms and workstations.

"Yeah. She told me the designers of the building didn't leave enough space for offices, so they've had to be creative over the years."

She was right, the space had no organization to it at all. As she led him down a few more turns, past cubicles and offices with no windows in sight, he listened for any hint of a security guard. Finally, she led him into a small conference room and headed for the back wall. She opened a door, then turned on her phone's flashlight. Nothing but boxes and easels inside. This remote closet would make a suitable hiding place.

But Eve didn't stop. She pushed the boxes out of the way then disappeared through the back of the closet. Blindly, he followed. Thoughts of Narnia popped into his head.

He emerged from the closet, trying to figure out where they were. They stood in a two-story space. Heavy curtains and ropes hung from the ceiling.

She turned in a circle, her arms spread wide. "We're now backstage of the Family Theater. Isn't that cool?"

The space was filled with racks of costumes and set pieces. *Very* cool.

He examined the construction of the sets while she wandered to a table full of hats.

"I think this one fits you." She tossed him a black top hat.

He set it on his head. "Well, let's see what we can find you." He rummaged through the scattered pieces and picked up a velvety maroon hat with peacock feathers attached.

"Oooh, pretty." She grabbed it and placed it on her head. She then reached for a feathery boa hanging on a nearby hook and wrapped it around her neck. "What do you think?"

He tossed one of the ends over her shoulder, further wrapping her in feathers. "It's perfect."

"Wait! There's a matching one." She reached for another boa. Stepping on her tiptoes, she flung it over his shoulders. "Love it!"

He blew at a random feather that tickled his face.

She laughed. "Selfie time!"

He smiled for the pic, wondering how she somehow got him to do these things.

When she removed her bonnet, he placed the top hat over her curls. "This will look much better on you."

"Well, then let's find you a new one." She shifted through the hats. "Look!" She held up a white sailor cap. "This would be perfect when you're in your little dinghy!"

He laughed. "You're a little dingy."

Her giggly snort got them both laughing uncontrollably. They were for sure going to get caught if they couldn't be quieter, but he was having too much fun to really care.

"Ah! A sombrero!" She flung it to him like a flying disc.

He plopped it on his head. "*Si, señorita.*"

She insisted on another photo.

Before they could try on any more hats, a voice boomed over the loudspeaker, announcing the center would be closing and all doors would be locked in ten minutes. They crept behind a rack of costumes to sit until they felt it was safe to emerge. He turned on his phone and pulled up the perfect distraction, a trivia game they could silently play while they waited.

Chapter Forty-seven

"Come on, loser. I think we'd better get moving." Eve would've preferred staying put, cozied up to Nick, playing games and being silly, but they had work to do.

"Who you calling loser? I had the highest score," he protested.

She bopped him in the face with the end of her boa. "Because you cheated."

He blew at the feathers. "I didn't cheat! I happen to know a lot of trivia."

"So do I, but it's hard to answer the questions when you're being tickled."

He stood, offering his hand to help her up. "Is it my fault you're ticklish and I'm not?"

She let him pull her up. "I call for a rematch. Someday, when we're not breaking and entering."

"Just to clarify, there was no breaking, only entering."

They put back the costume pieces, and she stuffed her sparkly sweater in his backpack. All black was a better option when you were trying to stay hidden in the shadows.

As she led him back downstairs, she questioned her sanity. Was she really sneaking around a sacred memorial, after hours, trying to protect a precious piece of art (which might hold a key to unknown treasure!) from being stolen by international criminals? Maybe this whole D.C. adventure was some elaborate hallucination, and she'd wake up in the Albuquerque Pizza Barn. But one glance at Nick and his warm smile, and she knew it was real. No dream could make your insides melt like that.

They moved as silently and stealthily as possible down the long Hall of States and through the Grand Foyer to the Opera House. No sign of a security guard anywhere. Thank goodness. When they arrived at the Grand Theater, they climbed over the velvet rope that indicated the theater was closed, then made their way up the stairs to the second-floor landing.

Near the doors to the theater, she stopped and pointed to the white sculpture known as the Uprising. Could it really hold the key? Literally? Nick nodded then searched around for a discreet spot to set up his camera. He headed to the opposite wall and knelt near a display of costumes to place the camera and set up the connection on his phone.

Eve paced around, listening for any signs of the guard. *Hurry, hurry, hurry.* Her internal chant was meant to calm her nerves, but it didn't seem to be helping. In fact, the butterflies swirling around inside her only seemed to be increasing their frenzy. From the dark below, a flicker of light stopped her in mid-pace. She squeezed his shoulder. They froze and listened. *Oh, no.* The security guard was about to find them. Would Nick be able to come up with some excuse to get them out of the situation?

But when she heard the voices, she clutched tighter, panic rising in her chest. That was not the security guard.

"Are you sure this is the right place?" She knew that voice. It was the blond guy that had been following them.

"He said it would be outside the Opera House on the second floor. And the sign says Opera House."

"Hurry, let's find it and smash the stupid thing before we get caught."

Nick slowly rose. Eve held onto him, her knees so weak she wasn't sure she could move on her own.

"We can't let them break it," she whispered.

"Or get the key." Before she could react, Nick was next to the sculpture. He looked over his shoulder at her then placed his hands on the glass cover. She nodded. Oh, boy, were they really doing this? He took a deep breath then lifted the glass.

Immediately, an alarm began to blare. Nick snatched the piece and spun back toward her. She needed to move but froze, unable to think clearly. He latched onto her arm and yanked her toward the theater door, pulling her inside. She scanned the cavernous Opera House. They were inside the theater on the second level balcony, trapped. Panic pulsed through every cell of her body.

Um, God? How 'bout a little help here?

As usual, Nick knew what to do. He rooted through his backpack and pulled out a dog's retractable leash. Why he'd thought to bring that, she hadn't a clue. He carefully placed the sculpture inside the bag then looped the leash's handle around the railing and extended the wide nylon leash. Was he thinking what she thought he was thinking?

He motioned for her to come closer. Yep. His plan was for them to climb down. *No. No way.* There had to be another option. But a quick scan of their surroundings proved there was no other way out. She instinctively took a step backward, but his reassuring nod gave her the spark of confidence she needed. With his help, she climbed over the railing, then carefully shimmied down the impromptu rope as the alarm continued to sound. Hopefully the security guard would come to investigate the alarm and find the two thugs.

She made it down safely. Now what? How were they going to get out of here? Going back out to the lobby was not an option with the bad guys and security both out there. A plan percolated in her head.

Nick was about halfway down to the main seating area when the leash broke under his weight. He crashed down next to her, landing on his hands and knees. He gave her a thumbs up, indicating he wasn't hurt.

"Stop!" An adrenaline-producing call came from behind them.

Eve started to raise her hands in surrender. The security guard had found them. An odd sense of relief washed over her. They might be in trouble but at least the sculpture would be safe from the thieves. Of course, they were holding the sculpture, so technically they were the thieves. But Nick would think of some way to explain it.

Nick yanked her arm down. "No. It's them."

She peered over her shoulder to see the bad guys staring at them. Fear knotted her insides. They must've escaped the alarm by entering the theater as well. Back to her plan.

Please, God. Let this work.

With a quick sign of the cross, she ran toward the front of the theater and crawled through the opening below the stage into the orchestra pit. Nick scrambled in after her. She spotted a door, yanked it open, then scurried down the stairs into the basement of the enormous complex.

She took a moment to get her bearings. *Think, Eve.* Which way to the loading dock? But concentrating was not helping; she was turned around and knew the guys would be following them. *Just move!* Desperate to flee, she pushed her way through the musicians' lounge they found themselves in, sprinted down the dark concrete hallway that ran the length of the Kennedy Center, past storage rooms and a giant industrial kitchen, with Nick on her heels. The slam of a door echoed through the hall. The men were close behind them. The alarms continued to pulse loudly, adding to the urgency.

Eve ran as fast as she could, ignoring the sharp pain in her side. She tried to concentrate on her plan and not on the beam of light from the flashlights of the two guys chasing them. Darting around a corner, she prayed she was right. But her flight abruptly stopped as Nick grabbed her arm and pulled her into the shadows behind some dollies and boxes. He placed a finger to his lips. Her chest heaved as she tried to catch her breath.

She watched in the dark as the two guys ran past the hallway. She should've been planning the next step of their escape, but being in such close proximity to Nick distracted her. Her ear rested on his chest, and she could feel the fast beating of his heart. She slowly looked up at him and held his gaze. In that moment, they were the only two people on earth, and she desperately wished it would last, but the slam of another door and angry voices startled them out of their reverie.

"Where'd they go?" One of the men grumbled.

"Start searching each room. They've got to be here."

"Are you crazy? This place is about to be swarmed by the police. We've got to get out of here."

"Do you really—?"

Before they could hear the rest of the plan, Eve silently led Nick down the hall, toward the loading dock. How was she even moving? Her legs felt like rubber. She inched open the entrance door adjacent to the enormous garage door and peered out into the night. D.C. police swarmed the complex. Sirens and lights flashed above them at the main entrance to the theater. Luckily, no one paid attention to where they were.

Nick grabbed her hand and led her toward the Potomac and the trail that would take them back to their boat. Behind them, the Kennedy Center glowed as all the lights blazed, ready for the place to be meticulously searched.

Thank you, God, for keeping us safe!

As they made their getaway, safely gliding down the Potomac, Eve finally relaxed a bit, her pounding heart slowing to a somewhat normal rhythm. They were only halfway to Georgetown when Nick stopped rowing. Startled, she turned to look at him.

"What's the matter?"

He leaned forward, his arms resting on his knees, hands clasped together. "Eve, there's something I've been wanting to say all day. I'm sorry about earlier, at the ballgame. I never want to do anything to make you feel uncomfortable."

They had avoided the conversation all evening. Guess it was time to deal with it.

She forced a smile. "It's okay. I know this whole situation is extremely odd and that I kinda freaked you out when we first met. But I've been having such an incredible time with you these past few months. I don't want anything that happened to mess up our friendship."

She meant it. As much as she liked him and couldn't stop thinking about their kiss, she didn't want to ruin anything and risk losing the one friend she had.

The light reflecting off the water sparkled in his eyes. Why'd he have to be so darn handsome?

He slowly nodded, his jaw firm and serious. "Do you think if I kissed you again, that would mess up our friendship?"

Her heart ricocheted around her chest. Did he just say he wanted to kiss her?

A slight grin formed on his face.

"I think it might complicate it a bit." Her voice caught in her throat, making her answer come out as a whisper.

He held her gaze. "I like complicated. It keeps things interesting."

Oh, wowzers. "Me, too."

He slowly leaned in toward her and—*Boom!* She jumped when a sudden loud sound rocked the boat slightly. She looked up to see a shower of sparkles fall from the dark night sky. The bright colors cascaded down, beautifully lighting the Key Bridge and the university spires. It was perfect.

"You certainly know how to impress a girl." She turned back toward his handsome face.

"I try." His hand traced her jawline, sending a quiver through her body. Then he leaned in and kissed her as fireworks lit up the sky behind them.

Chapter Forty-eight

Nick scanned the room, waiting for someone to talk, the whole scene surreal. He, Eve, her parents, and his dad were gathered in her living room, in the middle of the night, staring at the Uprising sculpture.

Mrs. Donahue broke the silence. "And why exactly did you steal a historic piece of art?"

"We didn't steal it, we rescued it." Eve's answer, while accurate, lacked any real explanation.

Maybe his brilliant plan to have them all come together to hear the whole story hadn't been so brilliant, after all. As he and Eve made their way back to the row club after the fireworks display, it occurred to him that Eve's mom would receive the news that the sculpture had been stolen; it was only a matter of time. She might already know. They were in this mess way over their heads. So, he called their parents and asked them to meet. At the time, the idea made sense, but seeing the bleary eyes of the adults now, he questioned the decision.

"You told us you were taking our daughter to your row club for a party. Now we find out you took her to commit a crime." Professor Donahue appeared to be on the brink of losing it.

Nick glanced at his own dad, who watched everyone but said nothing.

Eve leaned forward. "Dad, this isn't Nick's fault. First of all, we did go to the party, and it was great. Especially the fireworks."

Did anyone else notice the slight blush of her cheeks?

Professor Donahue snapped his head in her direction. "Then how did you end up with a stolen sculpture?"

She took a deep breath. "We tried to tell you earlier that the Uprising was in danger. We were afraid it wouldn't be safe until Monday, so we went over to the Kennedy Center and hid out until it closed for the evening."

She shifted and squirmed under the intense stares from the adults. Nick resisted the urge to hold her hand, pretty sure her dad would not appreciate the gesture.

Instead, he jumped in to help her out. "The plan was to leave a camera there, which I could monitor from home to make sure no one tried to steal the statue. And if they did, we'd have evidence of who had stolen it."

"Someone did steal it. You." Nick's dad calmly stated. Oh, now he contributes to the conversation.

Eve shook her head and repeated her earlier comment. "We didn't steal it. We rescued it." She turned to her mom, her eyes pleading for understanding. "They were going to smash it."

Mrs. Donahue reached for Eve's hand. "That doesn't make sense. Why would someone break in, just to destroy it?"

"We think there's something valuable hidden inside it." She looked at her dad. "A key."

Professor Donahue's forehead creased. "A key to what?"

Eve's gaze begged Nick to take over.

He took a deep breath, bracing himself for their reaction. "The Confederate gold."

Mrs. Donahue furrowed her brows in confusion, but the two dads frowned, annoyance knitting their brows.

"That's what this is about?" His dad's normally calm voice rose in frustration. "You two are on some treasure hunt?"

Professor Donahue's eye twitched. "There is no gold. You two should be smarter than this."

"Wait." Mrs. Donahue interrupted, bringing a moment of calm to the situation. "You said someone wanted to destroy the sculpture. Is someone else searching for this treasure?"

Eve nodded. "Yes, and they've been chasing us for a while."

"Someone's been chasing you?" Her mom's eyes widened.

Nick watched the adults' anger intensify. The situation was spiraling out of control. He needed to diffuse the growing tension. "Look, can we please start over and explain from the beginning?"

His dad clasped his hands together. "Fine."

Nick laid out the facts, explaining how after the dinner party at the embassy, Natalia had shown him the symbol on the grave. He omitted the fact that they'd sneaked into the cemetery but told them how he and Eve had began researching Barrett, Hamilton, and Meyers, and that they soon found another symbol at the Smithsonian.

As he talked, their angry burrowed eyebrows disappeared. They began to lean forward with interest.

Eve took over and described how, while studying her geometry, she determined where the third symbol would be. She glossed over the details of ditching the tour group at Arlington House to find the symbol but did tell them about the men following them.

Nick continued the tale, explaining how they deciphered the clues about the C&O Canal, drove to the cemetery in Cumberland, Maryland, found the tomb, and then were threatened by the two men in the parking lot.

His dad rested his elbows on his knees. "Who do you think these men are?"

"We think they work for either the ambassador or his chief of staff, Mr. Stoltz. We believe they're planning on using the money for the revolution you told me about. Natalia showed us the diary and letters from the original owner of the home. The letters state that Mr. Barrett gave him the key to the treasure before he died. He also cryptically wrote that the key was 'in the uprising.'"

Eve turned to her mom. "I remembered the sculpture at the Kennedy Center from Endelbourg was titled 'The Uprising.' Then we realized Mr. Stoltz's predecessor, who needed to hide the key for safekeeping, was around when the embassy gave the gift to the Ken Cen, so I thought it might be inside."

He continued their tag-team explanation. "We were planning on leaving it at that and telling you about it, but Natalia told Mr. Stoltz our theory. We were afraid they would try to steal it."

"And we were right," Eve added.

All eyes went to the art piece.

"You really think there's a key hidden inside this?" Professor Donahue leaned closer.

Mrs. Donahue carefully picked up the piece and examined it. She turned it upside down and stared at the open bottom.

Her eyes narrowed. "Strange. The edges aren't smooth and polished like the rest of the piece. It appears the bottom has been cut out."

Nick pulled a flashlight from his bag and handed it to her. She shone the light into the piece.

"Well, I'll be . . ." she breathed. "There may be something wedged in the top teardrop."

She headed to the kitchen for a few items to help remove the object.

Professor Donahue turned his attention to them again. "If there is something inside, who would it belong to? The Endelbourg Embassy, since they gave the sculpture?"

Eve fingered her cross. "Or our government and the Kennedy Center, since it was a gift?"

"Or Mr. Barrett's family, since the key was originally his?" Nick suggested.

His dad shook his head. "I have no idea."

Mrs. Donahue began the delicate work of removing the object. They watched in excruciating silence as she extracted something. She held up a brown cloth, slowly unwrapped the material and held up a large metal key.

They all stared at the old object.

"Unbelievable." Nick's dad rubbed his chin.

Nick reached over and squeezed Eve's hand. "We were right."

She beamed. "Next step, find the gold."

"Hold on. I don't think so." Professor Donahue reached for the phone. "We've got to call the police."

"Wait!" Everyone stopped at his dad's forceful command. "Let's think about this for a moment." He ran his fingers through his hair. "Nick's right. The new King of Endelbourg wants to cause chaos in the region, destroying a major trade agreement and aligning with some rogue nations. He wants power at any cost, including his people's freedom. This may be our chance to find out what's going on."

Professor Donahue didn't seem convinced. "I understand your point, but I don't like the fact that the kids are in danger. If whoever followed them escaped tonight, and they know the kids have the sculpture, they will come after them."

"They might not know we have it," Nick offered. "When we grabbed it and set off the alarm, those two men were still down on the main level, then went into the theater. I don't think they went up to check on the piece because there wasn't time. And when they saw us, the sculpture was already in my bag. They might suspect we have it, but I don't think they know for sure."

Eve continued his thought. "If we can keep that information quiet, they won't come after us."

"And it would give us more time to figure out what to do next." He loved how they always seemed to think alike.

His dad turned to Mrs. Donahue. "Would you be able to put the piece back on display, so the embassy doesn't know it was taken?"

She looked at the sculpture. "I guess. We could also put some extra guards at the Opera House and state there had been an attempted theft, but nothing was taken."

His dad nodded. "Let me work on this a little before we bring in the authorities. Maybe I can figure out who and what we're dealing with, and who the key and gold would rightfully belong to. Can we agree to keep this quiet for now?"

They all nodded.

"I can't believe you two may have solved a century-old mystery." Professor Donahue's bewildered expression went from Nick to Eve.

She smiled. "It was our mission."

"Your what?"

Instead of answering, she glanced at Nick. He knew they were thinking the same thing—their parents had had enough of a shock for one night. Mentioning a mission from God was probably too much for them to handle right now.

"Nothing. Never mind."

Chapter Forty-nine

"This has been the longest week of my life." Eve stroked Lizzie's back, and the gray feline purred in response. Girl and cat were cuddled together on Mrs. Grant's couch.

"I seem to remember you saying those same words every single day this week," grumbled Mrs. Grant.

"I did? Sorry. It's just been *so* difficult. Last week was unbelievably amazing, seeing Nick every single day and touring around to all those great sites. To go from that to another week of boring school has been hard."

She sighed. Why did their parents have to ground them? Sure, they had lied about where they were Saturday night and kind of did a few illegal things, but really, was it fair to be grounded for completing a mission for God?

She hadn't seen Nick since early Sunday morning at their little powwow with their parents. They'd texted and spoken on the phone, but she wished they could see each other in person. Of course, their parents had another reason to ground them: to keep them safe from crazy foreign bad guys. But she was *pretty* sure they weren't in immediate danger. Her mom had managed to put the sculpture back in its place, and somehow Senator

Hammond had been able to make the news of its near theft disappear.

As they all waited for the senator to come up with a plan, Eve visited Mrs. Grant every day after school. And every day, Mrs. Grant acted annoyed that she was there. But over the course of the week, she'd shared quite a bit about her life, her husband, and yesterday, even her son, who had died from a rare heart condition.

Upon returning to her apartment yesterday, after hearing about Mrs. Grant's son, Eve had received a response email from Father Romero. Earlier in the week, she'd sent him a long message describing, in great detail, all that had occurred. He had decided to check in to see how things had been progressing, and wrote something that made her think:

Eve,

I'm excited to hear about your adventure. You had a dramatic and unusual calling, but I feel I must remind you that God calls people every day, in smaller, more subtle ways, to do things for Him. Recognizing that call is difficult, but don't be so focused on some large mission and miss the small ways you can help people and bring them to God.

Father Romero

The priest had summed up exactly how she felt about Mrs. Grant—that Eve was the one who could reach out to her neighbor and guide her back to the Church. He was right, everyone could be called to help those in their lives who were hurting and in need. Eve had assumed

God called her for the big mission, but was she also meant to befriend Mrs. Grant?

Now, sitting in front of her elderly neighbor, Eve took a deep breath. No need to worry, God would guide her. He always had her back.

"Yesterday, you were telling me about Robert." She hoped to get Mrs. Grant talking about her son again. "He sounds so interesting."

"He was." Mrs. Grant's eyes scanned the family photos on the fireplace mantle. "He had a promising future and should not be dead."

Please God, give me the right words. She'd been trying to figure out how to reach Mrs. Grant all night.

"The loss of someone young never makes sense. We'll probably never understand God's plan."

"I hate when people say things like that," Mrs. Grant snapped. "What kind of God would take someone so precious from this world?"

Eve flinched. "You told me your husband went to church. Did Robert too?"

"Yes. He shared his father's faith. Some good it did him."

Deep breath. "Mrs. Grant, I know you're hurting, but isn't it more comforting to think of Robert and your husband up in heaven? They're together and neither of them are suffering."

"But why am I left behind here, to be miserable?"

Eve hoped the smile she offered conveyed understanding and sympathy.

"I'm sure they want you with them. I'm determined to keep working on their behalf, to make you a believer as well."

Mrs. Grant shot her a warning look. "I said I'd go to church with you on Sunday. Don't push your luck."

"Mrs. Grant, may I pray with you?"

"You are the most persistent child I have ever met."

Eve reached over to hold her neighbor's wrinkled hands. Lizzie shifted and purred even louder. "Dear God, please work on Mrs. Grant's broken heart. Help her to know You love her and want to be her comfort. Could You maybe send her a sign that her beloved son and husband are with You? Please show her how much they want her to come to know You so that she can join them one day in Your kingdom. Amen."

Tears glistened in Mrs. Grant's eyes before she pushed herself out of her chair and scurried away toward the window.

"You really don't know how to leave an old woman in peace, do you?"

Eve smiled. "Nope. Hey, did I tell you Brooke comes home tonight?" She changed the subject, not wanting to push her luck too far.

Mrs. Grant fiddled with the curtain. "Only about twenty times."

"I'm so excited. We've always been close. I can't wait to tell her all about Nick."

"Good. That will give you someone else to jabber to besides me."

A sharp knock on the door startled Lizzie, who leapt off Eve's lap and flew down the hallway in a blur of gray fur. Tyler only twitched his ears at the disturbance.

"Now what?" grumped Mrs. Grant.

She shuffled to the door and peered through the peephole, then opened the door a crack. "What?"

"I have a delivery for your neighbor, an Eve Donahue? I knocked, but no one's home. Can I leave this with you?"

Eve jumped up and ran to the door.

"I'm Eve." The delivery man held a large bouquet of flowers. Wow! She'd never had flowers delivered to her before.

He handed her the bouquet. She held them up to her face and breathed in the luscious scent. The delivery guy stood there awkwardly watching her. Why was he still here?

"Oh!" Duh. "Sorry. I don't have any money for a tip. But wait, I do have something for you." She hurried back to the coffee table, set the flowers down, and grabbed two brownies from the plate. She wrapped them in a napkin and took them to him.

"Oh, gee thanks." Sarcasm dripped from his voice as he stared at the napkin.

"You haven't tasted her brownies yet. Believe me, they're better than any two-dollar tip." Mrs. Grant shut the door in his face.

"These are so beautiful." Eve sat back down to admire the colorful bouquet of flowers.

"Are they from your beau?"

"Let's see." She pulled out the card.

Eve, I've missed you. It's time for this adventure of ours to have a happy ending. We'll meet you and your family at Rose Hill tomorrow. Can't wait to see you!

Nick

Chapter Fifty

"Nick, are you sure about this guy?" His dad kicked the tires of their car as they waited for Jeff Normandy to arrive at the Rose Hill Cemetery in Cumberland, Maryland.

Nick glanced at his phone for the tenth time. "You agreed it was probably the only way we could get into the tomb to check for the treasure."

"I don't trust him."

"Neither do I, but he agreed to all your terms," Nick reminded him.

All week he had begged his dad to let them take the key to the vault and see if it unlocked the gate, but his dad hadn't been convinced it was the right course of action. Finally, he relented but said they had to have a third party there videoing it all, to prove they didn't steal anything. Nick immediately thought of Normandy, and soon it had all been arranged.

If the treasure did exist, Nick and his dad did not want it to fall into the hands of the revolutionaries, or even the U.S. government for that matter. They wanted it to somehow help people. Mr. Normandy relented to taping the excursion instead of producing his usual live broadcast. And all parties agreed that if the treasure was found, it would remain in the Bank of Cumberland until the rightful owner could be determined. At that time, Mr. Normandy could air the footage in one of his television spectaculars.

As Grace and Olivia twirled around the tall trees, the rest of the Hammond family sat on nearby benches, waiting for the excitement to begin. No one had wanted to miss out on the big event.

Nick paced, one eye on the cemetery entrance, until he saw the Donahues' car pull into the lot. Eve waved at him through the window. Her smile made all his nerves disintegrate. He walked over to the car and held the door open for her. She flew into his arms. Just what he needed. It had been such a long week without being able to see her.

"This must be Nick." Another young woman climbed out of the car behind her. Her sister Brooke, of course.

She resembled Eve, but her hair was a darker auburn and lacked the unruly curls that he found irresistible. Nor did she share her sister's unique style. Brooke wore jeans and a t-shirt with her college logo, while Eve looked ready to participate in an excavation for an Indiana Jones movie. She sported khakis and a white shirt, with a scarf tying back her thick hair.

He smiled at the newcomer. "Hi, you must be Brooke. I've heard a lot about you."

She grinned. "And I was up half the night hearing about you."

Eve pulled herself from his arms. "I didn't talk about him *that* much."

"True. We did get one or two hours of sleep." Brooke winked at her sister.

Before Nick could say anything more, his siblings swarmed them, and introductions were made.

"Hey, gorgeous." Jace sauntered up to Brooke.

"Really, Jace?" Eve raised both hands in the air. "You dub me 'Stalker-chick' and she gets 'gorgeous'? Thanks a lot."

Jace raised one eyebrow, looking completely confused. "Hey, I wouldn't put the moves on my brother's girl. Give me some credit."

Finally, a white van pulled into the parking lot.

Ms. Selco and Jeff Normandy, along with two cameramen, emerged.

"Senator Hammond, you drive a hard bargain," Ms. Selco said as they shook hands. "But we're thankful for the opportunity to air the discovery, once you give us the all-clear. And you have our signed contracts stating we will not leak this story if something is found."

"Are you sure we don't need permission from the town or cemetery to be here?" Professor Donahue asked.

Dad shook his head. "I checked. If the key fits, we aren't breaking or entering. If it doesn't fit, then we'll need to bring them on board to open the tomb."

"Shall we get started?" Mr. Normandy rubbed his hands together.

For once, Nick couldn't agree more with the treasure hunter. *Time to do this thing.*

He and Eve led the way to the mysterious tomb. When they reached the area, everyone was allowed to scatter into small groups nearby while the crew prepped for camera.

Finally, a moment alone. Sort of alone, anyway. They sat together under one of the towering trees. He plucked a blade of grass. "Can you believe this is actually happening?"

Eve leaned her head back against the tree. "It's hard to believe. Think we'll find anything?"

"Only one way to find out. It feels like a lifetime ago that we were here last."

"It's a little more crowded this time around, that's for sure."

They glanced around at everyone. Their dads were huddled together, deep in conversation. The moms chatted while watching Grace and Olivia roll down a hill. Gabriella occupied herself by practicing her gymnastic routine in the soft grass. Jace tried to charm Brooke with stories of his sporting accomplishments, the three-year age gap not fazing him in the least. Dillon pestered the cameramen as they set up their equipment, asking a million questions. Ms. Selco helped Mr. Normandy apply his makeup.

Eventually, the perfect spot was chosen for the tripod and camera. The crew agreed a second camera would be handheld in order to get a better view inside the crypt. When everything was set and ready to roll, the entire group was called to gather around.

The cameras began to roll, and Mr. Normandy gave a beautiful speech about the gold, the war, and the men who'd protected the treasure for years. He then talked about the two teenagers who discovered it all, but something about the speech bothered him, so he repeated it three more times. Nick thought he'd explode from anticipation. This was ridiculous. *Just get on with it already.*

Finally, Normandy was satisfied. The time had come to place the key in the lock. The air sizzled with energy. Even the little ones stopped playing, anticipating the big moment of truth. Nick twitched from a ripple of nerves.

All eyes were glued on Mr. Normandy as he held the key, ready to insert it into the lock—

"No one move!"

Nick and Eve flinched in unison.

Everyone whirled around to find two men pointing guns at them. Nick's blood seemed to drain from his entire body. The women shrieked and moved in front of the children. Everyone else raised their hands in the air.

No! Why hadn't they thought to protect themselves? Now he'd put everyone in danger.

"We thought you two might be up to something." Taggert, the man with the buzz cut, sneered at Nick and Eve. "Shall we see what's inside of this tomb?"

Taggert snatched the key out of Jeff Normandy's hands while his blond partner kept a gun pointed at everyone else. Normandy didn't put up a fight. But he did subtly signal to the man with the still camera to keep filming.

Nick noticed the cameraman's slight nod as he backed away from the tripod. Neither of the criminals seemed to notice the red, glowing light on the camera.

Taggert reached for Eve and yanked her toward him.

Nick nearly quit breathing. He wanted to throttle the guy but didn't dare risk charging him. Taggert thrust the key into Nick's chest, then pushed Eve toward his partner. The blond thug wrapped an arm around her and jabbed his gun into her rib cage.

Eve's mom gasped. "No! Don't hurt her."

Taggert turned toward the crowd. "You all do as you're told, and no one will get hurt." His cold gaze shot to Nick. "Since you're the star of this show, go ahead and open it up."

Feeling helpless, Nick looked at Eve. Her terrified gaze sent a chill through him.

Please God, keep us all safe.

He took a deep breath then pushed the key into the lock. It slid in with only slight resistance. Swallowing hard, he twisted the key and was rewarded by an audible click.

Despite the tense situation, everyone released a collective gasp.

Taggert pushed Nick into the large vault while keeping his gun pointing around the crowd. "Come on, all men inside. We're moving the cover off this tomb."

Reluctantly, his dad, Jace, Professor Donahue, Jeff Normandy, and the two cameramen all crowded inside with Nick. They coordinated their efforts to push the heavy stone top off the tomb.

Nick breathed a silent prayer that their assumption was right and they weren't disturbing someone's final resting spot.

After several attempts, the stone moved enough to peer inside, but it was too dark to see anything.

"Well?" the gunman demanded.

Dad shook his head. "We need a flashlight."

"Everyone out," Taggert yelled. The men, hands raised in the air, started to leave the tomb. "Except you." He jabbed the gun at Nick as he tried to exit.

Nick made eye contact with his brother.

He tried to think of an escape plan but couldn't deny his curiosity. Was the gold indeed in there?

The gunman shone a flashlight into the dark, stone tomb. Nick peered in. Then, as Taggert focused on the contents, a rush of adrenaline coursed through Nick's veins. He hammered down on the back of the man's head with his fists, forcing the gunman's forehead to slam into the stone tomb. He slumped at Nick's feet.

Just as he grabbed the gun from the man's hand, a commotion arose outside. His mother screamed.

Nick's blood froze in his veins. He dashed out of the tomb.

The blond gunman was sprawled out on the ground. Eve lay next to him, with Jace on top of them both. Professor Donahue stood on the man's hand that held the gun.

"Jace!" Dad yelled.

Jace shrugged. "Just tackling the opponent, Dad."

"You could've gotten my daughter shot!" Mrs. Donahue screamed at him.

Jace shook his head. "No way. Didn't you see him turn his head and lower the gun a bit when we heard that sound from inside the tomb ... like a head cracking open? The guy was totally unprepared."

"Did you see that move?" Dillon jumped up and down. "Coolest thing ever!"

"Mom! You made me miss it." Grace squirmed out of her mom's embrace.

"Impressed?" Jace sidled up to Brooke.

"Mildly."

Nick helped Eve up while Jace and his dad threw Blondie into the vault with his partner. Nick locked the door, then handed the gun to his dad, glad to be free of the deadly weapon.

"Well?" Ms. Selco straightened her skirt. "Is the gold in there?"

Everyone turned to Nick.

Chapter Fifty-one

"Are you sure?" Eve stared at Nick's drawing.

"Yes, that's all that was there."

Everyone circled around as Nick showed them his sketch of what he had seen inside the tomb. Eve concentrated on the drawing. Three tridents forming a triangle inside a circle. The three men had definitely seen themselves as protectors of the gold.

"This symbol was the only thing in there. No gold." Nick looked around the disappointed crowd.

"No gold. What a waste," Jeff Normandy complained, sounding like one of the kids.

"But why would there be an empty tomb in a cemetery?" Her mom's hand kept rubbing Eve's back. Poor Mom. Ever since the men had been overpowered, she hadn't left Eve's side. Guess seeing her daughter held at gunpoint freaked her out. But Eve wasn't about to push her away. The protectiveness was comforting.

"Maybe the gold once was here but now it's long gone." Senator Hammond patted Nick's shoulder.

Something about the drawing tugged at Eve's mind. Something familiar . . .

It was similar to the symbol on the outside of the tomb they'd seen last week, but that wasn't what she was thinking of. She'd seen it somewhere else. But where?

"Well, that bites," Jace grumbled.

"We came all the way out here and almost died for nothing? So lame." Gabriella pulled out her phone, bored once again.

Grace stomped her little foot. "At least *you* got to see Jace's big tackle. I didn't see anything except Mom's shirt."

Nick's mom pulled Grace into her arms again. "I wanted to make sure you weren't injured."

Eve smiled at the two of them. Then it clicked into place. Oh! Bursts of understanding, excitement, and amazement exploded inside her like the beautiful fireworks that she and Nick had recently enjoyed.

She grabbed her dad's arm. "Dad, look at the symbol. Don't you recognize it? This isn't a dead end. It's another clue."

***

Dad eased the car out of the parking lot. "Eve, I can't believe it. Do you think it's possible the gold could be there?"

Nick had joined them while his family and the camera crew were following. Eve's mom and sister stayed at the cemetery to keep an eye on the men in the tomb until the police arrived.

"I'm positive it's the same symbol." She typed something into her GPS system, her hands trembling.

"Could you two please fill me in?" Nick leaned forward from the backseat as they sped away from the cemetery.

"I think all the concerns we've had about what to do with the money are about to be solved." She purposely kept her answer a bit cryptic, just as his often were. For once, she was the one with the knowledge, and it was downright fun.

A few moments later, the three vehicles pulled into a beautiful farm on the outskirts of town. Eve strode to the door, and everyone else trailed behind her. She took a deep breath, then pushed the doorbell.

A young woman answered the door.

Her eyes took in the large group of people on her porch. "Can I help you?"

***

"I'm still confused." The woman reached for her husband's calloused hand. Blond hair trailed down her back in a messy ponytail.

Aside from Grace and Dillon, who reminded Eve of little roadrunners as they chased chickens around the yard, everyone sat on the porch as Eve tried to explain the situation. They all did their best to ignore the camera's blinding light, capturing the moment.

Time to start at the beginning. "Was Charles Barrett your ancestor?"

"Yes, my wife's distant uncle." The husband's confused glance bounced around the crowded porch.

"Have you ever heard of Jonathon Hamilton or Alexander Meyers?" Dad asked them.

The man looked at his wife, who shook her head. "No."

Eve recognized the gleam in her dad's eyes. He always got that look when he was about to share a piece of history with someone. "For years, it was rumored that these three men were in possession of lost Confederate gold."

The young couple raised their eyebrows in unison. "Gold?"

"Yes." Nick jumped in to help with the story. She hadn't explained her realization yet, but she was pretty sure he'd pieced it together. "Most people thought it was only a legend, but Eve and I began to investigate and found clues that convinced us the gold actually exists."

"Okay. But what does this have to do with us?" The young woman still seemed baffled.

Eve scooched to the edge of her chair. There was no gentle way to prepare them for the news. "We think it might be here on your property."

The husband burst out laughing. "This house has been lived in for generations. If any gold existed, it would have been found by now."

"Can you tell us about this symbol?" Eve showed them Nick's sketch.

The woman took a look at the drawing. "Sure, it's the symbol we decided to use when we opened the farm as a rehabilitation facility for veterans. We're hoping to get it printed on a sign for the end of our lane."

Eve nodded. "Yes, I recognized it from the newspaper article about your wonderful program."

Nick shot her a slight smile, and Eve knew exactly what he was thinking. *Well done, Albuquerque.*

"Why did you choose this symbol?" he prodded.

"It's on the cellar wall. We always assumed it was a family crest or something."

Excitement moved over the group in a wave.

Ms. Selco stood. "Would you show us the cellar? Please?"

The entire group traipsed down a set of stairs into a damp, musty basement. All eyes fixed on the symbol carved into the stone.

Eve reached out and touched one of the tridents. A flood of emotion sent a shiver down her spine. This whole journey that started so many months ago with a crazy vision had led them to this moment.

Nick's dad knocked on the stone carving. "What's on the other side of this wall?"

The woman leaned against her husband. "Nothing."

"Are you sure?" Nick and Eve asked in unison.

Chapter Fifty-two

The young homeowners contacted a friend who showed up within moments, bringing tools to remove the carving. While the cameramen filmed the slow process of chipping away the century-old mortar, the others were given a tour around the property.

Eve's mom and sister eventually joined the group, informing them the local police would be by later to gather everyone's statements. As the tour progressed, Nick realized Eve was right—there could be no doubt where the money should go. Jim and Greta had been working for years to renovate the property in order to make a veterans' rehabilitation facility. They had installed a lift to the second-floor bedrooms, enlarged doorways to accommodate wheelchairs, and transformed their barn into a physical therapy gym. Their dedication and continuous efforts were amazing.

"This is all quite impressive," Professor Donahue said as they walked the grounds that would offer a special therapy program with dogs. "I read the article about your farm and your dream of making it a rehab facility for vets, but the pictures didn't do the place justice."

"Thank you." Greta slowed to walk next to him. "Our ultimate goal is to create a haven that heals the body, mind, and spirit with job training and spiritual counseling. Our local priest is almost as excited about the project as we are." She lifted one shoulder in a half-shrug. "We have lots of ideas but, well, there never seem to be enough funds."

Hopefully that would not be a problem for long.

"How did you get the idea to help veterans?" Nick's mom asked as her youngest children ran through the field.

"When we first married, we were living in Baltimore. We'd had enough of city life and wanted to move to the country. My parents planned on selling this property that had been in my family forever, and we thought it would be the perfect place to raise a family. As we were cleaning out the attic, we came across two letters from my distant relative, Charles Barrett. He had fought in the Civil War for the South and wrote to his wife Annabelle, who lived here with her family while he was away. His words about how much he despised the war and wanted to somehow help the soldiers stuck with us. We couldn't get that out of our minds and realized we could fulfill his wish."

What an incredible thing to do.

Eve reached out and squeezed Greta's hand. "That's beautiful. Do you think it would be possible for us to see the letters?"

"Sure, let's go back to the house. You can check out the letters while I get us all a snack."

Jace sprang to life. "Food, yes!"

***

As everyone gathered to enjoy cookies and lemonade on the porch, Eve read the two letters out loud to the captivated audience. Her eyes lit up as she read. She filled the words with such emotion that when she finished, everyone remained quiet for a moment, lost in the devastating descriptions of the war and Barrett's passionate desire to be reunited with his wife.

Nick couldn't wait any longer and broke the silence, anxious to piece it all together. "The friend he wrote about, the one he stayed with after he was injured in the war, must have been Jonathon Hamilton. Hamilton ranked high enough up in the Confederate Army; he somehow must have become the custodian of the gold."

"I still can't believe you think there could be treasure inside our home." Greta leaned back in her rocking chair.

"Well, we're about to find out." Her husband walked out onto the porch. "The plaque is ready to be removed."

Everyone scurried down to the cellar, leaving Nick and Eve alone on the porch. She smiled at him then rose to follow the crowd.

He stood. This might all be over in a few moments. There was something he needed to do first. "Eve, before we head down, I want to say something."

Her smile brightened, warming his insides.

"This has been a crazy adventure. And as much as I'm excited to find out what's behind that crest, I don't want it all to end." He stuffed his hands into the pockets of his jeans to keep himself calm.

She nodded. "I know what you mean."

"I think you know that I really like you. And, well, there's something I want to ask you."

"What is it?" Her eyes sparkled in the afternoon light.

He pulled his hands out and rubbed them together. Why was he so nervous? Things were good between them, but he couldn't let this journey end without making his feelings clear.

"I wanted to know if you'd maybe like to keep spending time with me and go out with me sometime. Like, you know, on a date."

She giggled, probably amused by his awkwardness. "I would like nothing more than to go out with you."

Relief rushed over him. "I was hoping you'd say that."

He glanced at the door to the house.

"Okay. Well, I guess this is it." He held out his hand.

She laced her fingers between his. "The moment of truth."

Together they made their way inside for the big reveal.

***

Ms. Selco ushered them to the front of the crowd surrounding the crest. Eve's knees wobbled. What would they find? Good thing she had Nick's hand to hang onto.

Jeff Normandy gave yet another speech for the camera then, in complete silence, the men pulled the heavy, chiseled stone out of the wall and eased it onto the floor.

Nick squeezed her hand then shone a flashlight into the dark space.

The beam of light shone on stacks and stacks of gold bars.

Eve gasped. She and Nick stared in silence at the treasure as everyone else cheered.

While Jeff Normandy rattled on to the camera, Nick leaned close and whispered in her ear. "We did it. We found the treasure."

She squeezed his hand. "We completed our mission."

Chapter Fifty-three

"I owe you much more than just my gratitude." Ambassador Schroeder vigorously shook Nick's hand.

Nick, his father, the ambassador, and Natalia were in his dad's office.

"I had no idea Mr. Stoltz was searching for the gold or that he had contacted Mr. Normandy." The ambassador shook his head and sighed. "The majority of my country wants peace, not the misguided ideals of this new king. Even though we're a monarchy, our people do have some say. Now that his plans have been revealed, I think he will be watched more closely."

Nick's dad nodded. "I know how you feel. I didn't want to believe Senator Abrams was capable of sabotaging our efforts to solidify the trade agreement. But when I started checking into the situation, it became clear there was a link between them, and that he was involved. It appears he was working behind the scenes with your new king. Now that the attempted trade embargo and dissention have been exposed, it will be harder for their plan to move forward. The Senate Ethics Committee will begin investigating the matter this week."

"I can't believe the Confederate gold really existed, and that they had been trying for years to find it for the purpose of destroying our country."

Natalia turned to Nick. "What will happen to all the gold?"

"Since it was on their property, and there is no proof of where it came from, it belongs to the Barrett descendants. After the government takes their share of taxes of course," he explained.

Dad reached over and squeezed his shoulder. "It'll help a lot of people. That dedicated young couple can now build a state-of-the-art rehab facility for veterans."

"It's perfect because, according to letters they had from Mr. Barrett, he was always concerned with the struggles veterans face, especially when dealing with their injuries."

"Well, I'm glad we had some small role to play in the happy ending. And now we should get back to the embassy." Ambassador Schroeder stood to leave.

Nick stood as well. "Sir, before you leave, there's something I wanted to discuss with you."

Natalia shifted uncomfortably in her seat.

"I promised Natalia I would help her talk to you." Hopefully he knew what to say.

"About what?" the ambassador asked.

"Well, umm . . ." Natalia's voice shook but she held her father's gaze. "I've been acting out because I'm unhappy here. I'd like to go back to the boarding school."

"Natalia, we talked about this and quite frankly, it is inappropriate to discuss with the senator and his son." The ambassador turned to leave.

"Please, listen," Natalia begged. "The only reason I've been misbehaving and dressing like this is because I want to get back to school with my friends and my boyfriend."

Her father sent her a sharp look. "We don't want you that far away from us."

She stood. "But I'm not happy."

He towered over her, but she held her ground.

The two stared at each other, the hard edge creeping back into Natalia's eyes.

Nick had promised her he'd help. He needed to at least try to diffuse the tense situation.

"Sir, I think Natalia feels like the two of you are unable to communicate and that you don't listen to her. And Natalia, I don't think you listen to your parents either. Ambassador Schroeder, I'm not trying to interfere, but I've seen a different side of Natalia, and I'm convinced she has been desperately trying to get your attention."

The ambassador stared at Nick then turned toward his daughter. "Is that true?"

Natalia shrugged, then with a glance at Nick, slowly nodded her head.

Her father watched her for a long moment. "I'm not sure your being so far away is the best thing for our family, but I promise I will listen to your side."

"Thank you."

The ambassador shook hands with Nick and his dad then squeezed his daughter's shoulder. They turned and walked out of the room.

Hopefully, they would work it out.

Nick glanced at the clock. "All right, I've got to get out of here."

Dad grinned. "Tonight is your big date, right?"

"Yep, our first official date."

Nick breathed in the scent of her hair. A hint of strawberries and citrus lingered in the vibrant strands.

At last, they had their happy ending.

Acknowledgements

I want to express my gratitude to:

First and foremost God, for guiding me on this incredible path to use my talents to encourage others in their faith.

The Mental family for their steadfast support of my writing and for inspiring me daily.

Perpetual Light Publishing for providing this opportunity to share my story.

My talented fellow authors at Catholicteenbooks.com. Working with these kindred spirits has been an incredible blessing.

Other Titles by Leslea Wahl

A Summer to Treasure
The Perfect Blindside
eXtreme Blindside
Into the Spotlight
Charting the Course
In Plain Sight
To Serve and Protect
The Mommy Mix-up

Contributing author in CatholicTeenBooks anthologies:
Secrets: Visible & Invisible

Discussion Questions

1. Have you ever felt God calling you to do something? Do you know anyone who has had this experience?

2. How does God "talk" to you?

3. Eve and Nick learned that we can all be called in big and small ways. They were proud to have helped Mrs. Grant and Natalia. Who in your life could use your help?

4. Eve confided in Father Romero about her vision. Do you have someone in your life you can turn to when you need guidance?

5. Eve was lonely when her friend and sister both moved away. Why did she isolate herself? Have you ever done this?

6. Both Eve and Nick pulled away from friends. How did they help each other decide to give friendships another try?

7. Eve felt like she was in another world after her move, since DC was so different than her home. Have you ever felt that way after moving or visiting somewhere new?

8. The book centers around Civil War history. What period of history do you find most interesting?

9. Should Eve and Nick have confided in their parents sooner?

10. Do you think you have the courage to say "yes, Lord?"

About the Author

Leslea Wahl lives in beautiful Colorado with her family. She strives to write teen and Young Adult novels that will encourage teens to grow in their faith through fun, adventurous mysteries.

She is the author of multiple faith-based teen novels. For more information on her award-winning Young Adult mysteries please visit her website at www.LesleaWahl.com.

Note from Author

The spark for this novel came to me twenty-five years ago with an idea that I felt would make a great beginning for a book. I didn't pursue it then, but after I published my first Young Adult novel, I pondered the idea again and wondered how it could be made to fit a teen novel. Eventually inspiration hit, and the story about recognizing a call from God finally came together.

Most of the things Eve experienced when she moved to Washington, D.C. are based on actual events that I encountered after moving there from Colorado as a newlywed. I loved our time inside the Beltway but felt overwhelmed by moving to a huge city on the East Coast. Those were very special years that I had fun reminiscing about while writing this book.

While inspired by some actual personal incidents, Where You Lead is a work of fiction. Names, characters, and historic events are the products of my imagination. Any resemblance to actual persons, living or dead, or actual events is purely co-incidental.

Dear Reader,

If you enjoyed reading *Where You Lead*, I would appreciate it if you would help others enjoy this book too. Here are some of the ways you can help spread the word:

Lend it. This book is lending enabled so please share it with a friend.

Recommend it. Help other readers find this book by recommending it to friends, readers' groups, book clubs, and discussion forums.

Share it. Let other readers know you've read the book by posting a note to your social media account and/or your Goodreads account.

Review it. Please tell others why you liked this book by reviewing it on your favorite site.

Everything you do to help others learn about my book is greatly appreciated!

Leslea Wahl

Keep reading for an excerpt from Leslea Wahl's *A Summer to Treasure!*

Chapter 1

Celia:
Sucked Into the Black Hole

This couldn't be happening.

Celia stared at her parents. *Are they serious?* They generally weren't known for their senses of humor, but still she held out a thin sliver of hope that their shocking announcement was some sort of weird experiment. A let's-freak-out-the-kids-then-break-it-to-them-that-it's-a-joke sort of prank. But they showed no sign of moving past the life-altering pronouncement. Okay, maybe not *life*-altering, more like summer-destroying. Either way, she had to admit it, this beyond-awful plan would make the perfect, cruddy ending to her disastrous school year.

The moment Dad had suggested the five of them talk in the formal living room, her internal bad-news radar started pinging. Nothing good ever came from a family meeting. Her gaze shifted to her brothers to determine their take on the whole situation.

Luke's forearms flexed as he clasped his hands. Celia's older brother always got his way. Surely, he could use his smooth-talking skills to persuade Mom and Dad out of this horrendous idea. He may be a royal pain and too cool to give her the time of day lately, but she'd learned over the years that it was best to let him schmooze the folks with his calm nonsense before she went into full freak out mode. This insight had come from years of being sent to her room for shrill outbursts, only to find out—after her punishment—that Luke, with his steady voice of reason, had miraculously gotten them to arrive at her desired outcome. The guy really should go into politics. He already had the clean-cut, all-American look going for him. When it came to reading people, understanding what made them tick, and using it to get his way, her older sibling was a pro.

Luke's favorite-child status was beyond annoying, but hey, if he used it to her advantage, then have at it, big bro. Take the lead.

He must've felt her desperate gaze given the annoyed look he shot her way before turning his attention to the folks. Celia wasn't sure if his grumpiness was aimed at her for staring, or at their folks for the bombshell announcement. Hopefully, the latter.

Luke's Adam's apple bobbed as he swallowed. "Umm. So, you're thinking we should spend our summer vacation driving around the country in an RV with Grandma?"

Celia's skin crawled when Luke gave voice to the stupid idea. Road tripping in some lame camper with her parents, brothers, and *grandmother?*

Um . . . don't think so. Come on, Luke, help a girl out. Time for his persuasive superpowers.

Dad clenched his jaw. "Yep. That is the plan."

Luke rubbed the back of his neck. "Wow. That does sound fun. Are you talking like a weekend trip or something?"

Mom shook her head, her dyed-blonde bob swayed with the movement. "No. It would be a bit longer than that." She nudged Dad with her knee.

The slight movement set Celia further on edge. *This can't be good.*

Dad ran a hand through his brown hair. A few gray strands flecked the boring shade that he'd passed on to his children. "We would be gone for a month. Or so."

"A month! No way! Not happening! *Ever!* I have plans for the summer." Celia couldn't stop the screech— it just flew right out of her mouth.

"Celia! That's enough."

You'd think she was five, the way Mom scolded her. Celia threw her head back against the couch cushion.

Luke pierced her with another scorching glance. This time she knew without a doubt who was the intended target. She bit the inside of her cheek to prevent any further outbursts.

Turning back to their parents, her older brother leaned forward, elbows resting on his knees. "I'm sure we could see a lot of cool things in a month. Can you get away from work for that long?"

Oh, good point! Why hadn't she thought of that?

Dad clasped his hands together. "Well, I have a lot of vacation time built up, so I arranged to work part time on my laptop. You all sleep later than me, anyway. I can get a couple hours in each morning."

What? Come on, Luke, you gotta do better than that! A flash of surprise flickered across her brother's face. "Oh, that's cool! Hey, sorry to be the one to put the kibosh on this plan, but I'm not sure I can get away for that long. Football pre-season starts up in mid-June, and you know how Coach is about missing practices—especially the seniors. I don't want to mess up my chance of being named one of the captains this season. Besides, I was planning on working a lot this summer."

He deftly ignored the other reason he wouldn't want to be gone for so long. Jenna. His clingy girlfriend could never survive without him for a month. Celia's quick glance at Austin to gauge his reaction only raised her frustration level. Her younger brother was slouched behind a pillow, eyes aimed at his lap—no doubt playing a game on his phone. The twerp couldn't even pay attention long enough to stay focused during one family meeting. Typical.

One swift kick to his foot made him jump, shaggy brown hair flopping over his eyes.

"Huh?" He brushed the messy mop out of his way.

She shot him a withering glare, which produced the desired result of him abandoning his phone, at least for a moment.

Luke motioned toward Austin. "Traveling that long would also cheat Austin out of summer camp. He's going into eighth grade. This is his last chance to attend. And Celia would miss . . ." His gaze flicked her way. "Whatever it is that Celia does."

Seriously? He couldn't come up with anything better than that? Unbelievable. He could take all the time in the world to understand everyone else, but his own sister? Forget it. Now that he was about to be a senior, his ego had ticked up a notch, from obnoxious to unbearable.

She resisted the tempting urge of telling him off. Right now, though, it was more important that he be the voice of reason to Mom and Dad.

Dad ran his hand along his jawline. Sunshine streamed through the kitchen window and gleamed off his wedding band. The weather outside in direct contrast to the dreariness that had suddenly infiltrated their home. "Look. I know this is not how any of you wanted to spend your summer. Honestly, it wouldn't be my first choice, either. But we're doing this for Grandma." Mom turned on the spousal support and rubbed Dad's back. "That's right. As you may have noticed, Grandma hasn't really been herself since her trip to visit her brother."

Grandma had always been close to her only brother, Harry. Over the years, she'd shared numerous stories about him, causing Celia to think how lucky her grand-mother was to have only one male sibling to deal with. He was a monk in some tiny town in Kansas, so they didn't see each other too often.

Now that Celia thought about it—Mom was right. Grandma hadn't been her upbeat self since she'd gotten back from that trip. Last weekend, when she'd been over for a barbeque, she'd been totally distracted. Grandma usually made family dinners much less stressful with her knack of including everyone in the conversation and re-laying funny stories about the folks at her senior living complex. Celia hadn't really thought anything of it until now, since she'd had more pressing matters on her mind.

"Is everything all right with her?" Luke's forehead scrunched with concern.

Dad's shoulder raised in a half-shrug. "Honestly, I don't know. She says everything's fine, but she's certainly not herself. I'm worried that maybe . . ." He shook his head then glanced toward Mom.

Mom cleared her throat, rescuing him from whatever he was about to say. "Apparently, Grandma wants to relive a vacation she and her brother took as kids with their parents. They spent several weeks driving through the Southwest visiting national parks." Her face hardened with determination as she took in her children's matching are-you-kidding-me expressions.

This was ridiculous. How would making the rest of them completely miserable help Grandma feel better? Dad leaned forward. "We don't know why she's so insistent on doing this. In fact, we also pushed back on the idea, but she wouldn't drop it." He reached over and grabbed Mom's hand. "After much discussion, we decided that maybe this is a needed wake-up call. Grandma won't be with us forever." His voice caught with emotion. Mom's hand tightened around his, giving him strength to continue. "Each year we have her is a blessing."

Austin's eyes widened. "Wait. Is something wrong with her?"

The gaze between Mom and Dad lingered for a moment before he shook his head no. "She claims that she and Harry were going through some items from their childhood and began reminiscing about their special trip out west. She insists that she's fine but, because she's getting older, thinks this could be the last big trip she can take, and she wants all of us to go with her."

Celia exchanged glances with her brothers, then swallowed her frustration. They'd all seen the extended look between their parents. Even Luke's smooth talk wouldn't get them out of this one. Something was going on, and none of them could possibly say no to Grandma's request. But a month in an enclosed space with the family? Pure torture.

Chapter 2

LUKE:
ROLL WITH THE PUNCHES

Jenna encircled Luke with her thin arms. He tried not to flinch or pull away, but the PDA in front of his family made him uncomfortable.

"I'm going to miss you terribly." The emotional strain in his girlfriend's voice filled him with guilt. *Don't be a jerk. She's going to miss you. Man up.*

So, instead of squirming out of her embrace, Luke pulled her close, breathing in the scent of her floral shampoo. "I know. I wish I didn't have to go." Since they'd started dating in the fall, they'd seen each other almost every day. Being apart for a whole month would be tough. "At least we can text and send photos."

Celia brushed past them on her way to the motorhome Dad had rented for their insanely long trip. Luke ignored the shake of his sister's head. Celia never even tried to hide the fact that she was no fan of Jenna. Granted, she didn't seem to be a fan of anything anymore. No, that wasn't true. There were a few things she enjoyed, such as sulking around, listening to music through her earbuds, and doodling in a stupid sketchbook.

He'd pretty much given up trying to figure out what was up with his sister. In the fall, things had seemed fine. Her freshman year began with her hanging out with all her middle school friends, but then something changed. She went from zero to weird in a millisecond and began infiltrating the fringe crowd. Luckily, no one at school made a big deal of his sister's aversion-to-color grunge phase.

"Thanks for coming by to see us off, Jenna." Dad's diplomatic words were clearly meant to end this goodbye scene. For once, Luke welcomed the disruption since he had no clue how to extricate himself from Jenna on his own without setting off the minefield of her emotions.

She pulled away and wiped her tears. "Of course. I couldn't let Luke leave without a proper send-off."

"Come on, gang. Let's hit the road," Dad hollered. He then leaned close to Jenna like he was about to reveal a big secret. "The beauty of traveling in a motorhome is that we don't need a million bathroom breaks."

"Siena, come!" Austin squatted down, and their goldendoodle cautiously shimmied up to him, heavy panting a sure indicator of her nerves.

"Oh . . ." Jenna reached down to pat Siena's soft head. "She doesn't want to leave, either."

Austin shook his head. "She loves car rides. Once we get moving, she'll be fine. She just gets worried when we start packing. I guess she thinks we'll drop her off at the kennel." He stroked Siena's back. "Don't worry, girl. This time you get to come along." The dog answered with a lick across his cheek.

Mom locked the front door of the house, then joined them in front of their home-on-wheels for the next month. "Okay. I turned off the water and set the alarm. I think we're all set."

"Good." Dad motioned toward the RV. "Pile in, everyone. Let's be on our way."

"Wait!" Grandma's head popped out of the motorhome window. Her wavy gray hair framed her smiling face.

Now what?

"We need a photo to commemorate the start of our journey." Grandma pointed at Jenna. "Will you take a photo of us, dear?"

"Sure."

Luke handed Jenna his phone, then waited patiently with the rest of the family while Celia slowly plodded out of the camper, her annoyance on full display. Hopefully, she wouldn't ruin the picture with her usual scowl.

After posing for a few shots, Luke pulled his girl-friend in for one last hug as the monstrous vehicle roared to life. His cue to leave. He smiled for a few more in-sisted-upon selfies, then climbed into the motorhome with the rest of the family.

He scanned the space. While he'd been being a good boyfriend, everyone else had staked out their spots. Dad manned the driver's seat, with Mom next to him assuming the role of co-pilot, a tail-wagging Siena perched between them, her front paws draped over the console. Celia and Austin had commandeered the two bolted-in-place swivel lounge chairs. Both hovered over their phones, Celia listening to something through earbuds, tapping her foot to some unknown song, and Austin already lost to his game du jour.

That left only one open seat—next to Grandma on the L-shaped bench at the table. Since the matriarch of the family had already chosen the short end, the seat with a direct line of sight to the front window, he plopped next to her on the bench that ran under the long window.

Outside, Jenna waved frantically to get his attention, then blew a series of kisses. He smiled and waved, touched by her emotional, although slightly over-the-top, farewell. Even though a casual observer might assume he were being deployed, not heading off for a family vacation—he found it sweet.

The mammoth camper lurched away from the curb, convulsing down the street as Dad grew accustomed to the touchy pedals.

"We're off on our adventure!" Dad honked the horn to emphasize the moment.

Luke squeezed his eyes shut. *This is going to be the longest month ever.*

The RV had barely made it out of their Colorado Springs neighborhood when his first text from Jenna came through.

I miss you already.

Luke grinned at the message. It'd only been six minutes since her tearful farewell. Grateful for the distraction from Dad's choice of road-trip music (who would want to relive the '80s?), he typed a quick reply to Jenna.

Setting his phone down, he glanced at Celia, her head swaying to the beat of her music. She had the right idea. If only he knew where he'd stashed his earbuds.

"Did Jenna send you a message already?"

He looked toward Grandma's smile. "Uh, yeah. She's going to have a tough time while I'm on this trip. We've only ever gone a few days without seeing each other." The phone buzzed with Jenna's reply.

Grandma pushed away the leather notebook in front of her. "Have you ever heard the saying 'Absence makes the heart grow fonder'?"

Luke shook his head. "Don't think so."

She nodded toward his phone. "A little time and distance can be wonderful for a relationship."

"Oh, yeah?" Jenna's newest message informed him that she'd already posted one of their goodbye selfies. He typed a quick reply.

"Did you know that your grandpa was in the military while we were dating? He was deployed, and we didn't see each other for a whole year."

"Really?" His phone buzzed again, but he forced himself to keep his focus on his grandmother. "A whole year? That must've been rough." Grandma was pretty tough, most likely she'd showed a lot less emotion than Jenna, even when her guy went off to war and not a simple road trip.

The skin around Grandma's eyes crinkled with a smile. "It was. And we didn't have texting or computers back then to help us keep in touch."

Hard to even imagine. "Were you able to call each other?"

She shook her head. "Believe it or not, it was too expensive. We wrote letters."

"Oh, wow. That must've taken a while to hear from each other." No instantaneous messages a hundred times a day. *What did they do with all their free time?*

A faraway look turned her eyes hazy. "I cherished his letters." She focused on her oldest grandson. "I bet Jenna would love to receive a letter from you."

"A letter? What would I write?" He pictured Jenna's confused face at getting a letter in the mail.

"Well, what do you type to her now?"

"I don't know. Nothing important."

"You could tell her about all that we see on our trip. And you could open up your heart and share your feelings." Her smile turned into a mischievous grin. "Girls like that sort of thing."

He shifted in his seat, glancing away. *Open up my heart? Like in some dumb romantic comedy? Don't think so.* "I'm not sure. I don't think I'd have enough to say to write a whole letter."

"Maybe a postcard then. You could send her one from each of our stops. That's what I'm planning to do; send postcards to update Harry on the trip." She grinned. "In fact, I bought a Pike's Peak postcard the other day so I can let him know we started our excursion."

Hmm. Postcards? Not a bad idea. That he could handle. "She might actually like that." If there was one thing he knew about Jenna, it was her weakness for rom coms.

He glanced at Jenna's newest query—wondering how far from home they'd driven. He peered out the window. Not far. And at their current speed, they might never reach the first destination. When semis zoom past, you know you're in for a long journey. He quickly answered the text, then stuffed the phone in his pocket. Enough for now.

He returned his attention to Grandma. "So, Dad said this trip is kind of recreating one you took as a kid?"

"Yes. Want to hear the story?" Her face beamed, obviously anxious for a trip down memory lane.

"Yeah, sure." Maybe she'd reveal what was really going on.

Before she could begin, Luke snatched two pillows from the bench and flung them at his siblings.

Austin glanced around for whatever he'd missed. Celia pulled out one earbud with an all-too-familiar scowl.

"Hey, enough with the phones. Grandma wants to tell us about the trip to the Southwest she took as a kid."

His siblings dutifully put their devices away, and all three turned their attention to their beloved grandmother.

"Well." The elderly woman rested her hands on the table. "I don't know if you know this or not, but my father was a professor of archeology."

"Cool! Like Indiana Jones?" Austin blurted out. "I loved that ride at Disneyland."

Grandma's gaze flicked off to the left as her face warmed with a smile. "Well, we did have some interesting adventures."

Huh. How have we never heard this before?

Grandma peered out the window before continuing. "He didn't teach summer classes, so every year, when school ended, we took a family trip. One year, we explored the Great Lakes. Another year, we ventured to Alaska. But my favorite trip was when we visited the national parks in the Southwest."

"Really?" Austin's face scrunched up. "Better than Alaska?"

Celia punched his arm. "Let her speak."

Grandma smiled at Austin, deftly ignoring Celia like they all longed to do. "Well, Alaska was special, too. But I think I enjoyed our trip to Arizona and Utah so much because Harry and I were old enough to explore a little without supervision, but we weren't too old to pretend and create our own adventures."

"How old were you?" Celia actually looked interested in something besides her sketchpad.

Weird.

"I think I was probably about ten, so Harry would have been twelve."

"You were two years apart like we all are." Austin brushed a strand of unruly hair away from his eyes.

Grandma nodded. "Yep."

"Did your mother go along too?"

Luke shook his head. When not immersed in a video game, his little brother couldn't stop talking. Hopefully, he wouldn't be breaking out the annoying puns anytime soon.

"Yes. She was an artist and would spend hours at each location sketching or painting, trying to capture the beauty of the landscape."

Celia sat a little straighter. "Are all those paintings at your apartment hers?"

Grandma's eyebrows arched like she was surprised Celia had noticed the artwork. "They sure are. I always thought she was very talented. She sold a few, but I think she had more fun creating than selling them. But as you can imagine, with my father doing fieldwork and my mother painting, it left Harry and me with a lot of free time."

"That sounds like a great childhood." Although, they'd miss out on all the organized sports camps and stuff.

"It was." That faraway look flooded her eyes again.

"Did your visit with Harry bring back all those memories?" Luke probed, still hoping to discover more about the reason for the trip.

Grandma focused her gaze on him. "Yes. In fact, we'd both forgotten so much from those years." She took a moment to look each of her grandchildren in the eye. "I'm not sure if you're all aware, but Harry and I lost our parents when we were in our twenties. They died in an accident—during one of their summer excursions."

Celia let out a little gasp. "How sad."

Grandma nodded. "Yes, it was very tragic. I suppose it was difficult to think about those trips after they'd passed away."

Luke's curiosity piqued. "So, why the sudden interest in recreating one then?"

Her mouth curved up into a small smile. "I'm glad you asked. When they died, I was a new bride. Charlie and I lived in a small house. Harry was discerning religious life. Neither of us had the room to store any of our parents' belongings, so our uncle kept several boxes for us." She folded her hands in front of her. "I'm not sure why, maybe it was just too painful, but neither of us ever retrieved those items. A few months ago, a cousin contacted us to let us know their family home is being sold, and he wondered if we wanted the boxes or if he should just throw them away. Harry and I decided we should finally face the past and go through them."

"That's what you did during your recent visit?" Austin pushed a wayward strand of hair out of his face.

Grandma's smile turned wistful. "Yes. And it was wonderful. We had such a good time reliving so many fond memories. There were notebooks with our mother's sketches, old photographs, our father's journals, and even the diary my mother had given me for our Southwest trip." She patted the notebook next to her.

Celia's mouth dropped open. "That's from when you were ten?"

Grandma ran her hand along the smooth leather. "Yes. It's been so fun to read through the entries." She closed her eyes for a moment before continuing. "It made me so sad that we'd forgotten how special our family trips were—like we'd dishonored our parents' memories. Those summers are truly some of my most cherished moments of my life, and I really want to share at least one of them with you."

Speechless, Luke glanced at his siblings. Celia seemed to be holding back tears as she bit her lip, while

Austin squirmed uncomfortably in his chair. Obviously, they were both at a loss for words as well.

"Umm . . . so, what's our first stop on this trip?" Austin, of course, was the first to break the heavy silence.

"Check your phone." Luke knew his tone was harsher than the occasion called for, but seriously . . . could the kid be any more incompetent? "Dad texted us all an agenda."

"You told me to put my phone away." There was no missing the "so there" look he aimed at Luke.

"He's got a point." Celia smirked, then reached out her hand to high-five Austin.

"We aren't traveling too far today." Grandma's response prevented Luke from launching a comeback.

The chances of surviving a month in this motorized prison with his siblings was practically zero. But he'd have to try—for Grandma's sake.

"We're camping near the Great Sand Dunes tonight," Grandma patiently shared. "Tomorrow, we'll see how far you can hike on them."

Austin's eyes bulged. "Sand dunes? In Colorado? No way!"

"You haven't been there before?" Grandma's forehead creased.

"We were there when I was, like, in third grade," Luke explained. "Austin probably doesn't remember it."

"Figures," Austin pouted. "They did all the fun stuff when I was too little to remember." He reached for his phone.

Grandma patted the table before the kid could disappear into his cyberworld. "Do you all want to play cards?"

Luke grinned. "Absolutely." Not only was she offering a distraction from the '80s rock anthems and the

RV's painfully slow pace, but Grandma had revealed the reason for the trip and was now back to her game-playing self. All was right in the world.

Grandma

Dear Harry,

I'm so thankful I was able to convince them to take this trip. We are now on our way, and the stage is set. Please pray we can accomplish our goal. I will keep you posted.

Your loving sister,
Grace

Chapter 3

Austin: Interface

"Do you think Grandma is dying?" Austin hadn't planned to blurt it out, but the thought wouldn't stop ricocheting around his brain.

Celia glanced over her shoulder. "Why would you ask such a thing?"

Unable to continue his forward momentum up the mountain of sand the three siblings were climbing, Austin stopped to catch his breath. He shifted the rope of the sled he was pulling to the opposite hand. *Who would have guessed it's so hard to walk through sand? Camels make it look easy.* "I dunno. I'm not sure I buy her explanation about the trip. She could have just shared pictures and told us about her childhood adventures. But instead, she suddenly wants to spend all this extra time with us? Something just seems off. And besides, she's always reading her Bible." Thankfully, his siblings stopped the uphill trek as well.

Luke wiped the sweat from his forehead. "She's always read her Bible a lot. But you have a point. I wonder why she was so adamant about the trip. It's not like when she suggested it Dad thought it sounded like a great idea. She really had to push for it—which isn't like her." He uncapped his water and took a long swig. Celia lifted the hair off the back of her neck. "Yeah, you're right. She's the most chill person I know."

Austin shivered as a wave of fear rippled through him. "So, you think it's true? She's dying?" They weren't supposed to agree with him.

Luke shook his head. "No. Don't you think Mom and Dad would tell us that?"

"Maybe if we spend time with her and get her talking, we'll figure out her real motive." Celia started trekking up the hill once again. "Come on, losers."

Geez, where'd she get her energy? Celia was the perfect-grades sibling, not the athletic one. Big brother had that covered. "What's your hurry? Someplace you need to be?"

"Yeah, anywhere away from you."

Just the set-up Austin needed. "You know, Celia, sometimes you can be nice, but right now you're being a total *sand witch*. Get it? Sandwich?" He grinned at his pun.

Celia's forward momentum didn't even slow. "Hilarious."

"I think you mean *hill*-arious." Austin stared past her to the top of the mountain of sand they were traversing, then back to where they started. *Ugh*. Only halfway to the top of this first dune.

"Come on." Luke nudged him. "We can't let her beat us."

"Why is there so much sand in the middle of a mountain range?" With a sigh, Austin adjusted the sled again and plowed forward. Sliding down the huge dune better be as fun as it sounded. "I don't get it. Where'd it come from?"

"How should I know?" Luke asked. "Guess you should read the brochure the park ranger gave us."

Austin continued his slow, stalwart march. With each step, his foot sank into the sand, then had to be pulled out. He could build an entire castle and surrounding village with the amount of grit in his shoes. Maybe Grandma had the right idea, waiting at the bottom with Siena. He and his siblings had declined the offer to join their parents on a smaller dune, thinking they knew better. He hated to admit that the boring adult choices now sounded much more appealing. Austin's aching legs screamed in protest, but somewhere deep inside, determination kicked in. If Luke and Celia could make it, he could too.

As they slowly neared the summit, Luke passed by with a few long strides. Show off. By the time Austin and Celia caught up, Luke stood enjoying the view.

Austin bent over, hands on his knees, sucking in gulps of air.

"Whew!" Celia leaned on his back to steady herself.

Luke chuckled. "You two really need to get in shape."

Here it comes—Luke's usual rant about what slugs we are and that we should join some sport. Mr. Football's mind was so full of himself, it never occurred to him that some people might not like sports.

Celia huffed out a breath. *Good, no need to say a thing.* Austin grinned, ready to enjoy the fireworks while she told Luke off for the both of them.

"Maybe you're right."

What? Austin tilted his head to look at the girl who seemed to have mistaken him for a leaning post. Surely, it was some imposter. A possible shapeshifter in their midst. Because clearly, it was not Celia. When the doppelganger removed her elbow from his back, he straightened.

"Whoa." The view before them made him forget everything. Massive sand dunes stretched for miles, ending at towering mountains.

The siblings stood in silence for a few moments before Celia shivered. "Wouldn't it be horrible to be lost out there?"

"Couldn't happen." Luke snapped a photo with his phone. "Your footprints would be easy to follow."

Rookie mistake. Austin shook his head. "One quick windstorm would make footprints obsolete. But don't worry, a drone could easily find you. You'd just better hope it'd be a search-and-rescue drone and not a bomb-dropping one."

Celia laughed. "Why are you so weird?"

Austin grinned, unable to look away from his sister. He hadn't seen her happy in forever. He'd even pondered if she was still capable of smiling, like maybe her facial muscles were no longer upwardly mobile. She turned and caught him watching her. He flinched, anticipating the punch or slew of insults that were sure to come his way. But oddly, her smile widened. Bizarre. Maybe he was onto something with the whole imposter thing.

Luke held up his phone. "Selfie time."

Austin's head snapped toward his older brother. What was with these two? Oxygen deprivation? "You hate selfies."

"Not when we're somewhere like this. Come on. We need to capture the moment."

They leaned together, and Luke lifted the phone, making sure the sea of sand behind them was visible. Why couldn't it always be this way when they hung out? Of course, there really hadn't been any hanging out lately. Austin had become quite used to the old glare-and-brush-off routine from his siblings. Could this trip possibly change that? Doubtful.

Luke stuffed his phone in his pocket. "Okay, let's do this thing."

Celia set down her sled. "Ready."

Austin's sled landed next to hers. "Fine and *sandy.*" Luke groaned at the joke, then plopped down his sled before taking a few steps back. "On the count of three." He rotated his baseball hat backward. "Three."

"Two." Austin took a deep breath. Celia leaned forward. "One!"

Together, they ran forward then leapt onto their sleds and plummeted down the steep dune of sand.

The wind whipped through Austin's hair, the breeze a welcome relief from the blistering heat. "Woohoo!" *This sand sledding actually works!*

Celia shrieked as she flew past him. Luke joined with a hoot.

Not to be outdone by the kids' screams, Siena's excited barks echoed through the valley. Grandma joined in by cheering and waving her sun visor as they soared toward her. She looked like Grandma always looked— not sick at all. Maybe she really did just want to recreate her favorite trip. Hopefully.

Too soon, the sleds slowed to a stop. Siena sprinted toward them.

"That looked amazing!" Grandma set her purple visor back on top of her wavy hair, which appeared silver in the bright sunlight.

"It was!" Austin glanced at Celia and Luke. He bit his lip. Should he ask? He hated to ruin the moment with his knack for annoying them. *Ah, what the heck. They were bound to get annoyed sooner or later anyway.* "Want to go again?"

"Oh yeah!" Luke called.

Celia scrambled off her sled. "Race you to the top!"

Pure awesomeness.